Son of a Smaller Hero

BOOKS BY MORDECAI RICHLER

FICTION
The Acrobats (1954)
Son of a Smaller Hero (1955)
A Choice of Enemies (1957)
The Apprenticeship of Duddy Kravitz (1959)
The Incomparable Atuk (1963)
Cocksure (1968)
The Street (1969)
St. Urbain's Horseman (1971)
Joshua Then and Now (1980)
Solomon Gursky Was Here (1989)
Barney's Version (1997)

FICTION FOR YOUNG ADULTS
Jacob Two-Two Meets the Hooded Fang (1975)
Jacob Two-Two and the Dinosaur (1987)
Jacob Two-Two's First Spy Case (1995)

HISTORY
Oh Canada! Oh Quebec!:
Requiem for a Divided Country (1992)
This Year in Jerusalem (1994)

TRAVEL
Images of Spain (1977)

ESSAYS
Hunting Tigers Under Glass: Essays and Reports (1968)
Shovelling Trouble (1972)
Notes on an Endangered Species and Others (1974)
The Great Comic Book Heroes and Other Essays (1978)
Home Sweet Home: My Canadian Album (1984)
Broadsides: Reviews and Opinions (1990)
Belling the Cat: Essays, Reports, and Opinions (1998)
On Snooker: The Game and the Characters Who Play It (2001)
Dispatches from the Sporting Life (2002)

ANTHOLOGIES
The Best of Modern Humour (1983)
Writers on World War II (1991)

Son of a Smaller Hero

MORDECAI RICHLER

EMBLEM EDITIONS
Published by McClelland & Stewart Ltd.

First published in Canada by McClelland & Stewart by permission
of the author and Andre Deutsch Limited, 1965
First Emblem Editions publication 2002

National Library of Canada Cataloguing in Publication Data

Richler, Mordecai, 1931-2001
Son of a smaller hero

ISBN 0-7710-7512-X

1. Jews–Quebec (Province)–Montréal–Fiction. I. Title.

PS8535.I38S6 2002   C813'.54   C2001-904143-8
PR9199.3.R5S6 2002

We acknowledge the financial support of the Government of Canada through
the Book Publishing Industry Development Program for our publishing
activities. We further acknowledge the support of the Canada Council for the
Arts and the Ontario Arts Council for our publishing program.

SERIES EDITOR: ELLEN SELIGMAN

Cover design: Kong
Cover image: Rosemary Porter / Graphistock, Inc.
Series logo design: Brian Bean

Typeset in Janson by M&S, Toronto
Printed and bound in Canada

EMBLEM EDITIONS
McClelland & Stewart Ltd.
The Canadian Publishers
481 University Avenue
Toronto, Ontario
M5G 2E9
www.mcclelland.com/emblem

1   2   3   4   5   06   05   04   03   02

For Cathy

Contents

Author's Note

Although all the streets described in this book are real streets, and the seasons, tempers, and moods are those of Montreal as I remember them, all the characters portrayed are works of the imagination and all the situations they find themselves in are fictional. Any reader approaching this book in a search for "real people" is completely on the wrong track and, what's more, has misunderstood my whole purpose. *Son of a Smaller Hero* is a novel, not an autobiography.

If God did not exist, everything would be lawful.

DOSTOIEVSKI

I

Summer 1952

NOAH'S ROOM WAS ON THE FOURTH FLOOR. THE PLACE
had been recommended to him by a taxi driver who worked for the
same company as he did. Mrs. Mahoney, the landlady, was a stringy
woman with hands which were brown and bony, like twigs. She eyed
him suspiciously as he set down his bags.

"Yer a young 'un, ain't yer?"

Noah nodded. He had a brown sceptical face and a narrow body
and long legs. He was twenty years old, but his forehead was already
wrinkled. His eyes, which were black, were sorrowful and deep and
not without a feeling for comedy. They had a quick tender quality as
well. He grinned shyly. He wanted Mrs. Mahoney to go.

"No wimmin. No parties," Mrs. Mahoney said. "Rent every Friday
on the dot."

Noah handed her a month's rent in advance. He turned away from
her and began to unpack, hoping that she would leave him. But
without looking he knew that she was still there. He unpacked his
books and dumped them on the bed.

Mrs. Mahoney picked up a copy of *The Naked and the Dead.*

"Medical student?"

"No," Noah said.

The walls were a faded green but there was a clean unfaded spot where a cross had used to hang. The nail was still there. Noah stared at the nail and lit a cigarette. The window was open, but it was very hot.

"I've been driving all night," Noah said. "I'm very tired. I'd like to sleep."

Mrs. Mahoney hesitated. The last young man who had moved in with books had turned out to be a ballet dancer, a homosexual. She was tempted to wait until Noah took off his shirt to see whether he shaved under his armpits, but – feeling the rent money freshly in her hands – she decided against that. "Well," she said. "I can't stand here all morning."

As soon as she left Noah lay back on the bed. He pulled a towel out of his suitcase and wiped his forehead clean of sweat. He was still angry about his last fare – a drunk and his girl. The drunk had worn a badge on his lapel. His name had been Pete somebody, and he had been in Montreal for the Lumbermen's Convention. Looking into the rear-view mirror, Noah had watched him make the first pass and then sprawl clumsily over the girl. She had groaned a lot, making it hard for him to drive. She had reminded Noah of his Aunt Rachel. He had imagined her, like his Aunt Rachel, entering a room full of people who had been talking heatedly for an hour or so, and saying: "Well, have you settled all the world's problems?" Anyway, when they had got in front of the Mount Royal Hotel, the man had insisted on tipping Noah ten dollars. Noah, inexplicably angry, had shoved the ten dollars back into the drunk's jacket pocket. Now he was sorry. Ten dollars meant a week's rent. He wanted to get a record player, too. Noah leaned over and squashed his cigarette on the floor. This is my room, he thought. He sighed, and he felt empty. There was little joy in that. He couldn't help thinking about his mother and how she had looked at him when he had said that he was going. He went over his reasons again. It was stifling at home . . . Melech . . . his father always apologizing. . . .

He fell asleep.

The ghetto of Montreal has no real walls and no true dimensions. The walls are the habit of atavism and the dimensions are an illusion. But the ghetto exists all the same. The fathers say: "I work like this so it'll be better for the kids." A few of the fathers, the dissenters, do not crowd their days with work. They drink instead. But in the end it amounts to the same thing: in the end, work in textile or garment factories. Some are orthodox, others void.

Most of the Jews who live at the diminishing end of the ghetto, on streets named St. Urbain, St. Dominique, Rachel, and City Hall, work in textile or garment factories. Some are orthodox, others are communist. But all of them do their buying and their praying and their agitating and most of their sinning on St. Lawrence Boulevard, which is the aorta of the ghetto, reaching out in one direction towards Mount Royal, and past that (where it is no longer the ghetto) into the financial district and the factory slums, coming to a hard stop at the waterfront. In the other direction, northwards, St. Lawrence Boulevard approaches the fields at the city limits; where there is a rumour of grass and sun and quick spurious love-making.

All day long St. Lawrence Boulevard, or Main Street, is a frenzy of poor Jews, who gather there to buy groceries, furniture, clothing, and meat. Most walls are plastered with fraying election bills, in Yiddish, French, and English. The street reeks of garlic and quarrels and bill collectors: orange crates, stuffed full with garbage and decaying fruit, are piled slipshod in most alleys. Swift children gobble pilfered plums, slower cats prowl the fish market. After the water truck has passed, the odd dead rat can be seen floating down the gutter followed fast by rotten apples, cigar butts, chunks of horse manure, and a terrifying zigzag of flies. Few stores go in for subtle window displays. Instead, their windows are jammed full and pasted up with streamers that say ALL GOODS REDUCED or EVERYTHING MUST GO.

Every night St. Lawrence Boulevard is lit up like a neon cake and used-up men stumble out of a hundred different flophouses to mix with rabbinical students and pimps and Trotskyites and poolroom sharks. Hair tonic and water is consumed in back alleys. Swank whores sally at you out of the promised jubilee of all the penny arcades. Crap games flourish under lamp posts. You can take Rita the Polack up to the Liberty Rooms or you can listen to Panofsky speak on Tim Buck and The Worker. You can catch Bubbles Dawson doing her strip at the Roxie Follies. You can study Talmud at the B'nai Jacob Yeshiva, or you can look over the girls at the A.Z.A. Stag or Drag.

Conditions improve on the five streets between St. Lawrence Boulevard and Park Avenue. Most of the Jews who live on these streets market what is cut or pressed by their relations below St. Lawrence Boulevard. Others, the aspiring, own haberdashery stores, junk yards, and basement zipper factories.

The employer and professional Jews own their own duplexes in Outremont, a mild residential area which begins above Park Avenue. They belong to the Freemasons, or, if they can't get into that organization, to the Knights of Pythias. Their sons study at McGill, where they are Zionists and opposed to anti-Semitic fraternities. They shop on St. Lawrence Boulevard, where the Jews speak quaintly like the heroes of nightclub jokes.

In the spring of 1952 the B'nai Brith published a report saying that anti-Semitism was on the decline in Canada and that the Jews joined with the great prime minister of this great country in the great fight against communism. The uranium market boomed. Dr. S. I. Katz, O.B.E., told the Canadian Club that "The Jewish beavers of this land will help make the Maple Leaf a symbol of greatness." But the spring passed fast. Those balmy days which had accounted for the melting of the snows turned longer and more hard. The sun swelled in the sky and a stillness gripped the ghetto. When the heat was but two days old everyone seemed to have forgotten that there had ever been a time of no heat. This was partly sham. For, secretively, the people of the ghetto gloated over every darkening cloud. They supposed that tomorrow there would be rain, and if not tomorrow then at least the day after that. But the sky was a fever and there was no saying how long a day would last or what shape the heat would assume by night. There were the usual heat rumours about old men going crazy and women swooning in the streets and babies being born prematurely. When the rains came the children danced in the streets clad only in their underwear and the old men sipped lemon tea on their balconies and told tales about the pogroms of the czar. But the rains didn't amount to much. After the rains there was always the heat again. The flies returned, the old men retreated to their beds, and all the missing odours of the heat reappeared with a new intensity.

The heat first appeared in June when it was still too soon to send the family up north for the summer. But, just the same, things were not too bad. Not too bad until the weekends came along. The weekends were hell. All week long you could at least work but when the weekends came along there was nothing to do. You were on your own. You were free, so to speak.

So on Saturday afternoons the well-to-do Jews walked up and down Queen Mary Road, which was their street. A street of sumptuous supermarkets and banks built of granite, an aquarium in the lobby of the Snowdon Theatre, a synagogue with a soundproof auditorium and a rabbi as modern and quick as the Miss Snowdon restaurant, neon drugstores for all your needs, and delicatessens rich in chromium plating. Buick convertibles and Cadillacs parked on both sides: a street without a past. Almost as if these Jews, who had prospered, craved for many lights. Wishing away their past and the dark. Almost as if these Jews, who had prospered, regretted only the solemn sky, which was beyond their reach. Sunny by day, and by night – star-filled: a swirl of asking eyes spying down on them. Watching. Poking fun at their ephemeral lights.

The neither rich nor poor Jews walked up and down Park Avenue – a few of the nervy ones attempting Queen Mary Road. The poor and the elderly kept to St. Lawrence Boulevard. Each street had its own technique of walking, a technique so finely developed that you could always tell a man off his own street.

The Queen Mary Road Jews walked like prosperity, grinning a flabby grin which said money in the bank. Notaries, lawyers, businessmen, doctors. They wore their wives like signposts of their success and dressed them accordingly. The children were big and little proofs, depending on the size of their achievements.

"Lou, meet the boy. Sheldon. He just won a scholarship to McGill."

"Don't say, eh? Mm. Hey, I hear talk you're gonna expand the factory. That increases your risk, Jack. You come round first thing Monday morning and I'll fix you like a friend. For your own good. You owe it to your family to protect yourself."

The wives exchanged small flatteries.

"Jack's going to buy a Cadillac. *You* try to stop him."

"Me, I don't live for show. Lou doubled his life insurance instead of buying a new car this year. He says you can never tell. . . ."

Park Avenue was different. It had once been to the prospering what Queen Mary Road was to them now. But the prospering had built a more affluent street for themselves to walk on, a bigger proof, where, twenty years hence, they would again feel the inadequacy of the neon, the need to push on and to flee the past and install brighter lights again. Meanwhile, the new ones, the intruding *greeners*, were beginning to move in around Park Avenue. Here, they mixed with the middling Jews. Knowing the right people was important. The aspiring walked without certainty, pompous and ingratiating by turns.

On St. Lawrence Boulevard the Jews, many of them bearded, walked with their heads bent and their hands clasped behind their backs. They walked looking down at the pavement or up at the sky, seldom straight ahead.

On that Sunday morning in the summer of 1952, as under a stern sun the split asphalt of St. Dominique Street showed quivering hot in spots, Melech Adler, his mottled hands lying big on his lap, sat on the kitchen chair on his balcony considering the prospects before him. Later, after he had eaten his lunch of roast beef and fried potatoes, his children and grandchildren would begin to arrive. Mr. Adler had ten children, six boys and four girls. All but the two youngest – a girl, and a boy of nineteen – were married. The married came with their young every Sunday. This Sunday, however, was special. There was going to be a family meeting. Even Noah was expected to come. Noah was Melech Adler's eldest grandson, Wolf's boy. Wolf was Melech Adler's first-born.

Melech Adler sat on his balcony wearing a worn skullcap, a *Jewish Star* folded under his arm and bits of egg clinging to his stiff short beard. He looked down at the weeds struggling up through fractures in the sidewalk and frowned. So the boy is coming, he thought.

Their argument was many years old.

Noah had been born in his grandfather's forty-second year, and whereas Mr. Adler had ruled all his own children by authority he had approached Noah, the first of his grandchildren, with kindness. Noah had responded by attaching himself to his grandfather like a shadow, leaping dreamily before him down the street and allowing no other to carry his prayer shawl. Then, one summer day in his eleventh year, Mr. Adler had taken Noah with him to the coal yard. He had allowed Paquette to take him for a drive in the Ford, and on his return had treated him with oranges and a bottle of Mammy and Halvah. Towards twilight a man drove a cart heaped high with scrap through the gates of the coal yard. Mr. Moore, who was an old customer, waved cheerily to Mr. Adler. Mr. Adler escorted him into his

office, and rolling back his swivel-top desk pulled a bottle of rye out
from behind a ledger. He placed the uncorked bottle and a clean
glass on the desk. Mr. Moore poured himself a drink. Here's to you,
Melech, he said, and tossed it down quickly. Then he began to cough.
Tears streamed down his cheeks and his broken, bony body quivered
and turned wet from sweat. Noah, unnoticed, drew away into a
corner. Mr. Moore had sharp prowling eyes and an insolent mouth.
He poured himself another and bigger drink, and this time consumed it easily. Afterwards he laughed hard and slapped Mr. Adler
on the back. Mr. Adler smiled. Several more drinks were consumed,
and then Mr. Moore asked Mr. Adler when his scrap was going to be
weighed. Mr. Adler said, you don't worry your head Mr. Moore, the
men are fixing. Mr. Adler was a coal merchant and only dealt in scrap
and old tires as a side-line. Noah, afraid of the stranger and dubious
of his grandfather, slipped out of the office. Paquette and his father
were unloading the cart. He noticed them pile several of the sacks on
the scales, hastily concealing others behind a stack of coal-bags. Two
of the sacks were quickly emptied and their contents strewn about
the yard. Finally Mr. Adler and Mr. Moore appeared in the yard and
walked over to the scales to check the weights. Only after they had
begun to haggle in a jocular way about prices did Noah realize what
had happened. He whispered to his grandfather that his father and
Paquette had hidden many of the sacks. His grandfather, his face
darkening, told him to please wait for him in the office. Noah
believed that his grandfather had failed to understand what he had
said, so he began his story over again. Mr. Adler slapped him. Noah
turned away from him swiftly and ran off across the yard, stumbling
on a rock and falling down. Mr. Adler chased after him but Noah
scrambled to his feet deftly and ran off into the dusk.

Things had never been very good between the old man and the
boy ever since that day.

But – reflecting now, on a full stomach and on his own balcony
under a stern sun – Mr. Adler remembered that Noah had not known

and had refused to understand that the *Goy* stole much of the scrap; that he mixed in cast iron with the brass and weighed down the sacks with earth; that he referred to him, Melech Adler, as a usurer when he made the rounds of the taverns.

The boy, he thought.

Melech Adler twisted in his chair, felt sweat like salt on his lips, knowing suddenly the fullness of all his sixty-two years. The brightest of the boys, Max, had left the coal yard to start out on his own in the clothing business. He had taken Nat and Itzik and Lou with him: the four of them were having a fine success. Faigel had married a *gurnisht*, a nothing, and Malka's husband would never earn a living. If he died who would find a husband for Ida? *He could have been the brightness of my old years. We could have gone for walks. Talking. I would have left him money.*

The children, who began to arrive shortly after lunch, congregated in the living-room. Mr. Adler sat in his armchair rubbing little Jonah's face up against his beard. The other grandchildren were grouped around him making raucous bids for his attention. Now and then he gripped one of them in a huge hand and, laughing gruffly, swung him into the air.

The women were seated around the table sipping lemon tea.

Goldie said that her Bernie, knock wood, had come rank-one again in school. But Sarah said that Bernie was a kind of sissy, that her Stanley was no rank-one boy all right but that she and Nat didn't mind so much. Nat had said, she said, that Henry Ford, *the* Henry Ford mind you, had been a Grade A-1 dumb-bell in school. So rank-one, in plain talk, was strictly for the birds. Period, Goldie said. Period.

The men were gathered around Nat, who was doing an impromptu take-off on James Cagney. When Wolf and Leah entered the room Nat whirled around, crouched, and pointed his finger at Leah like a gun. "I got yuh covered, doll," he said. "Covered, dreamboat – like a life-insurance policy. One move, and curtains."

Nat didn't like Leah. She was bringing up Noah to think he was a bigshot. She was always finding something wrong or looking at you as if you were a good-for-nothing.

Leah turned away from Nat coldly.

"She got me." Nat doubled up, clutching his stomach. "I'm a goner. Send for the D.A. I'm gonna sing. I'm gonna sing a solo. I'm gonna sing so low you won't hear me."

He collapsed on the floor. The others laughed.

Sarah turned around in her chair. "Nat, don't make yourself for such a fool in front of Paw. Get up, why don't you? The floor is damp."

"His Master's Voice," Nat said, crouching on all fours and barking.

Mr. Adler swept the grandchildren away from around his chair and glared darkly at Wolf. Wolf squeezed out a weak, frightened smile. He averted his eyes. He passed his hand through his black curly hair, and then stared at his hand.

"Where is the boy? Why have you come without Noah?"

All talk stopped.

Wolf fidgeted with his jacket. He turned to Leah, but Leah stared back at him firmly, without encouragement. Her eyes were red and swollen.

"Am I asking you a question?"

"He isn't coming, Paw."

One of the grandchildren, Bernie, giggled nervously, and Goldie yanked his arm. She held a finger to her mouth and made a hissing sound.

Melech Adler stood immediately before his eldest son, his eyes black with anger. "Why?"

"Paw, I . . . Paw, it's not my fault, eh?"

Why should *I* be blamed for what he does wrong, Wolf thought. Haven't I got troubles enough? And look at her. Some help she is.

"He's moved," Leah said. She was proud. But her eyes were heated and her voice quivered. "He's rented a room on Dorchester Street."

Mr. Adler did not say anything. He stared hard at Wolf, and then turned to the others. They were quiet. Only Max stared back.

All but the two youngest – Ida and Shloime – were married.

Ida knew why there was going to be a meeting. Mr. Adler had at last discovered that the boys hung around Panofsky's on Saturday afternoons, drinking cokes and eating chocolate biscuits, watching the pinochle games in the back room. They had found a way of getting around the sabbath. Panofsky marked down all their purchases and collected his money on Sunday. She knew what the boys would say. They would say that they hadn't actually violated any law. But Mr. Adler would reply that buying on credit was only one step away from buying, and if a Jew bought things on the sabbath he might as well go without a hat, and if a Jew went without a hat he might as well miss the evening prayer, and if a Jew missed the evening prayer ...

Lolling on her bed, nibbling peppermints, Ida read the *Silver Screen* magazine. The afternoon heat was stifling and all she was wearing was her soiled black slip. She was twenty-eight. Mrs. Adler made broad hints and Mr. Adler produced a progression of suitors, all pink-faced rabbinical students. Ida saw all the double-features which played at the Rialto. In her dreams there were many young men and she was no longer fat.

Suddenly Shloime stood dull and shapeless in the doorway.

"I'm going downstairs to the meeting. You coming?" he asked.

"No."

"Should I say you'll be down later?"

Ida made a show of throwing the bedspread over her slip.

"So what should I say?" Shloime asked.

"Don't say."

"Ha. ha, ha. I'm laughing."

"Don't be such a sissy, Shloime. Noah isn't afraid. Tell him if you want to go to Panofsky's on *shabus*, on the sabbath, that it's your own affair."

"I'm laughing. Look, I'm laughing."

Shloime was the youngest in the family. He was big for his nine-teen years and walked with a hulking gait. Embedded in his big head like beads, and half-concealed beneath drooping eyelids, were two sullen, malicious eyes. His oily, shaggy hair fell sloppily over his fore-head and stuck out around his lopping ears. He was forever trying to remember Nat's stories so that he could tell them to the boys in the poolroom but the punch lines always eluded him. Sometimes Ida let him see her, pretending that she didn't know he stood in the doorway, but that was only teaser stuff. Okay for kids. The boys called him Kid Lightning, and it was Shloime's ambition to own a blazer with the name KID LIGHTNING printed on the back of it. His other ambition was to stop being a cherry. But both ambitions required money.

Ida reached for a peppermint and saw that Shloime was still watching her. "You want to take my picture," she said.

Shloime grinned lasciviously. He shoved his hands into his trouser pockets and rocked to and fro on his heels. "Lend me a fiver and I won't tell Paw that I saw you doing you-know-what with you-know-who on a bench in Outremont Park last night."

Ida flushed.

"I tailed you," Shloime said.

"Beat it, mister."

"One fiver if you don't mind."

Ida got up and walked towards him. Shloime saluted, bowed, and said: "We'll do business later." Then he fled down the stairs.

The meeting had gone as Ida had expected. Only Max had stood up to Mr. Adler, but none of the boys had supported him. Melech Adler had been unusually stern with his family and when Noah's name had come up he had turned harder still. Max got up to defend Noah and Leah had quickly backed him up, but there had been more passion than reason to her argument, and the others – glad of an opportunity to show their good faith – had, following Itzik's example, rallied to their father's side. Brother outdoing brother in abusing their nephew.

When Melech Adler left the room after the meeting the others turned swiftly frivolous, giddy, like children running out to play after a great storm has passed.

Melech Adler was a short, swarthy man with smouldering black eyes and a greying grubby beard. All his gestures were quick and emphatic, as though he did not mean to waste any movements. He was strong with long, muscular arms and sturdy legs and nothing flabby about him. Even when he laughed with his grandchildren his eyes stayed solemn, watching them for any show of disrespect. He put some of his money in the bank, but apparently he had hidden the rest. Nobody knew where. Wolf was certain he had concealed it in the padlocked box which was kept in the office safe. He thought so because Melech Adler never took the box out of the safe unless he was alone and the office door was locked.

Melech Adler, who was the son of a scribe, was full of anger after the meeting. He stood in the kitchen doorway, watching his wife bake raisin buns. He saw the hairs on her face and the wrinkles under her eyes.

"Noah's moved away."

Mrs. Adler shuffled past him in her slippers, taking loneliness for granted and assuming the drudgery of her chores as a woman's proper legacy, studying her husband solemnly with her laconic eyes. She pinched a dollar weekly from the grocery money and was paying up on the sly for a lot in the Mount Carmel Cemetery. She did not bother too much about most problems. Melech will know, she thought.

"Are you not well, Melech?"

"I am well. But –" He broke off, and began to tug at his beard. Several hairs came out. He stared at them in his hand. "I work hard. I work hard for them. I am not a thief. I work hard."

"You work hard."

"He should respect me." Melech Adler sat down. "Your boy Max is waiting that if I should die he can run the factory on Saturday. Children I got. The youngest is a champion from de pool players and my first-born – Wolf – has a head like an I-don't-know-what. I don't understand what is? It used to be a man worked like a son-of-a-bitch but the children had plenty respect. Look at me, I'm a crook? All I ask is what is comink to me by right. Why should Noah move away from us? That boy will end up bad and that's a fact. He's got things comink to him he thinks. Such a squirt will tell me what I should and what I shouldn't. If Wolf was half a man he'd pull him down the pants and give him one-two-three wid a strap. What for a men do they make in Canada? Sons they make, not fathers. Gimme, gimme, gimme. You know what my paw gaime. A prayer shawl. Phylacteries. But I'll tell you plain we had a respect that was respect. Wolf says I should make him by me a partner. Why? 'I'm your son.' That's a reason! Leah puts him ideas in the head. She wears de pants. Why is? I don't pray? I don't work hard?"

"We are old. This ain't our country, Melech. Here they grow away from us."

"So now you are telling me something I don't know. *This is my house and I am the boss.* First, last, and always. The head of de family is de fodder. We are old – a new story. If I should die what would happen wid Ida? We are old. I pick up the paper to read so what is? – A friend is – has passed away. Funerals with funerals. Remember, Jenny, the weddings that used to be?"

"I remember."

"And the children one after the other? Did *you* go to the hospital?"

"No."

"No, is right."

"It is different now. The girls don't listen. I found for Ida a boy – remember Yidel Gold? Dis was a boy. So what happens? She don't like it he got a beard. Her fodder hasn't got no beard? She says it ain't de modern ting I should pick her out a husband. But if not me – who? And she's no prize package, let me tell you. So. So she'll do widdout. She thinks I don't know what for a business they make at their dances. She thinks . . .

"What? From this day no more dancing. Finished. No dancing, no movies. She stays every night in the house by us and quick up to bed at eleven o'clock."

Jenny Adler looked down at the dough she was kneading. It felt good and pliant in her hands. She was a thin woman with a narrow face. Her dense black hair was done up in a bun. On many a summer night in the old days, in the good days, he had used to twine it for her whilst she hummed tunes for him. She had borne him thirteen children, three of whom had died in their infancy. She enjoyed making raisin buns for her children to take away on Sundays. They adored her buns. So did the grandchildren. She had no money or wisdom to offer them, so when they were in trouble she baked them extra buns. She did not want Melech to alienate her from the children. He turned the other way when she undressed herself. Or, if he looked at all, his eyes were sorrowful. She wished secretly that he would touch her sometimes. Or look at her lovingly. He had used to do that.

"No, Melech. Don't be too strict again."

"Why? Didn't I teach Shloime a lesson? One-two-three with the belt and no more poolrooms until two in the morning. One Noah is plenty."

"You can't do that here, Melech. A different country. When we got married I didn't know from no fridges and no washing-machines or anything. Today a girl won't get married without. We are old. They are even ashamed for us."

"Who? Who is ashamed?"

"Never mind."

"Noah? Noah said something?"

"Noah, if you don't mind, is better than all the rest put together. All right, he moved. Who knows what for? But when he comes in the house he talks a Yiddish word. He brings flowers. He . . ."

"That boy he breaks my – Jenny, what did I do him? I wanted one of them at least should be a rabbi. An honour in the family. Of all of them he is the only one I offered money. So what does he say? No. No money. So Noah will tell me what to do. Me and him we are men together. *I am his grandfather, I tell you.* I don't understand what is."

II

Noah woke suddenly and looked at his watch. 5:15. The meeting is probably over by now, he thought. His room was downtown. Downtown usually means St. Catherine Street. But, more specifically, downtown Montreal is shaped like a rectangle. It is bordered on the west by Atwater Avenue and on the east by St. Lawrence Boulevard. The northern border is Sherbrooke Street, and the southern Craig Street. This rectangle, which immediately suggests a colossal pinball machine, abounds in frantic diversions and a squalor that glitters. Running plunk down the middle of it, shimmering, going from east to west and being the most important alley of all, comes St. Catherine Street. Every ten seconds or so somebody drops a nickel in the slot, pulls the trigger, and zoom goes a streetcar or seventy cars or three hundred pedestrians down the alley.

Noah's room was on Dorchester Street, a block away from St. Catherine Street. On a summer evening the men and women who live on Dorchester Street sit outside on the steps sipping beer and smoking. Sometimes they bring a portable radio or a gramophone out with them and listen to dance music. There's a grocery store at nearly every corner and most of them have big neon signs which wink the word BEER at you on and off in big red or green letters.

The rooming-houses vary. They range all the way from a place where you can take your girl for the night to tourist hotels. The tourist hotels usually have an American flag in the window. That, and a sign which says:

WELCOME NEIGHBOUR

JOHNNY CANUCK GREETS YOU

U.S. Money Accepted at Par

The street isn't too clean. The police often raid the more dilapidated rooming-houses looking for girls who take dope or men who drink too much. Sometimes they find suicides. Sometimes people complain about the police raids or the dirt. They write letters to the editor of *The Montreal Star* signed "Disgusted" or "Mother of Five." But most of the people don't mind the dirt too much. They are always planning to move away.

Noah got up. The couple in the room opposite his were quarrelling.

"If I wanna drink I drink. This is a free country. I pay taxes."

"When you work, you mean. You pay taxes when you work."

The old man, he thought, knows by now that I'm not coming. My mother, lonely in her kitchen chair, lonely even on a crowded street-car, sits among them defiantly, her white, chapped hands folded on her lap and her swollen eyes outstaring them. My father dares not think what is in his mind. He stares at the floor, or at a chair, or at anything that is not his enemy. The others are surely pleased. This week's anger, today's invective, is not against them. Everybody is free to join in. Everybody except her. *It is necessary, at times, to hurt others. But I'm hurting her very much. I'd better be right.*

The room began to cool, and the chunk of sky that showed through the window was greying. Noah sat down on the window-sill and remembered that evening, a Friday evening long ago, at the hall of the local youth group. The speaker, a messenger from Israel,

had been an angry Polish Jew with bad memories and piercing eyes.
He took off his jacket, Noah remembered, and spoke with one
foot propped up on a chair, stopping every now and then to wipe
his forehead.

"Look at me and think: How much can I do for Israel? I'll tell you
how much. *Not enough.* Do you know why? Because you are Jews, and
that's a crime in this world."

The audience was made up of boys and girls not yet twenty.
Children of an aspiring working class. Enthusiasts. Girls without lipstick and boys with bold notions of how they were going to fix their
tormentors. Pictures of the leaders hung on the walls. Herzl,
Weizmann, Ben Gurion. A map of Eretz had been pinned up on the
window behind the speaker and a huge white-and-blue flag hung on
the opposite wall.

"For the first time in two thousand years we are being given the
chance to die like men. Only the ones who pray will stay home. Do
you know them? The ones who pray. . . . If the Germans murder a
thousand they go to the synagogue. If the Germans murder two thousand they hold a special service. If the Germans murder ten thousand
they pray all day and all night. But they are noble, these men who
pray. They don't kill. The Messiah will lead *them* to Eretz. (Those
who are not yet burnt.) But the Messiah won't lead *you* to Eretz. The
Tommies only make way for bullets. Arabs aren't orthodox. But they
go down like flies before a machine-gun."

The speaker seized his crowd, held them with his heated eyes and
shook them in his clenched fists. They watched. Laughing when he
laughed, cursing when he cursed, glaring when he glared. He hated,
and they hated right back.

"Worse even than the Germans are the ones who think they can
become of them by shortening their names or their noses. Have you
seen them? They say that anti-Semitism isn't directed against them.
It is directed against the obvious ones. *They* go to good schools.
Even when the Gestapo broke into their houses it wasn't their fault.

It was *your* fault. You're the ones with accents. Big noses. Millions in the bank."

Noah watched. He looked into the wanting eyes of his friends. Duddie Felder, Gitel Shub, Gas Weiner, Faigie Rosenblatt, Yidel Kogan, Zalman Seigler, Hoppie Drazen. He looked, and they slipped away from him. Strangers in a smoky room. He turned to the speaker. A monkey-faced man with burning eyes. The leaders. Old men on fading paper. A magnificent black beard, a balding head, a swirl of white hair. Strangers. Old men.

All eyes were on the speaker. Noah touched his forehead, his hair was soaking wet. He had an idea of what was slipping away and gripping his hands together he tried to hold on. We're all of us Jews in this room, he thought. But a voice came back: All Jews and all strangers. He forced the conventional anguishes on himself. Quotas, Cyprus, Eretz, gas chambers. Gritting his teeth, he turned askingly to the speaker, demanding that he too be saved.

"Do you know what they are saying in the Foreign Office? The Jews are mad dogs. That's true, you know. Poor Mr. Bevin. Poor Mr. Churchill. The sheep have turned into dogs. Funny, isn't it? They want land. Aren't you amazed? I am. Poor Mr. Bevin. We were all right when we fought for him on the desert. Heroes when we died in the Warsaw ghetto. Now they'll read a new chapter. . . ."

That's when Noah began to laugh. Yidel Kogan poked him hard and Noah sobered up briefly. He stared at his friend, the stranger. We used to play ball together in Outremont Park, he thought. But Yidel could no longer be reached. He had already been committed to memory.

The speaker banged his fist down on the table conclusively. The deal had been made. The man, orphaned by a furnace, and swindled by memory, had drained away the innocence of others. From now on explanations, curiosity, intelligence, could be done without. The enemy, so long elusive, had been shaped.

"Comrades, let us join in and sing."

They came to their feet fast, answering him in full voices. Then they joined hands for the folk-dances. In the intense heat of the horah they seemed to shed their individuality like unwanted skins, trading in anguish and abandoning freedom for membership.

"Israel lives! Israel lives! Israel lives!"

Clammy hands, lolloping breasts. Arm in arm, locked in a circle ferociously, to and fro, this way, that way, they went, blurring themselves. One whoop between them, two took eyes, a shared soul.

"Who am I?"

"YISROAL."

"All of us?"

"YISRO-YISRO-YISROAL."

Noah smoked. He thought it obscene, ugly, to be watching but not taking part. Several times he started towards the dancers, but each time he turned back embarrassed. Finally, desperately, he tried to break into the circle. But they were whirling past too fast, and he was spun back and away from them defiantly, like a counterfeit coin from a cashier. The voices of strangers shouting, the boots of strangers trampling the floor. He watched, they danced. He slipped out and walked up to Park Avenue, where there were always crowds. Many of the coldly-lit store windows had been done up enticingly. He stopped for a long time in front of the 5¢ to $1.00 store, where he read the luncheon menu and the price tags on toys and an appeal for the blind. Then, working his way towards Bernard Street, he looked at lingerie, shoes, and hardware. Nobody he knew was in the Park Bowling Alley, but there were several free tables, so he played two games of snooker with a stranger. Upstairs, he watched them bowl. The loud clacking of the balls and the tumbling pins had a restful effect on him. Most of the bowlers were young couples. Several of the girls were pretty and when they ran up the alley their buttocks strained against their skirts. Outside, the snow came floating down in big lumps. He wandered back absently to the hall. The light from the window made a cold yellow block on the snow. From where he stood he could see the crepe-paper decorations around the light bulbs and a part of Theodore Herzl's head. . . .

The voices in the next room returned Noah to the present.

"How would you like it if I punched you on the nose? Not hard. Just enough to knock you out."

"You and what army?"

Stars began to spark in the deepening sky. Street noises were muffled, but when big trucks rolled by below, the yellow bulb shook in its socket and shadows swayed, swept towards him, and shrank back on the walls. Anger consumed him. He had expected that by moving away from home something wonderful would happen whereby he would end up a bigger and freer man. Instead, there was only this anguishing. He saw himself like that yellow bulb overhead, weak, nameless, and swaying amid rented shadows. At home his indignation had nourished him. Being wretched, and in opposition, had organized his suffering. But that world, that world against which he had rebelled so vociferously, was no longer his. Seen from a distance, it seemed full of tender possibilities, anachronistic but beautiful. Melech, at worst, was a dedicated man, not without love for his family. He had descended from a long line of scribes. Men who, if they were not quite rabbis, required a certain artistry and some nobility to proceed with their holy work – creating Torahs by hand on parchment. The house on St. Dominic Street, stifling as he had found it, was also rich in warmth and humour. All the dictums of the ghetto seemed unworthy of contempt in retrospect. I'll miss them, he thought.

Did I need them, he thought, the way my grandfather needs the *Goyim*? He wiped the sweat off his chest with a towel. It's not enough to rebel, he thought. To destroy. It is necessary to say yes to something.

Noah looked at his watch again. It was time to go to work. His taxi was parked round the corner. Perhaps I'll go and see Melech tonight, he thought.

III

Wolf Adler – Melech's first-born son and Noah's father – married
Leah Goldenberg in 1927. Melech Adler had been pleased. The
Goldenbergs were well known in the ghetto. Jacob Goldenberg,
who had also approved of the match, died in 1936. He had been a
Talmud Torah teacher and a Chassid. Everybody had read his wild,
yearning poems written in Yiddish that had celebrated fields and
forests that he had never known. Both families had been satisfied
with the match.

Only Wolf and Leah weren't satisfied.

Leah's brother, Harry, was a doctor. One day she had told him:
"We're a family of strangers."

Sometimes Wolf went to two different movies on Sunday nights.
Other times he went to an early movie and then to Panofsky's, where
he played pinochle with the boys. Occasionally Noah played pinochle
with him. Leah was vice-president of the Ladies' Auxiliary. She liked
the poems of Byron and Keats, and some nights, when she was feeling
lonely, Noah would stay home and read them to her in the kitchen.

The Adlers, who lived in a cold-water flat on City Hall Street,
spent most of their time in the kitchen. There was a big damp blotch
on the ceiling (Mr. Twersky, the landlord, was too cheap to fix the
pipes properly) and from time to time flakes of plaster spiralled
downwards, but it was warm and cosy there all the same. Leah,
however, was particularly proud of the parlour, which was restricted
to guests and meetings. A deluxe chesterfield set, end-tables and
antique chairs, a Persian rug and wine drapes, two bookcases with
glass doors, and a breakfront had all been crammed into this room.
The breakfront, which had taken two years to pay for, was a kind of
solace to her. She polished it often and felt every scratch like a wound
to her own person. The shelves swarmed with tiny china figures
and gold-trimmed plates and silver trays and china flowers. She
arranged and rearranged, and arranged again, her collection of odd

cups and saucers. She enjoyed looking after these possessions even more than she did watering the Japanese gardens on the various end-tables, something that she did every day. The bedroom which she shared with Wolf was simply furnished. There were two beds. She would have enjoyed doing more about Noah's room but he had objected to her fussing with the furnishings. The desk in his room, though, had been her father's and that gave her plenty of satisfaction. Showing friends about the room, she would say: "He uses my father's desk. You remember my father, don't you?"

The dishes cleared away, Wolf and Leah sat opposite each other at the kitchen table. They had just returned from his father's house about an hour ago. The door to Noah's bedroom was shut. Wolf, she knew, was impatient. This was Sunday evening and he would be late for the movies. The window that looked out on the lane was opened because of the heat. The cotton net that had been tacked up on the window frame to keep the flies out had been blackened by grit and smoke many seasons ago. Upstairs, Mrs. Ornstein's baby was crying. And downstairs, just below them, the Greenbergs were gathered in the back yard. Mort Shub was telling them jokes. Wolf could hear him.

"You haven't even got the spunk to talk back to your father," Leah said. "'He isn't coming, Paw. It's not my fault.' You should stick up for your boy. You call yourself a man?"

Waiting for her to begin always unnerved Wolf, even after all these years. But once she had begun he felt easier. He knew his role and played it without fault. The argument was constant. She said this, he said that. Neither of them cheated.

"Why should I talk back to Paw? He left so he left. Should I chain him to the door?"

"He left because you're common."

"Common. I worked like a nigger so that –"

"Don't say 'nigger.' Noah wouldn't like it. He recognizes the niggers!"

"Recognize. If you saw five niggers walking down the street you could recognize? A nigger is a nigger."

A voice came up from the back yard. "Hallo, hallo! HEY, ADLER. You got maybe by you a bottle opener?"

Wolf looked at Leah and Leah nodded.

"Waddiya think this is – Woolworth's?" Wolf yelled. "And you. You got maybe a bottle?"

"We got Jack Benny in person living upstairs yet," Mort yelled back.

Wolf got the opener off the hook and stepped out onto the balcony and tossed it down to Mort. All the Greenbergs were sprawled out in the yard. They had a watermelon and a case of cokes. They're having a lot of fun, Wolf thought. Mort winked, and motioned for him to join them. Wolf shrugged his shoulders, and returned to the kitchen. They're having a lot of fun, he thought.

"All right," Wolf said. "Have it your way. But he'll be back. Don't you worry. He'll find out that money doesn't grow on trees. It'll be an experience for him. Let's go to bed."

"Bed, bed, bed. He won't be back. He's got a job driving a taxi nights."

"You mustn't tell Paw."

"Look at him, afraid of his own shadow. *I'm a lady.* He left because *you're* common. You know what Mrs. Leventhal said to me at the Mizrachi meeting last Tuesday? You're a lady, she said. My Jack had one look at you and he said to me: 'She's a lady.' Some lady! I'm married to a coal dealer."

"If war was declared tomorrow I'd be the villain."

Leah tightened her fists. She stared at him, this man who epitomized all the injuries of her years, who had become the injustice and the hardship – stared, her eyes hardening, and was nourished. My father could see what he was, she thought. Why did he marry me to him? "For two cents even I'd leave you. Noah would take care of me. You bet your life he would. *He's* not afraid of your father."

"Noah's a fresh kid. He has no respect. I should have taken the strap to him long ago. . . . Leah – don't . . . Leah . . . Leah. . . ."

"I'm not crying!"

"I didn't say that you were crying!"

"If my father was alive I wouldn't have to go through this. If . . . He was a man! Not like you. A – a . . ."

Again from the yard. "Wolf! HEY, JEW-BOY. What, tell me, is de definition of an Eskimo with a hard-on?"

Leah scowled. It's not *my* fault, Wolf thought.

"*Nu.* Speak! YOU DEAF AND DUMB?" Mort yelled.

"I don't know," Wolf said weakly.

"A rigid midget with a frigid digit."

A burst of laughter followed. Wolf tried not to grin, but he made sure to remember the joke. And, from upstairs, Mr. Ornstein yelled: "Hey, Mort. We got minors up here. Keep it quieter. You want my missus should wash out your mouth wid soap?"

"Listen, Wolf, why don't you leave your father? You could start on your own like Max. I'd help. I could hold my head up when we walked down Park Avenue. Did you know that Max is going to buy a duplex in Outremont."

"Max married into the Debrofskys. What did you expect? He should live on St. Dominique? He had the breaks. Paw would have made me a partner if not for the depression."

"A partner! You should live to see the day. You're a truck driver for him."

"What's the good, eh? Okay, let's say I leave Paw. So what happens? I go to a *Goy* for a job. Go ahead and tell me that a *Goy* is gonna hire a Jew. So I go to a Jew for a job. Right away he thinks what does this Jew want to work for me for? In two months he'll be in business for himself. A wiseguy. *I* should teach *him* the tricks! The hell with him I should give him a job. So I go into business on my own. You can be a lady. Hold your head up. Comes the first depression and bang goes your head on the floor. Not me. No, sir. Did you read in the *Digest* last week what General Whats-his-name said? 'When I was twenty I thought my father was a fool. But when I was thirty I . . .'"

"Noah says the *Digest* is hooey."

"Noah says. If Noah knew better than the *Digest* he'd be a general too. Do you know how many million people read the *Digest*? Noah says. Pish-pish. I'm smarter than you think. I play it safe. Besides, look, not that I . . . But how long is Paw gonna . . . Well, you know. He has to leave the business to me . . . to us. . . ."

"You could start out on your own. Look at Max."

"Max? You should have half of what he owes on his factory. As soon as the slump comes bang goes Max's credit. That's a proven fact. I'm not so dumb."

"Excuses and excuses. You . . ."

"HEY! Here's one for you, ADLER. YOU LISSN'N, ADLER? This here guy meets his old pal, Cohen let's say, who manufactures brassières. Hey, Cohen, he says, how's business? Looking up, Cohen says. . . ."

Wolf pretended not to hear. He turned to Leah. "Why can't I do anything right? Do I beat you? I drink? I go with other women?"

"I wouldn't pester if Noah was with us. If – if Noah thought that I was sick he would come back. He loves me like anything."

"Meaning?"

"Go. Go to the movies. There would be another flood as sure as I'm sitting here if you missed a double-feature. Go play cards. I'm going to lie down with a book."

"ADLER. YOU LISSN'N? Answer a man a question, eh?"

Wolf retired to the den. He was a short, skinny man, and his head was crowned by a mass of black curly hair which was forever in need of cutting and always falling over his forehead. When he was nervous or afraid he pushed his hand through his hair, looked at his hand, then pushed it through his hair again. But he was seldom nervous or afraid in the den. The den was his. Wolf wore glasses. When he had to contend with the big drunken Irishmen who came into his office, haggling over prices with them, when he talked back to Leah, or when he was about to ask his father for more pay, he had a trick of wiggling his ears and raising his eyebrows and making his glasses go up and down on his nose. That way, if the others took what he said in the wrong spirit, he could always reply that he had been joking. He worried a lot, but the den was his. It was a clean, well-ordered room with many shelves and a nice smell to the wood. One corner was devoted to his hobby. Woodwork. That wall was lined with tools. The cabinet, which had been nailed to the wall, had many drawers. The drawers were all labelled and contained various sizes of nails, screws, and blades. He had made the cabinet and work-bench and tool-chest himself. He knew a lot about construction. Whenever he visited a house that was new to him he asked for a glass of water and set it down on the floor. Later, he would glance at it surreptitiously. That's how he could tell whether the foundation had settled in a level way. One wall of the den was completely taken up by his bookshelves. Here he kept his old copies of *Life*, *Popular Mechanics*, *Reader's Digest*, *True Crime*, and several volumes of scrapbooks. One series of scrapbooks contained his record of the war years, another his collection of data on coins and stamps clipped from the pages of various Montreal newspapers. Most of the drawers to his desk were locked. His diary was kept in the bottom drawer, which also had a false bottom where he kept personal papers and letters. Except for prosaic entries, such as family birthdays, dates of operations and graduations, the diary was kept in a code of his own invention.

Very often Wolf would lean back in his chair and brood about how much money there must be in the locked box that his father kept in the office safe. That box was very important to him and represented many things. Other times he would worry about the possibilities of another depression or of Noah doing something that would get him in trouble with his father. A depression would not be

such a bad thing. A small one, anyway, would certainly fix bigshots
like Seigler and Berger who had made a lot of fast money on the
black market during the war years. From time to time he fiddled
with various ideas for household gadgets. And then there was always
the possibility that he might pick up a small packet soon on one of
his investments – coins.

Two of the coins issued to commemorate the coronation of King
George VI in 1937, a dime and a nickel, had caught Wolf's attention.
Studying them with a magnifying glass, Wolf had discovered that the
King's nose was slightly crooked on the nickel. So he had invested
twenty dollars in the faulty coins. He kept them locked in his desk
where, he had decided, they would stay until 1960. I might make a
fortune on it, he often thought. And if I had money I'd be good. Not
like them. Wolf rubbed his jaw. Business was slow. Well, what could
you expect? The summer was always like that. Things would pick up
in the fall.

IV

When Shloime finally came home that evening his mother and Ida
were both waiting in the kitchen. Ida was leaning defiantly against
the gas stove, a spoon in her hand. She had prepared the dinner.
"Look at him," she said. "The Cat's Pyjamas, Jr. Only eight o'clock
and he's here to eat already."

"You shouldn't quarrel," Mrs. Adler said. "Paw will . . ."

Shloime sat down in his chair. There was a plate of meat and potatoes in front of him. He tasted the meat, tentatively, and then
slammed his fork down on the table. "The meat's cold," he said.

"What – did – you – expect?"

"All I am doing is stating facts. The meat is cold. Meat. M,E,A,T.
Cold. C,O,L,D."

"Maw, I'll kill 'im. I'm telling you I'll . . ."

"Eat your meat, *boyele*. Paw . . ."

"You call this meat?"

"You heard Maw. Eat your meat. I'll tell Paw."

"I will state another fact. Ida is twenty-eight. Ida needs a husband. Husband. L,A,Y."

"All right, Maw. All right. Fair is fair. I'm going to the movies."

"Children, children."

Mr. Adler stepped into the room and Shloime began to eat hurriedly. Ida smiled. Mrs. Adler looked at him pleadingly. Mr. Adler waited while the silence, which he had imposed on them, gripped the room, then he said: "What is?"

"Nuttin."

"Nothink? I heard shouting like animals."

"We were just kidding around, Paw. So help me."

"Why weren't you in the synagogue tonight?"

"I was sleeping, Paw. Tired. I . . ."

"He was in the poolroom, Paw. I'll bet you."

"Look what's talking? Fatso the first. Yeah. What do you do in . . ."

"Speak when you are spoken to. Both of you. Shloime, were you in the poolroom?"

"Paw, I . . ."

"Yes or no. Speak."

"I stopped in for a coke. *But that's all.*"

"Eat your supper. Afterwards you will do the dishes. Friday you give all your pay away to Maw. Finished."

Ida clapped her hands together. "Ha, ha, ha. I'm laughing."

Shloime felt a fluttering in his stomach. I'll fix them, he thought. I'll fix all of them. Mrs. Adler, passing him by, stroked his head tenderly. Shloime jerked away from her. His eyes flooded with tears, he leaped up and rushed out of the room.

"Crybaby."

"Don't talk so. Leave him alone. Ain't he your brudder?"

Ida shrugged her shoulders.

Mr. Adler sat down in the parlour and put on his glasses, spreading the *Jewish Star* out on his lap. The walls were lined with stiff, formal wedding pictures, and pictures of the grandchildren. There were also several framed graduation certificates, and a picture of Melech Adler in a top-hat and tails. That picture had been taken at Max's wedding.

A few days earlier Moore had come into the office. Mr. Adler, who had not seen him for several years, had been shocked. Moore had aged tremendously. Grey-haired, his body shrunken, he had stunk of alcohol: but when he had asked for a job, Mr. Adler had given him work in the yard. He had felt sorry for Moore, and standing in the shade of his office Melech had not been altogether displeased to see him sweating in the sun and dust, shovelling coal into sacks. In fact he had suddenly felt expansive. He had sent Paquette out to buy cokes for everybody and he had decided to make Moore his night watchman.

Noah, who at that moment was parked across the street in his taxi, wondering whether or not to go in and speak to Melech, occupied a unique position in the Adler family. He was, to begin with, Leah's son. Leah wasn't liked. He was the grandson of a man whom Melech Adler had deeply respected – Jacob Goldenberg, the Zaddik. The family never knew what Noah would do next. He ran away from home at seven years and again at ten, the last time getting as far as Toronto. Several years later he marched in political demonstrations. That was something that Wolf and the others could never do: they were Jews. At first Noah's boldness had given them pleasure, but later his enthusiasms frightened them. The Adlers lived in a cage and that cage, with all its faults, had justice and safety and a kind of felicity. A man knew where he stood. Melech ruled. The nature of the laws did not matter nearly as much as the fact that they had laws.

The Jews, liberated and led into the desert by Moses, had wanted nothing so badly as to return to slavery in Egypt. Noah broke the laws and was not punished. He flung open the door to that cage, and said, in effect, follow me to freedom. (Noah, at sixteen, had only understood that the laws were not true and that had seemed all-important. He had not yet known that laws in order to be true only required followers.) During the war he had tried, twice, to get into the army and once into the navy. He had threatened to report uncles and cousins for war profiteering, and the uncles and cousins had not been able to understand one Jew informing on another. They were, quite honestly, loyal to each other. As much as they might condemn one another in their own homes they presented a solid front to the *Goyim*. Melech watched and said nothing. Was he afraid? Did Noah have a grip over him? They didn't know. None of them, except possibly Shloime, was a malicious person, yet they waited anxiously for Noah's punishment. This particular cage, in order to prosper, required a gate that was clanged shut.

One Sunday when the family had been gathered in the parlour Noah had overheard Goldie scolding Bernie, who had just hit Yidel. "If you do things like that you'll grow up like Noah," she had said. In retrospect, the incident seemed ludicrous enough. But Noah had been deeply hurt. He wanted to be liked by the family, and he feared them as much as they did him. At weddings and *bar-mitzvahs* voices were lowered when Noah joined the group. Others, more straight-forward, turned their backs to him. They fed him with drink: and, briefly, he played the role of the drunkard for them. Then, when he abandoned that role, they began to think of him as a communist. For as long as he was a drunkard or a communist whatever he said was invalid and required no reply.

Noah was lonely. He visited them separately and read poetry or stories to them. He tried to explain why he did not follow Melech's laws. Immediately, they said: "C'mon, have a drink." They didn't drink with him, but watched approvingly. He offered to take their children to the circus or for walks on the mountain. They declined. "What? A guy who drinks like you?"

Noah realized that he had come to the end of something, and that he and the family could not meet again except as strangers suspicious of one another. That hurt him. He did not want or expect them to change their ways for him. He was not that selfish. But neither could he go on being an embarrassment and a sorrow to them. All that remained, he knew, was for him to speak to Melech.

He lit a cigarette and got out of the car.

The door opened.

Noah stood before him embarrassed, holding his taxi cap in his hands. "I had a fare near here," he said. "I thought I'd drop in."

Melech Adler took off his glasses and folded up his paper. But his eyes stayed solemn: Noah saw no tenderness, no response, in them.

"How are you, *Zeyda*?"

"You work on Saturday?"

"Yes."

Mr. Adler got up and walked over to the window. He cleared his throat, not trusting his own voice. Jenny is probably listening by the door, he thought, Ida, too. "You are no longer welcome here. Understand? Finished."

"But I . . . Can't you try to understand?"

"Understand? What should I try to understand?"

"Can't you see how everything is falling apart around you? Your sons are Canadians. I am not even that. Don't you think . . . I can't be something, or serve something, I no longer believe in. As it is, well . . . I'm sort of between things. I was born a Jew but somewhere along the way . . . You can't go back, *Zeyda*. It would be easy if you could."

"I don't understand what you talk."

Can't I see, he says. If I had told him about Moore that day, Melech thought, if I had explained it to him first, everything would have been all right. But he found out himself. Melech tugged slowly at his beard. His hands, he noticed, were clammy. He waited. He wanted Noah to ask him a favour. That would help, he thought. It would be a start.

"Take love, for instance," Noah said. "If you have never been in love then you still know that it's missing. Well, something is missing. But I don't know what it is. All I know is that it's missing."

"Other boys go to college. They make something from themselves."

"I can't make something of myself that way, *Zeyda*. I'm sorry. I think it's freedom that I want. I – I no longer have any rules to refer to the way you had. I . . ."

"Listen how he talks. You should study Talmud. You . . ." Melech turned away from him and spoke quickly, casually, pretending that he was not saying what he said: "If you came here to ask permission to come back I wouldn't mind you go without a hat. We could talk, the two of us. . . ."

Noah hesitated. He felt guilty, tempted. He had never heard Melech ask for anything before. "I'm sorry, *Zeyda*. I can't. I can't go back."

Melech stayed with his back turned to Noah. He had nearly said: "When I was young in Lodz I loved a girl, an actress, but –" But he hadn't been able to get the words out. He would have required Noah to have been weak before he could have shared such a secret with him. But Noah wasn't weak. He had refused him. My father was a scribe, he thought. He wouldn't let. *I am a strong man.* I didn't go against my family the way he does. I had respect. *Helga has blond hair and walks straight. She claps her hands together when she dances.*

"I wanted you to be a somebody. Something. Something not like them. All there is for them is money."

"But, *Zeyda*, if money doesn't worry you why don't you make my father a partner?"

"You too?"

"But it's such a small thing. It would make them both happy."

"Don't tell me what to do."

"I came to tell you that I'm going to college this autumn. I'm going to study at night."

"Go. Go, go. You go from here and I will give you nothink. You go so you go. Finished."

Melech Adler turned away from him again and sat down. *And she used to hold my hands in hers and clap them together when she sang. When I chopped wood for her father she came over with a towel and wiped the sweat off my chest.* Noah waited tensely, but his grandfather ignored him.

Melech Adler put on his glasses and picked up his paper again.

Noah got up. He touched Melech's shoulder and smiled lamely. "I'm sorry," he said.

Their eyes met briefly. A just man upright in a chair. Noah was shocked by the fury in his grandfather's eyes.

"Go! Get out!"

Melech watched him go. He wanted to call him back, but he also wanted to punish Noah because he, Melech, had loved Helga and had deserted her. Up until that moment Melech had felt that he hadn't quite deserted her, that he could, when he wanted to, return to her. But now he realized that he was too old. Noah had unwittingly condemned him as a coward again by walking out on him. Melech stared at the picture of himself in a top-hat and tails. That was taken ten years ago, he thought. If I die, they will have it enlarged.

Noah sat in the car and rubbed his eyes. He was shaken. He felt that he had seen his grandfather for the first time. Melech was old, but he was full of justice and not to be pitied. *Yet I had nothing but apologies to offer him.* Noah did not feel triumphant. He felt small. He started up the car and drove off into the night.

Afterwards Mrs. Adler brought in a glass of lemon tea for Melech. She sat down on the sofa, but he didn't say anything. She looked around the room. The furnishings were cheap. Mobile. Jenny was not stingy, but she was used to the idea of moving. If there was suddenly trouble, if they had to flee quickly to another country, if . . . Better not to invest in things that they would have to leave behind. Finally, she said: "Noah was here?"

"So?"

"You sent him away?"

"I sent him away."

"Why did you send him away?"

"I sent him away, that's all."

Each man creates God in his own image. Melech's God, who was stern, just, and without mercy, would reward him and punish the boy. Melech could count on that.

"I don't understand . . ."

Melech noticed, for the first time, the bowl of flowers on the mantelpiece. Jenny must have put it there when she had brought in the tea. Undoubtedly, it was a gift from Noah. Melech frowned. Flowers for her, impudence for me. When Jenny had been ill several years ago, Noah had come every day to read the stories of Sholem Aleichem to her.

"Look, Jenny, he tells me that he ain't a Jew. What, tell me, is a Jew? It is like belonging to the club where all the members got a crippled foot. So what does he say? One cripple is different from the other. So? Finished. You should let me read my paper."

Mrs. Adler sighed. "Would you like maybe a bun wid . . .?"

Melech heard. He understood and he was alarmed. But he didn't answer.

2

Autumn and Winter 1952

MRS. MAHONEY, IT TURNED OUT, DIDN'T OBJECT TO women or to parties either, as long as she was invited. She was awfully lonely. Noah ate with her once a week and took her to the movies whenever he could. He also got to know the couple next door, Mr. and Mrs. Joey Nowacka, and that friendship inadvertently cost him his record player. Joey drank a lot and played the horses, Bertha was pregnant. Before long, Bertha became Noah's special charge – and that accounted for his savings.

Noah was lonely too. He talked about his family a good deal to the Nowackas and Mrs. Mahoney. Often, when business was slack, he drove through the streets of the ghetto, remembering places and things that he had done there. He weakened once, and thought of going back, but a visit with his mother taught him quickly that there was no going back. He did a lot of reading. He walked. His room was peopled with dreams, and he was not happy. College, for instance, was another disappointment.

The principal of Wellington College was a small man with eyes of no colour at all who would be remembered and celebrated for having feared God and been tolerant of men. He never forgot the face of a Wellingtonian. Everybody respected him. The dean had compiled a huge mimeographed bibliography which listed the dimensions, title, number of pages and illustrations, author, and subject, of all the books that had ever been published in Canada. Dr. Edward Walsh, the assistant dean, had a splendid smile: nobody could outdo him as a host. He began his lectures in Political Science I by writing on the blackboard:

I. SYSTEMS OF GOVERNMENT
a. monarchy
b. totalitarianism
c. democracy
d. others
(Canada is a parliamentary democracy)

Most of the students came to Wellington because their marks weren't high enough for them to get into McGill. Many of them were Jews who couldn't get into McGill because of the quota system.

Into this benign backwater of mediocrity came a young professor of English literature named Theo Hall. That was in the autumn of 1952, about five years after he had married Miriam Peltier. Theo, who had been hired to run the English department, inherited a staff of superannuated high school teachers, middle-class housewives with a penchant for poetry, and old graduates who were writing their autobiographies. He could have got a better job at a big American university. He could have stayed on at Magdalen College, Oxford, and become a fellow. But Theo had faith. Three hundred years before him the Jesuits had paddled up to Hochelaga to pitch their Bibles against the tomahawks of the Iroquois and the Sioux. Since then Hochelaga had become Montreal. The pagans had been banished and the Christians held the fort. Theo was made of the same intrepid stuff as those Jesuits. Armed with the texts of Wilson, Trilling, and Leavis, he hoped to wrest Montreal from the grasp of the philistines.

He was a tall man with tired eyes and a small mouth. His smile was wan, condescending, like the smile of a novitiate showing a group of peasants through St. Peter's. He would have liked to have been a poet but he was not morbid about his limitations and did not envy the success of others. He had gone the other way, using the word Art like a man at his prayers. He hoped to organize the English department of the college along saner lines and to found a little magazine that would print the best in Canadian writing and criticism. Theo began with the college library. He went over it catalogue by catalogue and before a month had gone by he had ordered seven hundred new books. He overhauled the curriculum of the English courses and by the end of his first academic year had managed to get rid of a lot of faculty dead wood, replacing them with bright young lecturers of his own choosing.

Disappointments were plentiful. *Direction* did not inspire or proselytize in Canadian academic circles. A lot of material came in but no forceful talents emerged. After the third issue, the magazine settled down to a circulation of about seven hundred copies. Two hundred were sold in the United States, a hundred or so in England, and the rest in Canada. The Russian Embassy took three copies. But among smart people his magazine was known as *No Direction*. Theo's students proved yet another disappointment. Most of them did well enough in examinations but Theo had a compulsion, almost neurotic in its intensity, to surround himself with disciples and to discover talent. So when he chanced on a more than usually bright student his enthusiasm leaped. He brought home his prodigies one after the other and one after the other they turned out ordinary spirits. His hopes thwarted, he turned cruelly on his would-be talents. Susceptible to the exasperations of spirit which characterize most reformers, he tended to suffer vulgarity in smaller spirits as a personal affront. He was a social democrat. Encounters with almost any amusement designed for the crowd made him choke up and clench his fists. He did not find it easy to cope with society.

Miriam tried to help. She pampered him when he was depressed and when his enthusiasm was at its most feverish she tried to calm him down. She adored him for his angers and helped in all his exploits against bigotry without complaint or second thoughts, but she believed in him rather than in his causes. If someone, among their friends, remarked that marriage didn't work the inevitable reply was: "But look at the Halls."

That afternoon, in the first week of November, Theo came home early from classes. He chucked his briefcase on the sofa and grinned boyishly. "I've got somebody coming for drinks."

"Oh-oh. Here we go again."

They kissed in a perfunctory way.

"You look all in. Bad day?"

"So-so."

She smiled helpfully. Theo slumped back on the sofa and shut his eyes. Sometimes, when she smiled at him like that, he felt hopelessly inept. In the past few months their intimate moments had been characterized by a poverty of sorts. She seemed bored, her enthusiasms were rehearsed. Perhaps we should have a child, he thought.

Miriam served tea. "All right. Tell me about it," she said.

"He's a taxi driver. Evening College student. Noah Adler. Jewish with accent. Living in a rented room on Dorchester Street, hangdog look."

"What time you expecting him?"

"Four. In twenty minutes."

"Shall I ask him to stay for dinner?"

"Only if you like him."

Theo sipped his tea quietly. Miriam got up, put Beethoven's Fifth Symphony on the gramophone, and then sat down again. They were listening to the symphonies in order. After the symphonies they would turn to the concertos. Theo slumped back on the sofa with his eyes shut and reached out for her hand. She accepted it wordlessly, like the morning paper. She watched him. When he relaxed his long body went limp, dead, as if he was grateful for any kind of respite. Miriam, however, couldn't sit still. She let go of his hand and walked over to the window. She felt as though she wanted to rip something apart. Herself, perhaps. She squashed her cigarette in the ashtray on the window-sill.

When Noah arrived, about three-quarters of an hour later, Miriam opened the door for him: Theo had gone out to do a bit of shopping.

"Is this Professor Hall's apartment?"

"You must be Adler. I'm Mrs. Hall. But Miriam will do."

Noah followed her into the living-room. The walls were grey and the furniture functional. One wall was papered pink. Two walls were lined with bookcases made up of bricks and unfinished pinewood boards. Other books spilled over onto the floor. Several prints by very modern painters hung on the walls. The room had a curious quality that made him expect to be led into another and more oppressive room as soon as his papers had been verified. Miriam frightened him. He wished that she would do something wrong, knock over a chair or rip her stockings. She was quite tall with warm brown eyes and black hair. Her skin was dark. But she seemed awfully clean, fresh, as if she had just stepped out of a bath. She was wearing a brown sweater and a green corduroy skirt and moccasins. Her glib poise seemed calculated to undermine him and he hung back sullenly. She was the first modern, sophisticated woman whom he had ever met. A woman entirely unlike his aunts, cousins, and former girlfriends. He found it difficult to believe in her. There seemed to be no flaw or error in her manner. He felt dazed, and couldn't remember what to do with his hands, whether it was proper to sit down or pick up a magazine or what. In desperation he pointed at a Jackson Pollock. "Did you do that?"

"Oh."

"What's wrong – I'm sorry . . ."

"Nothing. Here, let me take your jacket. Theo's gone out to get some soda-water. Sit down, I won't eat you. Here, have a cigarette."

He accepted the cigarette and put a match to it before he remembered that he was supposed to light hers first. He put out the match swiftly. Lit another one, and pushed it towards her.

"Theo says that you drive a taxi."

"That's right."

"Is it fun?"

"It's not bad."

She bit her lip. "Cold, isn't it?" she said.

"Yes."

"Would you like a drink?"

"Yes."

She tossed a copy of the *New Statesman & Nation* at him. "Here, I won't bother you."

Noah pretended to read. Panofsky had used to get the *New Statesman & Nation*, and he sometimes glanced through it in the library. He enjoyed the classified section most and he had once sent them an ad.: "Fascist meat-eater coming to settle in London will exchange fencing lessons for furnace-room with prejudiced family" – but he had had no reply.

She handed him a glass of sherry and he gulped it down quickly. Already too late he noticed that she had only sipped at hers. She refilled his glass and this time he drank more delicately. She watched him. He was dressed shabbily. Poor Theo, she thought. He doesn't know what he's let himself in for. He felt her eyes on him like a humiliation. He looked down at his hands and saw that his fingernails were dirty. He hid his hands in his pockets.

"There's an interesting article on the Jewish question in it," she said. "I think Theo would like to discuss it with you."

Briefly, Noah was tempted to go into his they-used-to-beat-me-up-on-my-way-to-school routine, but instead, he said: "Which Jewish question?"

"I beg your pardon?"

Noah jumped up and began to walk up and down the room. "Why couldn't he be here when I came? Why do you look at me as if I was a freak or something?"

"You didn't have to come."

"That's right. I think I'll go."

"Go ahead."

He hesitated.

"Go on. Nobody's stopping you."

"My manners are bad, eh?"

"Atrocious."

He began to make excited circles with his hands, groping for words. "I'm nervous. I guess that's it."

"Why?"

"I dunno. Can . . . *May* I have another drink?"

"Scotch?"

"Yeah. *Yes*, I mean."

"Will you stay for dinner, Noah?"

She did not invite him to stay because she liked him. But, immediately, she had recognized that he came from a poor family. She wanted to impress him. She, too, had come from a poor family.

"Are you being polite or . . ."

"Oh, stop being such an ass!"

There was another pause. Their anger had embarrassed both of them. She must be very well-educated, he thought, rich. He wanted badly to say something that would fit. Finally, he asked for the toilet. She indicated the door.

Safely in the toilet, Noah briefly considered an escape through the window, then he began to study his surroundings. The bathtub and toilet bowl were made of green enamel. There were many taps over the tub. The floors and walls were made of green tiles. Numerous huge pink bath-towels hung in racks. They were all initialled. He opened the medicine chest. Salts. Perfumes. Nylon brushes hung on hooks. The bathtub, he noticed, was sunk into the floor. Noah was amazed. He remembered that several years ago Hoppie Drazen had bragged that he had been in such a toilet at one of Claire Kinsburg's parties in Outremont. But Noah hadn't believed him. I must visit Uncle Max, he thought quickly. He's just the kind of guy to have something like this. *But he'd be joking.* He saw, for the first time, the roll of toilet paper half-concealed in an opening in the wall near the toilet bowl. It was pink. Quickly, obeying an old school instinct, he ripped off a few sheets and shoved them into his pocket. He flushed the toilet before leaving just to keep up appearances.

Theo had arrived.

"H'lo Noah. Sorry. But I had a bastard of a time getting what I wanted."

On special occasions Theo tried to speak colloquially but the effect was usually embarrassing.

"I've asked Noah to stay for dinner."

"Wonderful."

Gradually, Noah began to feel easier with them. Theo had meant to probe him about his background and ideas but Noah asked most of the questions. Theo told him about London, Paris, and Italy. He talked to him about books and music. Noah listened. Names stuck to him. Pound, Klee, Auden, Kafka. Names he did not know. Words also. Words like rococo, jejune, *déjà vu*, and *avant-garde*. Words he did not know the meaning of. He saw Theo as a kind of hero. His talk drugged him. Theo was happy too. The give-and-take talk of Oxford had had small rewards. Most fellowship students were beyond wonder. But Noah was different. Talking to him Theo suddenly got an acute notion of his own powers. I will mould this man, he thought.

I will make him big. Knowing. (I will make him grateful.) His head flooded. He talked on and on ecstatically.

Theo talked. Noah listened. Miriam watched.

Noah felt her eyes on him. He felt her body as a living, yearning thing, and that embarrassed him. He did not dare to think of her in that way.

Miriam, most of all, was conscious of the excitement. She felt vibrations in the room that had more meaning than only drink or only talk. Theo mustn't be hurt, she thought. This thought alarmed her. Why should he be hurt?

She watched Noah, not liking what she saw, but feeling herself drawn to him all the same. He was a raw man with hurt eyes and a clumsy kind of vigour about him that she had not encountered before. She smoked and drank thoughtfully. Something which had stayed dim and uncomplaining within her for years was beginning to stir. She hoped to purge it with drink and memory. But drink sharpened the images and memory counted against her. She recalled the affairs with faceless men that they had all had in Oxford. Loving being highly recommended for ennui, like a glass of water in a gulp for the hiccups. But Noah, she thought, I don't even know how to talk to him. He would find my sophistication hard. Poor Theo doesn't realize what's happening, she thought. Noah's a ruthless man.

Noah seemed to be absorbed in Theo's talk. But she felt that he was in no way personally involved or friendly. He shrugged off Theo's smiles, his generosity, in a superfluous way, as if he had guessed – or had known beforehand – that Theo's kindness was the kindness of a baffled man. She hated Noah at that moment. He frightened her.

Poetry had been denied Theo. Love also. But the long frugal years of study and scholarships, of frayed jackets and hand-rolled cigarettes were behind him. He had consumed the books. But who knows at what cost? What does he think of when he is alone in his study?

Does he detest the books? Suddenly she saw the books that lined the walls as a great weight pressing down on him. Burn them, she thought. Burn them, Theo. She looked at him and despised him for his simplicity. He's happy, she thought. He doesn't know what's happening. Theo had struggled, and this impudent boy will pick his brains for a few months and walk away with Theo in his pocket. He will read what he needs and turn instinctively away from the rest. But even *he* doesn't realize what's going on. Imagine, she thought, he looks up to Theo. He will come to hate him. "Hall? A plodder. Well-meaning, but no insights." She turned to Noah, looking at him as if he had already said that.

"How do you feel about it, darling?"

"What? . . . I'm afraid I . . ."

"I was just telling Noah that we could fix up the study for him. He's paying ten dollars a week rent where he is. Here, he'd have books. The opportunity to meet people. He can't get on with his studies driving a taxi eight hours a day. We could manage wonderfully. He could mark my papers. He – what do you say?"

She didn't say anything.

"Well?"

"Would you mind sleeping on a cot, Noah?"

He wasn't aware of the irony in her manner. "No. Not at all. But I'd have to pay rent. I wouldn't think of it otherwise . . ."

No. You wouldn't, she thought. You're not that generous. "We'll discuss that later."

"The sooner you move in the better, Noah," Theo said warmly.

Theo turned to Miriam in bed later that night. "I suppose I should have asked you first. About his moving in, I mean."

"Oh."

"What's wrong?"

"Nothing."

"No. Tell me, darling."

"Nothing I could explain."

He put his hand on her arm. Her flesh was warm.

"I hope that John doesn't make an advertising man out of him," Theo said.

"John? Noah wouldn't have anything to do with *him*."

"You say that with such certainty. How would you know?"

"Let's go to sleep," she said.

A half-hour later he felt for her in bed but she wasn't there. Her body was a habit, a comfort, to him and he found it difficult to sleep without her. She was standing by the window and smoking.

"What's wrong, Miriam?"

"I don't know."

"Coming to bed?"

"Soon. You go to sleep."

He waited. There was that flicker of expectancy in her eyes. He knew what that meant. An ordeal – a pretence – for him; and for her – frustration. Afterwards neither of them would sleep. She would comfort her defeated man. A woman unsatisfied – but triumphant. He waited fifteen minutes, and then said: "I was just thinking. Remember that night before I went overseas, the night of my last leave . . . You were Chuck's girl then, weren't you? I mean . . ."

"Chuck is dead."

"I didn't mean *that*. I was just trying to . . . I'm not jealous, darling. Besides, that sort of thing doesn't mean anything. I know that!"

"Yes. I know you know."

"Marrying a woman doesn't mean you own her."

"Theo. Are you happy with me? Seriously."

"Why, certainly. Of course, darling. I don't know what I'd do without you."

"I'm happy, too. I am. I'm coming to bed."

II

Montreal is cleanly defined on cold autumn nights. Each building, each tree, seems to exist as a separate and shivering object, exposed to the winds again after a flabby summer. Downtown the neon trembles like fractures in the dark. Fuzziness, bugs, groups of idlers blurring cigar-store windows, have all retreated together. Whores no longer stroll up and down St. Lawrence Boulevard, but beckon from the shelter of doorways or linger longer at nightclub bars. The mountain, which all summer long had seemed a gentle green slope, looms up brutal against the night sky. Streets seem longer, noises more hard.

Autumn is stingy, Noah thought unhappily.

Walking back to his room, down St. Catherine Street, he stopped several times to blow on his hands. He peered into the window of Dinty Moore's restaurant where sporty men sat around telling masculine jokes and cleaning their fingernails. Later, he thought, they will move on to various nightclubs where they'll drink cool drinks with bored, anonymous women. But they won't drink too much.

A man yelled: "GZET! Layst noos! GZET! Payph! GZET! GZET!"

Bums sprawled on the concrete seats on Phillips Square, and across the street in Morgan's windows, cool mannequins like all our next-door neighbours prepared to pass this and every night on Beautyrest mattresses.

The sign in Rand's Clothing window said:

SMILE AT PEOPLE
It takes 72 muscles to frown – only 14 to smile

When he got back to his room he began to feel that something was wrong. She doesn't want me to move in, he thought. He got out his pad and wrote down, Pound, Eliot, Kafka, Auden. Then, remembering Theo's library, he got up in disgust. There must be some other way, he thought. It would be crazy to read all those books. There isn't enough time. Noah rubbed his jaw thoughtfully. She's perfect, that woman. They're *Goyim*.

Noah's first encounter with the *Goyim* had been in Prevost, long ago. Prevost is in the Laurentians, about ten miles past St. Jerome. . . .

That bright, cloudless Friday morning in the summer of 1941, Noah, Gas, and Hoppie were to meet on the balcony of Old Annie's candy store. They were going to climb the mountain behind the Nine Cottages to get to Lac Gandon, where the *Goyim* were.

Hoppie turned up first.

Old Annie, who was a tiny, grey-haired widow with black, mournful eyes, looked the boy up and down suspiciously. A first-aid kit and a scout knife were strapped to his belt. "What is?" she asked. "A revolution? A war?" Hoppie grimaced. "He who hears no evil, speaks no evil," he said. Old Annie's store was a yellow shack that was all but covered with red-and-green signs advertising Kik and Sweet Caporal cigarettes. She wasn't called Old Annie because she was sixty-two. Long ago, in Lithuania, the first three children born to her parents had not survived their infancy. So the village wise man had suggested that if another child was born to them they should call her *alte* (old) immediately, and God would understand.

Gas arrived next. He had a BB gun and a package of sandwiches.

"Knock, knock," he said.

"Who's there?" Hoppie asked.

"Ago."

"Ago who?"

"Aw, go tell your mother she wants you."

Behind Old Annie's store was the yellow field that was used as the market. Early every Friday morning the French Canadian farmers arrived with poultry, vegetables, and fruit. They were a hard, sceptical bunch, but the Jewish wives were a pretty tough crowd themselves, and by late afternoon the farmers were worn out and grateful to get away. The women, who were ruthless bargainers, spoke a mixture of French, English, and Yiddish with the farmers. "So *fiel*, M'nsieur, for dis *kleine* chicken? *Vous* crazy?"

Pinky's Squealer saw the two boys sitting on the steps, waiting for Noah. He approached them diffidently. "Where you goin'?" he asked.

"To China," Gas said.

When the Squealer's mother wanted him to go to the toilet she would step out on her balcony and yell: "Dollink, dollink, time to water the teapot." Pinky, who was the Squealer's cousin, was seventeen years old. His proper name was Milton Fishman. He was rather pious, and conducted services at Camp Mahia. The Squealer was his informer.

"I've got a quarter," Pinky's Squealer said.

"Grease it well," Gas said.

Those Jews who lived on St. Dominique Street, St. Urbain, Rachel, and City Hall clubbed together and took cottages in Prevost for the summer. How they raised the money, what sacrifices they made, were comparatively unimportant – the children had to have sun. Prevost has a very small native population and most of the cottages are owned by French Canadians who live in Shawbridge, just up the hill. The C.P.R. railway station is in Shawbridge. Prevost, at the foot of the hill, is separated from Shawbridge by that bridge reputedly built by a man named Shaw. It is a confusion of temporary clapboard shacks and cottages strewn over hills and fields and joined by dirt roads and an elaborate system of paths. The centre of the village is at the foot of the bridge. Here are Zimmerman's, Blatt's, The River-View Inn, Stein the Butcher, and – off on the dirt road to the right – the synagogue and the beach. In 1941 Zimmerman and Blatt still ran highly competitive general stores on opposite sides of the highway. Both stores were sprawling dumpy buildings badly in need of a paint job and had dance halls and huge balconies – where you could also dance – attached. But Zimmerman had a helper named Zelda and that gave him the edge over Blatt. Zelda's signs were posted all over Zimmerman's.

Over the fruit stall:

> AN ORANGE ISN'T A BASEBALL. DON'T HANDLE WHAT
> YOU DON'T WANT. THINK OF THE NEXT CUSTOMER

Over the cash:

> IF YOU CAN GET IT CHEAPER BY THAT GANGSTER
> ACROSS THE HIGHWAY YOU CAN HAVE IT FOR NOTHING

However, if you could get it cheaper at Blatt's, Zelda always proved that what you had bought was not as fresh, or of a cheaper quality.

The beach was a field of spiky grass and tree stumps. Plump, middle-aged women, their flesh burned pink, spread out blankets and squatted in their bras and bloomers, playing poker, smoking, and drinking Cokes. The vacationing furriers and pressers seldom wore bathing-suits either. They didn't swim. They set up card-tables and chairs and played pinochle solemnly, smoking foul cigars and cursing the sun. The children dashed in and out among them playing tag or tossing a ball about. Boys staggered between sprawling sun-bathers, lugging pails packed with ice and shouting: "Ice-cold drinks. Chaw-lit bahs. Cigarettes!" Occasionally, a woman, her wide-brimmed straw hat flapping as she waddled from table to table, her smile as big as her aspirations, gold teeth glittering, would intrude on the card players, asking – nobody's forcing, mind you – if they would like to buy a raffle in aid of the Mizrachi Fresh Air Fund or the J.N.F. Naked babies bawled. Plums, peaches, watermelons, were consumed, pits and peels being tossed indiscriminately on the grass. The yellow river was unfailingly condemned by the Health Board during the last two weeks of August, when the polio scare was at its worst. But the children paid no attention. They shrieked with delight whenever one of their huge mothers descended into the water briefly to duck herself – once, twice – warn the children against swimming out too far and then return – refreshed – to her poker game. The French Canadians were too shocked to complain, but the priests sometimes preached sermons against the indecency of the Jews. (But as Mort Shub said: "Liss'n, it's their job. A priest's gotta make a living too.") At night most of the Jews crowded into the dance-halls at Zimmerman's and Blatt's. The kids, like Noah and Gas and Hoppie, climbed up the windows, and, peashooters in their mouths, took careful aim at the dancers' legs before firing. Fridays, the wives worked extremely hard cleaning and cooking for the sabbath. Everybody got dressed up in the afternoon in anticipation of the arrival of the fathers, who were met in Shawbridge, most of them having arrived on the 6:15 weekend excursion train. Then the procession through Shawbridge, down the hill and across the bridge, began. That event always horrified the residents of that village. Who were those strange, cigar-smoking men, burdened down with watermelons and Kik bottles, yelling to their children, laughing, slapping their wives' behinds and – worst of all – waving to the sombre Scots who sat petrified on their balconies?

Noah showed up last.

"Pinky's Squealer wants to come with us," Gas said.

"Did you tell him where we're going?"

"Ixnay," Gas said. "You think I'm crazy?"

"He's got a quarter," Hoppie said.

Pinky's Squealer showed Noah the quarter.

"All right," Noah said.

Old Annie, shaking her head sadly, watched the four boys start off across the fields. Noah led. Hoppie, who came next, was Rabbi Drazen's son. He was a skinny boy with big brown eyes. His father had a small but devoted following. Hoppie hung around the synagogue every evening and stopped old men on their way to prayers.

"Gimme a nickel and I'll give you a blessink." He didn't do too badly. "I'm holy as hell," he told Noah one evening.

"What's the difference between a mailbox and an elephant's ass?" Gas asked.

"I dunno," Pinky's Squealer replied quickly.

"I wouldn't send *you* to mail my letters."

Gas was plump, fair-haired, and covered with freckles.

They turned up the dirt road that led to the Nine Cottages, the sun beating down ruthlessly on their brown bodies. They passed Kravitz's cottage, Becky Goldberg's place, and the shapeless shack that housed ten shapeless Cohens.

There was still lots of blue in the sky but where there were clouds the clouds got very dark. The tall grass at the foot of the mountain was stiff and yellow and made you itch. There were also mushy patches where bulrushes grew, but they avoided those. The mountain was cool, but the boys had a long climb and descent ahead of them. The soft plump ground they tramped on was padded with pine cones, needles, and dead leaves. Sunlight moved deviously among the birch and maple and fir trees and the mountain had a dark, damp smell to it. There was the occasional cawing of crows: they saw two woodpeckers: and, once, a humming-bird. They reached the top of the mountain around one o'clock and sat down on an open patch of ground to eat their lunch. Gas chased around after grasshoppers, storing them in an old mayonnaise jar that had two holes punched in the top. After they had finished their sandwiches they started out again, this time down the other side of the mountain. The foliage thickened, and in their eagerness to get along quickly they scratched their legs and arms in the bush, stumbling into the occasional ditch concealed by leaves and bruising their ankles against stones. They heard voices in the distance. Noah, who had been given the BB gun, pulled back the catch. Gas picked up a rock, Hoppie unstrapped his scout knife. "We'll be late for *shabus*," Pinky's Squealer said. "Maybe we should go back?"

"Go ahead," Hoppie said. "But watch out for snakes, eh?"

"I didn't say anything!"

Voices, laughter, too, now, came splashing loudly through the trees. The ground began to level off and, just ahead, they saw the beach. There were real canoes, a diving-board, and lots of big crazy-coloured umbrellas and deck-chairs. The boys approached the beach cautiously, crouching in the bushes. Noah was amazed. The men were tall and the women were awfully pretty, lying out in the sun there, just like that, not afraid of anything. There was no yelling or watermelon peels or women in bloomers. Everything was so clean. Beautiful, almost.

Gas was the first to notice the soft-drink stand. He turned to Pinky's Squealer. "You've got a quarter. Go get us Pepsis."

"Gas should go," Hoppie said. "He's the least Jewish-looking of the gang. Look at his nose – Christ! They'll take him for a *Goy* easy."

"You can have my quarter."

"Aw go water your tea-kettle," Gas said. "Maybe I don't look as Jewish as you or Noah, but they can always tell by pulling down your pants . . ."

They all giggled.

"It's not so funny," Hoppie said. "That's how they found out about my uncle, who was killed in Russia."

"You're all chicken," Noah said. "I'm going. But I'm having my Coke right out there on the beach. If you want anything to drink you'll have to come too."

A convertible Ford pulled away, and that exposed the sign to them. Gas noticed it first. Suddenly, he pointed. "Hey! Look!"

THIS BEACH IS RESTRICTED TO GENTILES

That changed everything. Noah, who got very excited, said that they should hang around until evening, and then, when the beach was deserted, steal the sign.

"Yeah, and walk back in the dark, eh?" Pinky's Squealer said. "It's Friday, you know. Ain't *your* Paw coming?"

Gas and Hoppie looked puzzled. Both of them had been forbidden to play with Noah by their mothers. Pinky's Squealer made sense, but they did not want to be associated with him and if Noah intended to stay, they would look foolish having left him behind. Noah wanted to stay. Having his father up for the weekend usually meant two days of quarrelling.

"Aw, in a hundred years we'll all be dead," Gas said.

Pinky's Squealer waited, kicking the stump of a tree absently. "If you come with me, Hoppie, you can have my quarter."

"Watch out for snakes," Hoppie said.

Pinky's Squealer ran off.

They waited. The afternoon dragged on slowly. But at last the sun was lower in the sky and a stronger breeze started up. Only a few stragglers remained on the beach.

"Is a Gentile a protestant and a catholic too?" Hoppie asked.

"Yeah," Noah said.

"But they're different," Hoppie said.

"Different," Gas said. "You know the difference between Hitler and Mussolini?"

Noah said that as it was getting late they would have to chance it, stragglers and all. The few couples that remained were intent on each other and wouldn't notice them if they were smart. Noah said that he and Gas should stroll out on to the beach, approaching the sign from different directions, nonchalantly. It didn't look like it was stuck very solidly into the sand. Hoppie was to yell if he saw anybody coming for them. He had stones and the BB gun.

So the two boys walked out innocently on the beach. Noah whistled. Gas pretended to be looking for something. The wind kicked up gusts of sand, and the sun, quite low now, was a blaze in the opposite hills. Suddenly, frantically, the two boys were yanking at the sign. Gas roared with laughter, tears rolled down his cheeks. Noah cursed. They heard, piercing the quiet, a high-pitched yell. "Look out!" Gas let go, and ran off. "Hurry!" Noah persisted. A man was running towards him with a canoe paddle in his hands. Noah gave one last, frenzied tug, and the sign broke loose. The man was about twenty feet away and already swinging his paddle. His eyes were wild. "You son-of-a-bitch!" Noah swerved, and raced swiftly for the bushes. A shower of pebbles bounced off his back. The paddle swooshed through the air behind him. But he was fast. Once in the bushes he scampered madly off into the mountain. He ran and ran and ran. Until finally, clutching the sign in his hands, he tumbled down on the pine needles, his heart thumping wildly. . . .

Noah sat down on the window-sill of his rented room. I couldn't find Gas, he remembered, but Hoppie was waiting for me in the bushes. It got dark fast, and – of course – we got lost. I wasn't frightened. I had the sign, didn't I? But Hoppie was scared. We didn't have a flashlight. For all we knew we might come out of the woods again back at Lac Gandon. We had stopped climbing and had reached a level bit of ground when suddenly we heard many voices. Light beams shot through the darkness. We hid the sign under a mess of leaves and climbed up the nearest tree – our pockets filled with stones. The voices and the lights came nearer. Remembering, Noah laughed warmly. I think every Yid in Prevost was on the mountain that night. Where they got all those pitchforks and clubs and sticks, God knows. Hoppie and I never thought we'd be grateful to Pinky's Squealer, but we were that night. We slid down the tree and uncovered the sign, and that was our night of glory in Prevost. Nothing was too good for us. Sunday morning, Noah remembered, he, Mort Shub, Gas, and Hoppie had planted the sign on the beach. They had got some paint first. When the people had come out to swim, they had read:

THIS BEACH IS RESTRICTED TO LITVAKS

That was some time, Noah thought fondly. It really was. He leaned back on the bed, and smiling almost imperceptibly, smoked with his hands clasped behind his head. Pinky's Squealer, he thought, is studying to be a rabbi now, like his cousin Milton Pinky Fishman. Noah got up. Miriam, he thought, resembles those pretty women on the beach at Lac Gandon. *I did not make my mother to suffer or my father bewildered, or my grandfather hard. I should have had the right to begin with my birth.* He sat up and rubbed his jaw absently. *It's all absurd, but here I am.* Glancing out of the window he saw a blackboard of sky with several stars chalked up in yellow and an imperfectly rounded moon done up in orange. It would be all right, he thought, to reach out and pull down a star or two to look at. They can't be as big or as far away as they say. They're only stars, he thought. If you were tall enough you could pick them like berries. "Miriam," he said softly.

III

Something was happening to the old man. His anger and his words were still law for the family, but Shloime and Ida disobeyed him behind his back, something they would not have done so freely before. He complained of rheumatism and a weight on his heart and sometimes he did not go down to the coal yard in the mornings. He had a nap after lunch. He felt the damp November days in his bones. During the afternoon he read Talmud and in the evening he studied with the other old men in the synagogue. Had I been willing to let my children fend for themselves, he thought, had I followed my natural bent, I could have been a scribe – and Noah would have had respect. . . .

"Max wants for us to move into an apartment in Outremont. I should retire, he says. What should I do, I ask, if I retire. What . . ."

"He means only good, Melech. Thank God we haven't got for children such bums as Edelman. You know de Edelman boy was in jail again? A Yiddish boy. Now they will say we are robbers on top of everything. As if we didn't have enough. So what would you like? Sons like Panofsky has? Communists yet. You see his Aaron? Everybody loved Aaron. So. What is? He sits in front of de store in that wheelchair smoking cigarettes like a chimney. Where are his legs? His legs are in Spain. At least we have boys who are pushers. Max, you watch. Maxie will be all right."

"Max. A lot he knows."

Autumn had come swiftly to the ghetto. The leaves had turned briefly red and yellow on the trees and then tumbled downwards dead. Black clouds swept by fast in the lowering sky, and the prosperous who lived in Outremont, Max among them, brought their families back from their summer homes in the Laurentians. The McGill freshmen among their children wondered whether they would be asked to join a good fraternity or sorority. The boys bought pipes and blazers and the girls tried on party dresses. Meanwhile those who had already graduated began to exchange pipes for cigars: party dresses brought in a good return in engagement rings. He who had failed opened up an insurance office, or, if she were a girl, went in for social service work or nursing.

Ida couldn't hear her parents talking. Upstairs, she sucked impatiently on a peppermint and listened to the Make-Believe Ballroom.

> "Right now, folks, we've got a swell ditty coming up from the King of Sobs. *I Believe*, number 2 on your CJAD Hit Parade. Plug. My salary goes up each time I mention CJAD. Can you hear me, boss?"

Don Bishop laughed. So did Ida.

> "*I Believe* by – you guessed it! – Johnny Ray. This one is from Ida to Stanley. Are you listening, Stanley? I'll bet he is! Let's have that platter, Lou."

Ida had gone to Goodman's hotel, in Val Morin, for her summer vacation and that's where she had met Stanley. But Stanley did not come from an orthodox family and Ida was worried about introducing him to her father, so they saw each other secretly.

A shaded yellow light hung low over each of the eight tables in the Royal Billiard Room. Smoke, eight clouds for eight suns, thickened under and around the bulbs. The long and narrow room reeked of french fried potatoes, the walls were heavy with soot. Men watched the players from the benches that flanked the walls. Occasionally they made derogatory remarks: but otherwise they did not talk much. The snooker balls clacked together again and again making a hard, clean sound. Shloime, who was also known as Kid Lightning, was playing The Sleeper on the second table. The game was for five dollars, Shloime, who was a good player, was up twenty-two points and they were already on the coloured balls. The Sleeper, who in his wakeful hours had been arrested four times, once for arson, twice for petty larceny, and another time for shoplifting, cursed each time he shot and always watched to make sure that Shloime kept one foot on the floor. Each time Shloime made a run he accused him of fluking. Shloime was excited. Not because of the five dollars, no, but because he was being watched by Lou The Hook Edelman. Each time he sunk a difficult shot Shloime looked up at The Hook and grinned. The Hook had his boys with him. It could mean anything, Shloime thought.

"You waitin' for Christmas? Shoot," The Sleeper said.

Shloime took aim patiently, and sunk the green ball in the side pocket. The cue ball swerved back and rolled into perfect position behind the brown ball. Shloime knocked the brown hard into the corner pocket and the cue ball zoomed fast down the cloth, nearly scratched in the far corner pocket, jumped clear and rolled lazily up towards the blue ball which was frozen against the band. Shloime leaned his cue against the table and rubbed the chalk off his hand. "Pay up," he said.

"You blind? Dey're still three balls on the table."

"This jerk believes in miracles yet," Shloime said, turning to the others.

The Sleeper flung his cue down on the table and rushed towards Shloime. "Who's a jerk, eh?"

"You tell me. I'm lissnink."

The Hook got up and came between them. He turned to The Sleeper. "You're a jerk. Okay? Now give the kid his five fish."

"Dis is our business," The Sleeper said, beating his chest.

"I just made it mine. Okay, *jerk*. I'll count ten."

The Sleeper flung a five-dollar bill down on the table and then grabbed his coat and rushed towards the door. He stopped in the doorway. "You can't count no higher'n ten, Hook. You ex-con you. Hankink is too good fur you." Then he slammed the door and rushed down the street.

"Heroes." The Hook shrugged his shoulders and turned to Shloime. "You play me now. Okay, pal?"

"Sure. But it's on me, Hook. I'll pay."

"Naw. We'll play for the fin. But you and me, we're pals. We got business to talk to you after de game. Me, and the boys."

"I'll be right back."

Shloime washed the chalk off his hands and combed his hair in the toilet. Various comments had been scrawled over the urinals.

"The next Guy who comes In may be Barefoot!"

"Jeanne sa 2146."

And written in yellow chalk:

"A merry xmas to all our readers."

Shloime hurried back to the table and chalked up his cue joyously. A whole new world seemed to be opening up to him.

Wolf was always grateful for the night. But in recent years he had spent less and less time in Leah's bed and he did not know whether that was the usual thing or not. He would have liked to ask his brothers, but he was too ashamed. Nat, he remembered, had tied a cow-bell to the bedsprings on his wedding night. Wolf giggled. He had paid Nat back by placing a huge carrot and two onions between the sheets on *his* wedding night, arranging the vegetables just where Sarah couldn't miss them. Remembering, Wolf nearly giggled again. He stopped himself just in time, afraid of waking Leah. Leah had to be watched. She had had a difficult summer. She complained of headaches and pains in her shoulder, insomnia, and shortness of breath. She had had her spectacles changed, but that hadn't helped. Her brother Harry, the doctor, had put her on a diet. Once, when she had been laid up for a week, Wolf had suggested that he should phone Noah, but she had said no, absolutely no. Wolf hadn't argued. Why should I look for trouble? he had thought.

But things weren't so good, anyway. She didn't even argue with him, and business wasn't so hot. Well, the autumn was always slow. What could you expect? Things would pick up during the winter. They always did.

"Leah. You sleeping?"

"No."

"You want an Aspirin?"

"No."

"It might do you good?"

"No."

"Leah. I want you should listen. I mean not to interrupt. I . . ."

"Who's interrupting?"

"No. What I mean is you should listen without being angry or stopping me to put in this or that. All right?"

"Go ahead."

"I spoke to Paw today. I said to him just like that how I am the oldest boy and it's not so nice for people that I shouldn't be a partner. We should be Wolf Adler & Son. With a new sign and everything. Well, he didn't say no, Leah. He didn't say yes but he didn't say no.

You know what else? I said Max is younger than me and he lives in Outremont. That's what. I said to him, Paw. Paw, I said. You should retire and I'll take care of everything. We could split fifty-fifty. You should see the way he walks around the yard these days, Leah. A regular dreamer. Anyway, Leah, what I mean to say is he didn't say yes but he didn't say no. That's a start, you know. Other times he would walk away as soon as I started to talk. I was thinking, Leah, that after he – well, you know. I'll sell the business. Don't think I haven't got ideas. I read in the *Digest* last week how a man made a fortune in the gift business. You start a club which costs ten or twenty dollars a year to join. Each member when he joins sends in a list of occasions he mustn't forget. His wedding anniversary, family birthdays, and so on. A week before each occasion you send him a letter saying next week, for instance, it's your wife's birthday. 'Choose from the following gifts and return form with your choice marked X. We'll attend to the rest.' You can make a pile, I'm telling you."

"My husband is waiting for his own father to die."

"Who said? Don't talk like . . ."

"I'm going to sleep."

"Leah. . . ."

"I'm going to sleep. I don't care any longer, Wolf. You're yes a partner, no a partner, I don't care. My life is over – finished. For that I have my father to thank. And Noah – Noah . . . I'm going to sleep, I said."

Leah stared at the wall, her eyes wet. If Father were alive, she thought, Noah wouldn't have left. They would have had a lot to talk about. *The old man, the poet, came in and sat down at the kitchen table. Nu, Leah, he said, Nu. She sat down on his lap and laughed. He kissed her and rubbed his beard against her cheek. When Noah came in from school she made tea for both of them, and then sat down and listened to them talk. Noah had won another scholarship, everybody was talking. I am his daughter and his mother. From time to time one or the other of her men turned to her and smiled.* Wolf began to snore, and that awakened her.

That night he had undressed in front of her. She had wanted not to look but the very revulsion she felt for his body had compelled her to, and so she had watched, surreptitiously but fascinated. She had watched him scratch his back and then slump down on the edge of his bed and pick his toes. He had seemed deeply satisfied but, as the light was bad, she had not been able to tell if he had actually been smiling. She had seen him scratch under his armpits and then smell his hand. That's when she had turned to the wall. Turned quickly, repudiating him.

Wolf snored. He dreamed that his father was dead. A mysterious woman handed him a key. He didn't ask her what it was for. He knew without asking.

The next morning, Friday, Melech Adler did not come into the office, so when people rang up and asked for "Mr. Adler" Wolf said "Speaking" instead of "Hold on a sec." It was a grey, cold day. Wolf stood by the window watching his workers. He and the men played pranks on each other. One day, for instance, Wolf fixed a wire to Paquette's lunch pail and attached the wire to an electric switch. When Paquette reached for his pail he got an electric shock. The next day Armand blew up a prophylactic and secured it to the tail of Wolf's jacket. But they had to watch out for old Mr. Adler: he seldom approved of their antics. Wolf walked into the inner office and sat down at his father's desk. Leaning back in the swivel chair, he stared at the wall safe. That's where the money is, he thought. The building was really something of a shack. The outer, and larger, office was filthy. Bits of scrap were strewn in corners and worn tires leaned against the walls, sacks of rags were piled in the rafters. There was a long counter, and behind that a desk for Wolf. Wolf had taken photographs of the workers, the derrick, and the truck, and had arranged them on the wall to form the letters "W.A." There was a larger, more imposing desk in the inner office. Wolf had painted these walls in two colours: blue for the first six feet and white the rest of the way up. An Israeli flag hung behind the desk. There was also a portrait of Weizmann, and a framed certificate which proclaimed that "Melech Adler & Family" had paid for the planting of forty orange trees in Israel. Wolf twirled around in his chair. Afterwards, he thought, I'll paint the outer office too. After Wolf had finished his lunch he went out into the yard. That afternoon they were going to clear the yard of a year's accumulation of scrap. Wolf was the only one who could work the derrick properly. There were to be four loadings at intervals of an hour each, which was the amount of time it took the Ford to get to the C.N.R. sidings and back. The second loading finished, Wolf came back into the office and stood by the radiator blowing on his hands. Suddenly he noticed his father's coat hanging on the wall. The door to the inner office was ajar. Walking over to his desk, Wolf peeked briefly in the door. The safe was opened. The strong-box was on the desk. Also opened. The desk was littered with papers. His father was writing. There was a strange and peaceful expression on his father's face, a look – almost beautiful – that Wolf failed to recognize. Melech seemed a stranger. Wolf sat down and rubbed his jaw: It's his will, he thought. But how come the office door isn't locked? Wolf fumbled with the papers on his desk. Now or never, he thought. He got up, knocked, and entered the inner office. Melech gathered up his papers swiftly and clamped the box shut. He was trembling. "What do you want?"

"I didn't know, Paw. . . ." Wolf passed his hand through his mass of hair, looked at his hand, and passed it through his hair again. "I wanted to talk. Leah is not so good. She's in bed again."

"So."

"It means doctors."

"You don't have a doctor?"

Wolf continued to stare at the box. I am locked out of everything, he thought. Everything. "Doctors cost money. I . . ." Wolf wiggled his ears and made his glasses go up and down on his nose. "What would happen if you gave me a raise, Paw?" Wolf laughed. "I mean, you know, Paquette earns nearly as much as I do – your own son. The oldest. I'm just asking, though . . . I mean you don't have to do it. . . ."

Melech Adler banged his fist down on the table. "Everything I did I did it for your sake. You see Moore outside? I had to make monkey-business with him. Why? Why? I'll tell you why. For you and the others. Me, the son from a scribe. I could have been a scholar too. Haven't I got de brains? No, I worked for my children. So what do I get? Max I get. Your Noah for a grandson. Paquette is a truck driver, you are a truck driver. But you get paid more money. Finished."

"I was just asking, anyway," Wolf said, looking at the floor. "But is that a way to talk?"

"Liss'n here, Wolf. You got no head. If not for me you'd be out on the street without a job. You tell me who would hire you for a manager? Be grateful for what you got. Don't tell me no stories from raises. Who's the boss in your family – Leah? Go. Finished."

Wolf staggered out. He swayed, then collapsed in his chair in the outer office. He held his head in his hands.

Melech followed him. "You don't feel good?" he asked softly.

"I feel good."

"You can have twenty-five dollars for a bonus this week," Melech said. He looked down at his son contemptuously, but with sadness and some tenderness too. "You mustn't come in the office when I'm with the box. Understand."

Wolf walked out into the yard. Okay, he thought. At least I know where I stand. You, and your box full of money. Okay, he thought. He walked over to the derrick and sat down in the cab to wait for the truck. I won't go to his funeral. What does he mean talking about Leah that way? His eyes clouded and his heart beat quickly. Rain began to fall. Maybe I'll catch pneumonia, he thought. Then they'll be sorry. The cab roof leaked. Drops plunked down on his leather cap. That wild world of his, which was filled with enemies and the anger of strangers, that world, which was a plot against him, began, for the first time, to assume a definite design in his mind. All his years the enemy, unknown, had been waiting to leap up at him out of the convenient dark, but today he recognized his persecutor. The truck backed into the yard. Automatically Wolf started up the motor and began to work the pedals. The boom creaked. Two tons of twisted scrap scraped against the dirt then came free of the earth, swaying this way and that. When Wolf had lifted the load higher than ten feet his father appeared under the boom. Wolf's eyes ached and his heart beat quicker. Sweat loosened him. He stared dumbly at the gear, which, once released, would send the whole load tumbling downwards. He began to sob. *It's not my fault*, he thought. He shouldn't have talked to me that way. A big raindrop plunked down on his cap and Wolf jumped. His mouth was dry. *I didn't want to do it*, he thought. Melech Adler knelt down to pick up a hunk of brass and the load swayed over his head. Paquette started towards the cab. He wants to know why I don't clear the load, Wolf thought. He stared at the necessary gear. He shut his eyes. Swaying dizzily, he reached for the gear. Paquette saw Wolf lurch toward the window. He leaped up into the cab and pushed him clear of the gears.

"Mr. Adler. Quick! Come quick! Wolf has fainted!"

Wolf slumped forward in the cab seat, his face contorted and his eyes squeezed shut. He waited. Waited for the crash and the scream. Waited, mumbling to himself.

Paquette couldn't make out what Wolf was saying.

"It was an accident," Wolf said. Said again. "It was an accid . . . Not my fault."

His father, all the world, was bleeding. Paquette shook him and Wolf passed out gratefully.

IV

A week after he had moved in with the Halls, Noah was sorry about the whole thing. He gave up his job as a taxi driver, and worked in the college library and corrected papers for the English department. He meant to visit his parents, but he kept putting it off. Time dragged. Noah had renounced a world with which he had at least been familiar and no new world had as yet replaced it. He was hungering for an anger or a community or a tradition to which he could relate his experience. He began to understand that God had been created by man out of necessity. No God, no ethic: no ethic – freedom. Freedom was too much for man. I was wrong to worry about God, he thought. I don't believe in Him so He doesn't exist. My grandfather believes in Him so He does exist. Theo is an atheist. But belief or non-belief amounts to the same thing in the end. Non-believers are only fugitives from God. He is still a factor in their thinking. Worse still, he becomes a *reason*. In order to be liberated from God one must *forget* him. But can one forget?

Whenever Theo went out to evening lectures Miriam and Noah were left alone in the apartment. Noah would retreat into his own room, pretending that he had work to do – but he wouldn't work. He would lie down on his cot and listen to her movements in the living-room. She wasn't beautiful. But there was something about her. Something human, warm, something that astonished him and something that he cherished. He felt a great need of her. And that need was physical and logical, and also transcended both these things. He began to go over his memories as if they had been shared with her. Or, other times, he remembered what had happened to him only as a story that he would have to tell her one day. There was a quality of suffering about her, a kind of beauty truer than her acquired poise, that touched him deeply. He wanted a share of it. He longed to touch her. To feel her hair or hold her hand. The idea of love-making had not yet occurred to him. When he heard her in the living-room he would leap up and come in himself, under one pretence or another, hoping to see her in passing. She seldom looked up. But he would return to his room, his longing briefly nourished, and he would lie down aching with a fresh and tender image of her all his own to manipulate in his mind. Oh, she was lovely. He would have liked to do things that would amaze her. Once he came out and surprised her darning his socks. His first impulse had been to rip them away from her. He had not wanted this kind of contact – the kind that he had had with his mother.

"You can't walk around with holes in your socks."

"Oh. Thanks. Thanks a lot."

On such nights he hoped fervently that Theo would not come home until after ten, for at ten she invited him into the living-room and they sat down together and drank tea.

Their tea talk was always jerky.

"Do you like it here, Noah?"

"Yeah, *Yes*. Very much."

"I'm glad. Because Theo is very fond of you."

Or another evening.

"Why don't you bring any of your girlfriends around?"

"Oh, I . . ."

"Surely you have *one*."

"Sure. What do you mean?"

"Are you very fond of her?"

"Of course I am."

"Then bring her around one night. I'd like to meet her."

When Theo came home they would both greet him effusively and with embarrassment. She would kiss him in a way that he was not used to and Noah would slap him on the back and grin stupidly. Theo did not understand these sudden outbursts, but it pleased him immensely.

The nights were a terror to Noah. The study, his room, was right next to their bedroom. When she laughed that throaty laugh of hers he would clench his fists or grip the head of his cot. He would get up and walk up and down the room shivering and cursing and not knowing what to do with himself. Remembering, maybe, that wild but stricken light in her eyes – the fullness, the yet unspoken child, of her lips; or remembering the imprint of her bare feet on the bathroom floor; that night when she had slipped in the snow and had grabbed his arm, falling against him so that their cheeks touched. Christ, he thought. Doesn't she understand? *I need you.*

He was in a frenzy. But Miriam did not have an easy time of it either. Whenever they were left to themselves in the apartment she meant to do this and she meant to do that. Usually she meant to go out. But she could seldom give up being alone with him. Each time they were forced together like that she meant to make the first gesture that she knew would have to be hers. She did not doubt that she loved him but she was afraid because she had never loved before and she did not love easy and the young, she thought, are callous. She had no plans. But she was tender with Theo. She seemed to be saying to him: "I can't help what is coming. But afterwards when you are hating me I want you to remember that I was kind first." She was kind to Theo and cruel to Noah. But this cruelty, she thought, did not matter much. I love him, she thought. I can be cruel to him if I want to. But she was already dependent on him. None of his remarks eluded her. She waited for him impatiently to come home from lectures or the library, and once he did come home they did not talk much but felt each other's presence in the room and could not concentrate on anything. When he left her alone to go out to a movie, she was furious but she doubted whether she would have gone with him had he asked her. She dressed and talked and cooked for him. She was thinking of having a party because she wanted him to know how well she was liked and that her friends were people of quality, artists and intellectuals. She also wanted him to bring his girl around because she knew that the girl would not be much, really, and that she would appear fine in comparison. All that remained was for her to touch him. That, and the talk that comes after passion.

There were times, however, when she resented and feared him. And at such times she hoped that she could get him out of her system quickly. She, who had striven so hard to build a world that was proof against fire and storm, was not going to let Noah destroy it. So she did not think that she would leave Theo. She did not dare think that. But at night in bed she no longer minded his passivity. She sobbed quietly and had many dreams. Theo, if he appeared in them, was a man to pity.

But Miriam's abstruseness was fast becoming too much for Noah. She had taken to passing smart remarks about "his girl" when Theo was around, and Noah was expected to bring her to the apartment soon. They both believed that there actually was one and Noah did not want Miriam to think that he was the kind of man who could not have lots of girls.

That was Tuesday. Noah spent that afternoon drinking beer in the Bar Vendôme.

The Bar Vendôme was a small basement bar on Drummond Street, not far from Wellington College. The crowd varied. There were the clean-faced young men in brushcuts and bow ties with their pretty, well-dressed girls: and then there were the women, who, having been courageous enough to rebel and to seek "bachelor" apartments and to compete with men for jobs, were, now that they had both, unable to speak of their jobs, except cynically, and unable to contend with their apartments, except when drunk or accompanied or both. A few dissipated men, regulars, sat at the bar consuming drink after drink without expression, watching the newly scrubbed girls who sat with younger men. A French Canadian girl who wore a lot of jewellery and painted and who went to Paris every summer with her mother came in nearly every night. She sobbed when she had more than six drinks, and that, also, was nearly every night. There were many bright young journalists and lawyers and commercial artists.

Noah finally got up enough courage to call her.

"I'm in the Vendôme, Miriam. Would you like to come around for a drink?"

"I don't see why not."

"Swell. I'll wait."

"I'll leave a note for Theo. He can join us later."

"Oh yeah, sure. Good idea."

"Are you drunk?"

"No. Of course not."

"You sound drunk."

"You sound like my mother."

There was a pause.

"All right. I'll see you in twenty minutes."

He noticed that her voice had cooled. "I'm sorry," he said.

"Sorry? Sorry for what?"

"Never mind."

She hung up.

Three-quarters of an hour later she stood soaking wet in the doorway. He watched her whip off her kerchief and fling her hair clear of her neck with a quick, defiant toss of her head. He waited impatiently, and at last she came up to him. They looked at each other and grinned. He laughed richly. He reached out and fingered her wet hair and touched her lips and cheeks impetuously. Then he flushed deeply and withdrew his hand. She pressed his arm and smiled as if nothing out of the ordinary had happened. "You *are* drunk," she said.

"Am I?"

She grabbed his chin and turned him towards the mirror. Her fingers felt cold. Looking into the mirror, he saw that his eyes were glossy, red. "All right. But I'm not drunk."

"Neither am I."

They laughed again, together, and then turned away from each other embarrassed.

Two tables away Jerry Selby turned to a man with heavy jowls and rimless glasses and said: "The way I look at it, Mr. Corby, give us another twenty years and we'll be as big as you guys in the U.S.A. This is one market you can't afford to miss up on. Your product is the best on the market. And believe you me I'm not saying that just because you're sitting here with me. But you can't afford to be shy. Even when you've got the best. Look at Bishop Sheen, for instance. He's got God, and you can't do any better. But even he knows that you've got to get out there and sell."

Noah ordered two whiskies. Now that they were together he did not know what to do. He drank his whisky quickly and ordered another. She seemed calm, indifferent, too, perhaps, and he longed for an excuse to touch her again. He clasped his hands together and tapped them against his chin nervously. I'm afraid, he thought. She turned to him as though she anticipated some remark or instruction. He wanted to hit her. "Would you like another drink?"

They drank again.

She watched him. She felt light on her feet, young, and she wanted to hurry him into a taxi and back to the apartment. But she knew that she couldn't do that, that afterwards he would not forgive her. She knew that she must wait.

"I was drunk, I guess," a lean man said thickly. "I thought that after this war there was going to be a big fiesta. I believed in Taft shaking hands with Browder. I believed in the war and I believed in 1945. And now, what? Your best ticket to prosperity in Germany today is . . ."

"I don't know anything about politics," the woman with him said.

"Let's go," Noah said.

"What about Theo?"

Noah frowned. He wished that she wouldn't keep throwing him in his face that way. Besides, he was suspicious of Theo. He was suspicious of Theo because although Noah believed that you could love one man or two men or ten men he did not believe that you could love man. Not man, and not mankind. Such generalities, such loves, were the tormented inventions of those who loved with much facility and no truth.

"Theo can go to hell," Noah said.

Suddenly, he felt her hand soft and restraining on his wrist.

"He won't get away for hours, anyway," he said. "We can come back."

St. Catherine Street glistened in the rain. Up towards Peel Street and under a play of darting neon, long queues formed waiting to get into the first-run movies. Yellow streetcars clanged by. The loudly human street smelled of exhaust fumes and other bodies and drowsy lights. Noah grabbed her hand swiftly and held it in a laconic grip. He decided that after he had counted up to ten he would tell her that he loved her. What will happen then? She'll get into a taxi, he thought. She'll tell Theo. Tell him in bed. And, Christ, they'll laugh. He counted up to sixteen and then he turned to her. "Let's go back," he said. "I want another drink."

This time they sat at a table in a dim corner and ordered two whiskies from Emil.

"Carter is having a thing with Edna," a girl said.

"But Edna is the *end*."

Emil slammed his tray down on the bar. "I told you that I wanted two gins and tonic with lemon and three without. Not three with and two without."

Noah and Miriam didn't talk. As the crowd thickened they were pushed closer and closer together on the red-leather bench. Perry sang "La Vie en rose." They drank whisky, and they held hands. He allowed himself hope but he felt her eyes on him like a threat. "I love you," he said. "I can't help it. I love you."

She laughed. She wiped her eyes and kissed his hand. He looked at her and he could not bear the deep, hurt thing in her eyes. Suddenly, everything had changed. Her upturned face was full of expectations. He felt that something still remained to be done. His joy was tremendous, but so was his sense of frustration: his anger increased. He eyed her yearningly and understood, briefly, the nature of madness.

"What's wrong?" she asked.

"Sometimes I'm so happy that I don't know what to do with myself. There seems to be no way of expressing it."

"I've always wanted a man with whom it would not be necessary to talk. So that when we were together – silent – we would be full."

"There are so many things I must tell you."

She nodded obediently.

"I would like to be something really fine for you."

She touched his lips with her fingers. She thought, briefly, of the others in the bar, but then she realized that she no longer minded them. "I don't know what to say. I've waited so long."

Jerry Selby and his heavy-jowled client got up to go.

"You sleep on it. It may sound crazy but I don't want your business if I have to talk you into it. I want you to do what *you* think is best."

"Noah, do you worry about being a Jew? You know what I mean. . . ."

"No. I don't. The guy who wants to get into a restricted golf course or hotel and the other guy who won't let him in are really brothers. The fact that one is inside and the other outside is an accident. They could switch places just like that. Besides, there is a certain kind of Jew who needs a *Goy* badly. And then . . ."

"And then there's the kind like you, the worst, who turns all the way around and becomes an anti-Semite himself. What about Germany?"

"The important thing is not that they burned Jews but that they burned men. It didn't have to happen in Germany, either. A Zionist, who I know very well, sold scrap to Japan right up to '41. He didn't see the connection. Nobody in the family protested against non-intervention in . . ."

The room was full. Talk swayed like the candlelight. There were red girls in green dresses, pink men in blue suits, and brown girls in yellow dresses. Women with tanned backs and men with pallid faces and women with flaxen heads.

"What, darling?"

"Against non-intervention in . . . Isn't that what you call *him*?"

Miriam didn't reply. Noah scratched his head and began to make quick circles with his hands. "Christ, I feel stupid. I can't think."

A swaying man grabbed Perry, the West Indian pianist, by the arm. "Your people deserve a break," he said.

They left.

They walked aimlessly up St. Catherine Street, past the Loew's Theatre and the Chicken-Coop and Ogilvy's department store. The sign at F.D.R.'s said: "WE SELL 4½ TONS OF SPAGHETTI A WEEK." They got caught up by the traffic lights at Guy Street, and overheard a man say: "Did you know that the human head weighs thirty-five pounds?" They looked at each other and laughed. Miriam pressed Noah's hand. "I want to kiss you," he said. She giggled. "Not here," she said. A tattered man in steel-rimmed glasses was distributing pamphlets at the next corner. "Put God in your will," he yelled. "You're sure to be in His." Noah stopped and lit a cigarette, and she stood close to him. He touched her cheek. "God," he said. She smiled. "Your eyes are wet," she said. "I know," he said, taking her arm again. They walked for a bit without saying anything, then Miriam stopped him and took a puff of his cigarette. They couldn't look at each other without laughing. There was a big poster of Yvon Robert over the doors of the Forum. He was going to wrestle Sir Harry Northcliffe next Wednesday night. A world's championship match. The poster made them laugh, too. Everything did. Finally, Miriam said: "We'd better get a taxi."

They got into a taxi, and that's when her mood changed – changed swiftly. I still love Theo, she thought. I don't want to hurt him anyway. Noah, she noticed, was sulking. She kissed him, but he didn't respond. I can't have them both in the apartment, she thought. I'll go crazy. Noah was thinking just about the same thing. He was thinking that he would have to move. But what if she won't come with me, he thought. She hasn't said that she would.

When they pulled up in front of the apartment Miriam was quickly transformed into an efficient, modern woman. She let go of his hand and made up her face. Then she checked to see if there was any lipstick on him. He pulled away from her abruptly. "I'll tell him right now," he said. "We'll go away tonight."

"Are you mad?"

"Miriam, Miriam. You were serious. You weren't . . ."

"I love you," she said.

"Don't . . . I'm in the next room. I hear things. I . . ."

"Don't torment me, Noah, please don't."

"I can't go in now. I'm going for a walk. I'll see you later."

"All right," she said.

Sadly he watched her walk away from him.

Earlier that evening Theo had come home from his lecture and found Miriam's note. He had been vaguely pleased that the two of them had gone out together, for he was troubled, and he wanted time to think. His days, from the very beginning, had been ordered. When he had been a small boy his mother had ordered them for him, just as she had ordered his father's days, hardly allowing him time enough for death. Dr. Hall had, in fact, died most inconveniently. Had he held out for just another two weeks he would certainly have been chosen the C.C.F. candidate for Verdun. But Mrs. Hall was conditioned to disappointments. G.B.S. had answered none of her letters: her daughter, Beatrice, had married a Catholic and did not practise birth control. She wrote Theo weekly letters from Toronto, as lengthy as they were erudite, dealing with political and population problems and criticizing *Direction*.

His days, from the beginning, had been ordered in the nature of a preparation. Ever since he had been ten years old Theo had kept several sheets of paper tacked over his desk. One of them, a chart divided up into hours, listed things to be done on a particular day. Another listed books to be read: a third music to listen to. Through boyhood and adolescence and into manhood he had hurried through his days trying to catch up with his self-imposed schedules. He had seldom had moments for unscheduled pleasures, so now, slumped back on the sofa with his eyes shut, he could no longer remember what he had wanted to think about when he had the time. He felt guilty. So he switched on the reading-lamp and began to read. He read for an hour or more, not really absorbing anything, before he fell asleep on the sofa. He woke suddenly when his book fell to the floor. The crash startled him. Where are the students? Miriam! I'll be late for lectures! Slowly, he became aware of his surroundings. He slumped back into the warm, snug sofa. 12:15. I wasted a half-hour sleeping, he thought.

He heard the key fumbling in the lock.

Miriam opened the door and Theo smiled calmly. She was surprised, almost insulted, to find him unchanged. The familiar room whirled around her. She allowed herself to be kissed in a perfunctory way.

"Are you drunk, darling?"

"I don't really know," she said. "Why? Would that be funny?"

"I'll make you some black coffee."

"Will you stop being so understanding! If I'm drunk perhaps I'd like to stay that way."

"Oh. I'm sorry. All right."

Oh God, she thought. She got up and kissed him, clinging to him tightly. Her ardour distressed him. "I'm a bitch, Theo. An awful bitch. I'm so sorry."

"You'll be fine, darling. You've had a bit too much, that's all."

She moved away from him coldly. "I need a shower. You go to bed, Theo. I won't be long."

"Oh, Miriam. What's happened to Noah?"

But, shutting the bathroom door behind her, she had pretended not to hear. Theo shrugged his shoulders. Something was wrong, but that something, which was certainly oppressive, eluded him. He sat down and tried to read again, but he couldn't concentrate. Looking around the room he saw all the familiar possessions and heard all the familiar noises and thought, *This* is what I have striven for, but found no comfort in the thought or in the possessions. His eyes filled with the ineffable terror of those who, drowning, search an empty hostile sea for something, anything, to hold firm to: whether that thing be true or not. Nothing's wrong, he thought. I'm tired. He tried to read again, desperately, but the print blurred. The books can be sold, he thought. So can the furnishings. *Everything I have is rented.* "Miriam . . ."

The shower drowned out all other noises. She could not hear him call out and he could not hear her sobbing. She realized quickly that, as far as Noah was concerned, Theo was just a thing in the way. But she knew differently. She recalled with some disgust the exhibition that she had made of herself in the Bar Vendôme. Then she relented. She felt that she was betraying Noah. I *do* love him, she thought. But if I don't betray him I must betray Theo. She ripped off her cap and turned the tap on harder, surrendering herself to the water like a punishment. Drying herself, she meticulously avoided looking into the mirror. An ageing woman's lust, she thought. I can't. He must know that I can't. That I was drunk.

Theo was still up when she got into bed with him. The room helped. She lay her head child-like on the pillow, newly rich in an acquired belief and intent on falling asleep before Noah returned.

Theo kissed her cheek. "Miriam. Let's have a child."

"Oh. Oh, no!"

"Why?"

"Oh, Theo, I . . . Remember? We said that we wouldn't until you . . ."

"Until I was earning enough money. Well, I am now."

He waited, but she didn't reply. Miriam stared into the familiar, habitual dark of their room. Then, sadly, she turned to him.

V

The first time Noah had been to a concert the orchestra had played *The Four Seasons* of Vivaldi and he had been so struck by it that he had felt something like pain. He had not suspected that men were capable of such beauty. He had been startled. So he had walked out wondering into the night, not knowing what to make of his discovery. All those stale lies that he had inherited from others, all those cautionary tales, and those other dreadful things, facts, that he had collected like his father did stamps, knowledge, all that passed away, rejected, dwarfed by the entry of beauty into his consciousness. The city, the gaudy night, had whirled around him phantasmagorically but without importance. I didn't know about beauty, he had thought. Nobody ever told me. When he had next been aware of his surroundings he was sitting on a bench on the mountain. It was dawn. People were getting up to go to work.

Later Noah had found out that there were booths in music stores where customers could try out records. So for weeks he had wandered from store to store sampling different symphonies and concertos, but always coming back to Vivaldi.

There had been other incidents, too. One afternoon, when he had still been in high school, he had decided not to go to classes, but to go for a walk instead. For suddenly he had realized that nothing they thought horrible could really hurt him. They could strap him. Fail him. Throw him out of school. What did it matter? All their threats, all of Melech's laws, were like autumn leaves that, once flung into the wind, scattered and turned to dust. He had not done anything special with that afternoon of freedom. He had walked, but not in beautiful places. Yet somehow the whole city had seemed to be illuminated by the fire that burned within him. Walking, he had danced. Loitering on benches, he had suddenly, inexplicably, burst out into great peals of laughter. He had not been able at that time to think of anything reasonable or unremarkable or sorrowful. Finally, he had felt absolutely exhausted.

When he had got home his mother had said: "Where have you been so late?"

"Walking."

"Where, walking?"

"I dunno."

She had looked at him, surprised, and he had been swiftly overcome by a deep and unyielding sadness.

"It was beautiful, Maw. Honest."

That night, after he left Miriam, Noah had been filled with something of that old awe, a touch of that first-discovered beauty, and he had walked along happily – dead sure that life was a perfect thing – for several hours. Then, suddenly, it was morning. The lowering sky was chill and without promise or much light. Over towards the left of the Sun Life Building a dripping cloud was stained bright yellow. That would be the sun, he thought. Christmas decorations were going up over Eaton's. *When My Baby Smiles at Me* was playing at the Princess Theatre, across the street. He crossed. He looked at an enticing cardboard figure of Doris Day. Somebody had shoved thumbtacks into where her nipples ought to have been and Noah reached up and pulled them out. Dour people, standing at the corner and waiting for streetcars, watched him critically. Noah grinned at them. I'm never going to die, he thought. Dying would be stupid.

When Noah got back to the apartment Miriam and Theo were still eating breakfast. She did not give him any sign, but Theo asked him to sit down. "How's your girlfriend?" he asked knowingly.

"Fine."

"You look all in, boy." Theo stubbed his cigarette and got up and put on his coat. Noah avoided Miriam's eyes. "We're not prudes,

Noah. No need to rent a room. Bring her around here for the night if you want."

He looked away when they kissed.

After Theo had gone Miriam looked at him sorrowfully and then slipped into her bedroom, shutting the door behind her. Noah waited. He waited fifteen minutes, and then he knocked on the door. She didn't answer. He knocked again.

"All right. You might as well come in."

She was seated before the bureau combing out her black hair. She could watch him in the mirror, but he couldn't see her face. The bed was unmade, and he noticed their pyjamas tangled up together on the sheets. There were no chairs. He didn't want to sit on their bed, so he stood. "Would you like to go for a walk?" he asked.

Her pyjamas were pink, and his were grey with red stripes.

"Aren't we speaking?" he asked.

"I think you'd better move, Noah."

"Oh. Oh, I see."

Watching him in the mirror she thought, Go. Go, she thought. Please go. Go now.

"I'm beat. I'll go back to Mrs. Mahoney's. She'll have a room for me."

"All right."

"I'll get my things tomorrow. Okay?"

"Okay."

He hesitated. Then he flushed, and walked up nearer to her. "You know when to stop, eh? That's a damn good thing."

"Please, let's not have a scene. *Please*. If you were older you would under . . ."

"You mean we could part friends. That kind of crap, eh?"

"Theo and I are going to have a . . ."

"Listen," he said, twisting her around. "You look at me when you talk to me, understand? I'm no animal."

"I can't give this up, Noah. Not even for you. You don't know what my life has been like, you . . . I want security, that's all."

"All right."

The door slammed.

She walked over to the window and watched him walk away. She picked up an ashtray and smashed it on the floor. I hope you have an accident, she thought. I really do.

VI

Mrs. Mahoney had been glad to have him back. But Bertha, she said, had returned to her mother in Sherbrooke, and Joey had disappeared. Noah knocked off his shoes and undid his collar and lay back on his bed. I knew that she wasn't real from the first, he thought. He recalled all the ordinary, clean-washed things that he had eaten in their apartment and suddenly, sleepily, he longed for properly spiced food. Christ, if I were back on City Hall Street I could tell Hoppie and Gas some real stories. And Theo, the bastard, always trying to get me to talk about my family when people are around. I'm colourful, he thinks. Hell.

He fell asleep.

He slept soundly and without dreams through the rest of the day and the night that followed.

Finally, a knocking came to him faintly. . . .

Noah stumbled out of bed and noticed, half-consciously, that it was morning. He was surprised, for he had thought that he had only been sleeping for an hour or so. He walked over to the sink and splashed cold water on his face and wrists. The door opened.

"May I come in?"

Miriam was wearing her brown tweed coat. A green silk scarf accentuated the vulnerability of her throat. Her hair was brushed back hard and held tight by a gold clasp, but there was something of the child in her sorrowful brown eyes. She smiled boldly but without conviction.

"Sure. Of course you can."

She flung her coat down on the bed like a rebuke. She was wearing a green woollen dress. He felt a fluttering in his stomach again and he brushed back his hair nervously.

"I won't have you talking to me the way you did yesterday."

"Is that what you came to tell me?" he asked.

"I think you're a son-of-a-bitch. You're young and you don't know what you're doing. I think Theo is a much nicer guy than you are. Understand?"

He moved towards her compulsively and took her in his arms and kissed her tenderly first and then with passion. He felt her quiver and yield against him. He undid the clasp and dug his hand into her hair and pressed her scalp, saying poignant things softly, and feeling her lips like a burn on his neck. He kissed her eyes and her nose and her throat and then slowly, together, they stumbled back on the bed.

Afterwards they touched each other tenderly and without caution.

"I love you when you're angry," he said. "I love you, anyway. But I love you best when you're angry."

"Noah, I'm not fooling. I – I thought a lot before I came here."

"I guess you did," he said.

"It wasn't very good without you around."

"You're really beautiful. Christ, I didn't know you were beautiful. I mean you look kind of severe when you're dressed. I trust you better this way."

"I like the feeling of your voice. I like your hands, too."

Noah laughed, and stared at his hands. "If I were Jelly-Roll Morton," he said, "I would look at my hands all the time. I would walk down the street and look at them and put them in my pockets and pull them out and look at them and laugh like hell."

"Jelly-Roll is dead."

"Yes. So's L. Trotsky and Mr. Vivaldi," he said. "So that makes us both greater than them. Really, it does."

"Oh, Noah. Christ, Noah."

Miriam wanted to tell him about other men – about how long she had waited for loving and how frightened she was now that she had it. She waited to say something that would bind him to her irrevocably. But each time she tried, a lump formed in her throat and all she could do was to touch him and smile weakly. She wanted to tell him about her father. Chuck. She was afraid and she wanted time to stop – to stop right then.

"You think being alive is fine, don't you?" she asked.

"Yes, I do. I think being in bed with you is fine, too. Finer than anything I have ever known."

"I haven't got your capacity for happiness. I won't mind dying at all. Being out of it, I mean."

"That's just so much crap," he said.

She giggled. "That's just so much crap," she said.

He touched her hair with his hand. He felt relieved for he did not know much about love-making and he had been worried that he would do the wrong thing, that she would burst out laughing because he was such an inept lover. He was intoxicated. Full. He kissed her again and laughed. "God, it must be real crazy to be a woman. Do you look at yourself all day long?"

"Don't be silly!"

"If I were beautiful like you I'd walk around naked always. I'd lead parades and dare people not to –"

"Are you happy?"

"I'm better than happy. You?"

She was sobbing. Suddenly, just like that. Her swift changes of mood baffled him.

"What's wrong?" he asked quickly.

"Nothing. Nothing, you fool. Nothing."

"Are you sure?"

She laughed and wept, and laughed some more. "I've waited so long, Noah, I'm so afraid."

Noah woke first.

She was sleeping with her head resting on her arm. He got up without disturbing her and pulled down the shade a bit to keep the afternoon sun out of her eyes. He sat down and watched her. He wanted to shout. Her beauty hurt him, and he could not understand why.

Noah hurried downstairs and bought smoked meat sandwiches and salad and four bottles of beer. When he got back she was sitting up in bed and smoking. He grinned foolishly. "Food," he said.

After they had eaten she turned to him and said: "What are we going to do, Noah?"

"I'll get a job. Then we'll get an apartment of our own."

"You make it sound so easy. What kind of job?"

"Wal, I could go out West and get work poking cattle, or whatever it is they do. Or I could stay East and sell filthy sonnets and gold-mine stocks, corner Peel and St. Catherine. Or I could become a rabbi. You'd have to shave your head and wear a wig. Would that be okay?"

"Will you please try to be serious?"

"Worried about Theo?"

"Yes."

"You don't love him. I don't even think he loves you. He's got no rights, Miriam." He began to make excited circles with his hands. "Some foolish minister read a few foolish words over you."

"We've been married five years."

"All right. What do *you* suggest?"

"First of all I suggest that you don't shout. Second of all – you can't keep these things a secret. People will talk."

"A guy like Theo marries so that he can have someone to blame his failures on. I don't understand. What if they do talk?"

"I don't want to be talked about. Not again. I'll have to do it my own way, Noah. I'll tell him. But give me a couple of weeks."

"And meanwhile?"

"Meanwhile you come back. I'll need you."

"I go back into that apartment and you've got all your memories and all your habits together. Like you said, you've been married five years."

"Please, lover, let's leave it for now. Today has been so good. I've never had such a day."

Noah stood by the window sipping beer and watching the sky turn pale and then dark. Stars twinkled, first weakly and then with more assurance. Cars zoomed away into the night anonymously. Suddenly he felt her arms go around him and her head resting on his back. He did not feel any tensions in his body the way he had earlier in the afternoon. He embraced her tenderly.

"Why did you marry Theo? Did you love him?"

"No. I liked him. I still do. I wanted to be respectable, I guess. I was lonely." She laughed her throaty laugh, but it sounded sad and forced to him. "I'm ten years older than you. Did you know that?"

"My left leg is longer than my right. If I were a pinball machine 'tilt' would be lit in red on my forehead."

She laughed more gladly, and he grinned.

"Can you stay the night?" he asked.

"You know I can't."

"Then I'm not coming back with you. Not tonight."

She kissed him. "Why don't you ever visit your parents?"

"It's too painful all around. But I will – soon." He turned away from her. "The guys I used to go around with as a kid talk about irrigation problems in Israel now and make ideal son-in-laws."

"And you, my love?"

"Christ. I used to march down St. Catherine Street with placards. Sing songs. Wave flags. But I've stopped reading comic books and going to Roy Rogers movies and . . ."

"I would have liked to have seen you in one of those parades. I would have laughed."

He reached out for her and kissed her urgently. "Hey, just between the two of us, did the earth move?"

She giggled. "Noah." She held on tight to him. "Noah. Oh, Noah."

VII

One evening a couple of weeks earlier Mr. Adler dropped into Panofsky's for a lemon tea on his way home from the synagogue. Mr. Adler passed by Panofsky's every evening, but previous to that visit he had not been inside the store for fifteen years. When Panofsky had seen him come in he had got up and sat down beside Mr. Adler.

"How is it by you, Melech?"

"I can't complain."

"You should drop in more often."

So Melech Adler began to drink lemon tea at Panofsky's every evening.

When Panofsky had gone into business for himself in 1919 he had named his store The People's Tobacco & Soda, but the people had thwarted him. His store became known as "Panofskys." The back room, which he had fixed up as a chess club, was used for pinochle and gin rummy games. Panofsky had two boys, Aaron and Karl. If not for Karl the business would have failed many years ago. Karl had invented the 49-cent luncheonette and the Panofsky Special, which was the favourite meat sandwich of the ghetto. He had also brought in the pinball machines and got the boys interested by paying off five dollars to the high score of the week.

Panofsky was a shaggy-faced man with big pleading eyes who liked to sit outside his store on Yom Kippur eating ham sandwiches and smoking his pipe because he wanted the others, like Melech Adler, to know that religion was bad and that Samuel Panofsky had figured things out for himself and was not afraid of God or anything. When Aaron had been away fighting in Spain he had hung a sign over the cash:

O ye that love mankind! Ye that dare oppose not only the tyranny, but the tyrant, stand forth! Every spot of the old world is overrun with oppression. Freedom has been hunted round the globe. . . .

The sign, like Spain, had been smudged by the years. Other signs, like the one which said OPEN UP A SECOND FRONT, had faded.

Aaron had been Panofsky's favourite boy. But for several years now they had been avoiding each other, like lovers after the affair has ended. Karl wanted to sell the *Herald* in the store but Panofsky said he wouldn't have a lying, capitalist paper on the premises. Karl said: "A guy buys the *Herald* for Palmer and the sports. He buys the *Herald* so he sits down and has a coffee. Does he have a coffee only? No. He has a sandwich with. Maybe cigs, too. If he can't get the *Herald* here he goes to Levy's. There he has his *Herald* and his coffee and his sandwich and his cigs."

But Panofsky was adamant. No *Herald*.

They both suffered. But there was a fundamental disagreement between Melech Adler and Samuel Panofsky.

"Don't talk stories, Sam. Comes the New Year a Jew, even the *cackers*, puts on a hat and goes into the synagogue to pray. What, tell me, do *Yoshke's* children do on New Year's? Drunk they get – like pigs. You listen, Sam. A Jew dies so all his sons pray. What happens when one of theirs dies? The family is happy yet because now they got de chance to sleep with the widow. So. So they got the nerve to call *us* dirty Jews. Why? We're too smart for them, that's why."

"Look. Once and for all a Jew is no smarter and no dumber than a Goy. All right. We're persecuted. Why? Because it is the interest of the capitalists to divide the workers. And who, tell me, fights the anti-Semites? *Only* the communists. Adam and Eve you believe in? You just tell me how the Jews crossed de Red Sea. . . ."

"What are talking? You never heard de word Siberia? They got fridges? Fords? A Cossack is a Cossack. You mean to tell me there are no pogroms?"

"Who? All I ask. Who? Who was the other woman? Eve died and –"

"Who, who, who. What is written is written. We are de Chosen People. We . . ."

"Chosen. You tell me what for we were chosen? Soap? Furnaces?"

That evening, Thursday, Melech Adler left Panofsky's at eight o'clock. He noticed Shloime and two other boys standing in a doorway across the street. But at the time he didn't think anything of it.

That evening, Thursday, Shloime Adler, Mort Sacks, and Lou Weinstein loitered in a doorway across the street from Panofsky's. When Shloime saw his father come out of the store he turned the other way quickly. The Hook was parked around the corner.

Miriam and Noah had had a difficult week. She had not spoken to Theo yet. But that evening, Thursday, Theo had gone out to an evening lecture and the two of them had decided to go out for a drive in Theo's car. Noah had driven down to the ghetto and wandered in and out of the familiar streets between Park Avenue and St. Lawrence Boulevard.

"That was my old parochial school we just passed."

She didn't say anything.

"Wait. That's Panofsky's!"

"What . . ."

Noah parked the car and leaped out without a word. The store window had been smashed. A police siren wailed from away off. He pushed through the crowd and into the store. Panofsky sat on the floor, his head propped up against the wall. His grey hair was damp with blood. Cigarette cartons, books, were strewn on the floor. Noah knelt down beside Panofsky. The old man, groaning, opened his eyes and stared dimly at Noah. "Noah. Noah, you're a good boy. I . . ."

Hoppie Drazen tapped Noah on the shoulder. He looked at Miriam and then back at Noah and grinned. "Don't worry. The doc's on the way."

"Noah . . . Noah . . . I saw . . . I . . . Your poor grandfather."

Hoppie walked away towards a corner of the store and motioned to Noah.

"Miriam. You hold him, eh? Watch his head." Noah turned to Panofsky. "You'll be all right, Mr. Panofsky. The doctor's on his way."

Hoppie spoke in a whisper. "He's hiding in the lane. I saw him. You . . ."

"Who? What are you talking about?"

"Sh!" He pressed Noah's arm warmly. "Get out of here quick. Here come the cops. Turn down the lane and you'll find him."

"Miriam! Come on." Noah turned back and smiled. "Thanks, Hoppie."

They got into the car and drove slowly down the lane. Noah saw him standing stiff in a doorway, trying to avoid the headlights. Then on a mad impulse he broke out of the doorway and raced down the lane. A rock bounced off the bonnet of the car. You damn fool, Noah thought. He stepped on the gas.

When they caught up with him he was standing on a garbage pail, trying to get over the top of a fence.

Shloime leaped into the back seat. "Noah. I didn't do it. Honest."

They finally came out on St. Lawrence Boulevard and Noah turned towards the apartment.

"He saw you, Shloime."

"I don't care. You can all go to hell. I wasn't in this alone. I can make trouble." Shloime grinned. "Who's the broad?"

"Never mind that now. Who hit him?"

"Hit him? *I* hit him? You crazy?"

Miriam lit a cigarette and passed it to Noah. "He can stay at our place tonight. I'll fix it with Theo."

Noah parked on Sherbrooke Street, his hands felt slimy on the wheel. He shivered. You've read books on sociology, he thought. "No," he said. "I've got to do this myself. I don't want Theo smirking. I . . ."

"Theo doesn't smirk."

"All right. But I'm driving you home and then we'll go back to Dorchester Street. I'll phone tomorrow morning. Oh, this is Shloime Adler. He's my uncle. My father's the oldest. He's the youngest. Shloime, meet Miriam."

They parked in front of the apartment.

"You keep the car," she said. "I'll phone in an hour, Noah. I'll tell him I'm going out for a walk. I'll phone from the corner."

Noah turned back towards Dorchester Street. He had paid Mrs. Mahoney two weeks' rent in advance, so – technically – the room was still his.

"Your car?"

"No," Noah said.

"Your goods?"

"Sort of. Like her?"

"Liss'n. What should you expect – television?"

Inside, Shloime wandered around the room clacking his tongue appreciatively. He and Noah had gone to Baron Byng High School together. There were two regular high schools in the ghetto, Baron Byng and Strathcona Academy. Strathcona was a fine-looking school in Outremont, but Baron Byng was on St. Urbain Street, a shapeless brown brick building surrounded by tenements. Baron Byng, however, had a long tradition behind it. A previous generation, that of Aaron Panofsky, had produced a number of brilliant scholars and had gone out on strike when the Protestant School Board had raised school fees. Students during the depression, that generation had not only rebelled against authority but had fought for what it had considered to be the political truth. Noah and Shloime had gone to school during the war, when their fathers first began to earn a decent living. They didn't produce many scholars and never took any political or moral action. They resented authority, and reacted against it by aggressively doing everything forbidden. They smoked and gambled and drank. Aaron Panofsky's Baron Byng apprenticeship had led to the loss of his legs; Shloime, a student of the same teachers, was a petty thief with still grander prospects before him. Noah was still doubtful of his directions.

"It's the berries," Shloime said. "The car belongs to a pal. The broad is hitched. We've got a lot in common, you know. I don't care what Paw says. We should talk."

"What do you mean, we've got a lot in common?"

"We're both lone operators, eh? We both like *shiksas* – dames – and we both don't give a damn about eating kosher and . . ."

"We've got nothing in common," Noah said sharply.

"At least I admit what I am," Shloime continued. "At least I don't pretend to be a *Goy* or . . ." Suddenly, Shloime began to tremble. He choked. Tears ran down his cheeks. "The cops are after me, Noah. I'm . . . What if Paw finds out? I . . . They send you to a kind of reform school. They . . . I'm telling you, I . . ." Shloime collapsed on the bed and sobbed wildly. Noah turned away from him. He felt that his concern, his willingness to help, had been an affectation. I'm not free yet, he thought. I had to help him, in spite of everything. No, I'm not free yet. He turned around, and Shloime faced him contritely. "She'd hide me," he said. "She offered to. I heard. She'd do anything for you. She . . ."

"I'm not going to help you. I don't like you, and I don't give a damn. I . . ."

"You're scared of me," Shloime said. "Ashamed."

"I'm not scared of you," Noah said quickly. "Now – if you don't mind – you can clear out of here. You . . ."

"You know what," Shloime said, getting off the bed. "You remind me of Paw."

Noah stared at him, horrified.

"You remind me of Paw," Shloime said, smiling confidently. His fear seemed to have passed. His long hair was greased back to his head and his dim eyes were darkly ringed underneath.

"You might have killed him, Shloime," Noah said.

"Hey, hey. Liss'n, *ockshmay*. Don't give *me* the business."

"He saw you. So did the others. You'll probably be arrested. I'm not worried about you. But it would be hard for *Zeyda*."

"Look what's suddenly worried about *my* father. He threw you out of the house, didn't he? Listen, big-boy. He's more ashamed of you than he'll ever be of me. Don't give me no sermons, if you don't mind. We're not good enough for you. Your own mudder's sick in bed you go to see her? A lot you give a damn." Shloime grinned maliciously. He sensed, instinctively, that Noah had been defeated. He was not sure of how he had done it, though. "Besides, Max would never let me get pinched. He can't afford it. Okay?"

"What makes you think that?" Noah asked weakly.

"Didn't you know? Max is gonna run for alderman. That's not all, either. He'll go to Quebec yet. Member for Cartier. How would it look – I ask you – if his own brudder was pinched?"

"Not too good." Noah sat down on the bed. "How's my father?"

"Dumb as ever."

Noah stiffened. His father was the oldest, Shloime was the youngest. It suddenly occurred to him that Shloime was his father turned inside out. "I guess it's safe for you to go now," he said. "But I'm going to see Panofsky tomorrow. If anything happens to him I'll . . ." Noah stopped. He felt stupid.

"You'll what?"

"Nothing." Noah wiped his brow absently. "What can I do to help you?"

"I need money."

"Money?" Noah sensed a way out. We send flowers to the sick. Money. He had thirty-five dollars in the bank. He knew it was cowardly of him, but all the same, he said: "I can give you thirty dollars."

Shloime nodded, and Noah wrote out a cheque.

"I'm going," Shloime said, taking the cheque. "But first I'll tell you something. I don't care a shit in hell if the old man finds out. I hate him. So do you. We got a lot to talk together. Look, you come out with me one night. You bring your broad and tell her to bring a friend. You . . ."

A voice came booming up the stairway. "Telephone for Mr. Adler."

"Coming," Noah yelled. He turned to Shloime. Once more, he was tempted to offer him something more tangible than money. A hand. Friendship. But the desire to be rid of him proved stronger. "I'm sorry, Shloime," he said.

"Sorry?" Shloime paused at the door. "Hey, I wonder if it'll be in the papers? Did you notice any photographers around? I mean – Christ . . . What time does the *Herald* come out? We call ourselves The Avengers."

Noah had been sharp with Miriam on the phone because he needed her and she had not been able to come to him. He felt disorganized. He remembered that when they had been boys, he and Shloime had used to sit down on the cold concrete steps outside the synagogue to take off their roller-skates before going in for evening prayer. Inside the tattering Jews had used to pray in a failing light. Once the two of them had forgotten to go to the evening services, Melech had found them, his son and his grandson, playing chequers in the basement. He had ripped the chequers board to pieces and smashed their roller-skates against the wall.

Panofsky, his head bandaged, sat up in bed and sucked on his pipe. His grey, melancholy eyes were without their former unwavering quality. Aaron sat nearby in his wheelchair reading a book. He was a gaunt man with intense black eyes and an honest mouth. He had used to be quite lively.

The room was papered yellow and three pictures hung on the walls. One of Marx; one of Lenin; and one of Mrs. Panofsky, who was also dead. The bureau was stained and scratched and several drawer knobs were missing. The room was warm. Warm, and worn out.

The doorbell rang. Rang again.

"It's him," Aaron said.

Noah stood in the doorway smiling lamely.

"How are you, Mr. Panofsky?"

"Fine, fine. Come, Noah. Sit down here by me."

Noah sat down on the foot of the bed.

"How long do you have to stay in bed? What do the doctors say?"

Aaron wheeled over closer to the bed. "The doctors say that had he been hit just a bit harder he'd be dead. You tell him that."

"Who? Who should he tell? I told you to stay quiet." Panofsky turned to Noah. "I'm in the pink. Only one trouble I got. I can't remember who hit me or what happened. The doctors say this is often the case when an old man is hit hard on the head. Enough. You tell us about you. How does it go?"

"Fine. Fine, Mr. Panofsky."

"You studying?"

"Yes. Yes, I am."

"He's nervous," Aaron said. "I wonder why he's nervous?"

"You stay quiet, I said."

Aaron wheeled himself furiously out of the room. His face was taut.

"Aaron – you know – he's not so well. You mustn't pay attention."

The evening Aaron had left, Noah remembered, there had been a big party at Panofsky's. Many songs had been sung. Several of the girls had wept, for Aaron had been the tallest in the ghetto and he had known many of them well. The people of City Hall Street had clubbed together and had bought him a typewriter. *Salud*, Panofsky had said. Don't forget you should send us news. *Salud!*

"So, say a few words."

"I don't believe you," Noah said.

Panofsky leaned over and banged his pipe on the side of the bed. He pointed at the tin of tobacco on the bureau and Noah got up and fetched it for him. Panofsky began to fill his pipe slowly. He would have liked to have been able to explain to Noah, and to explain to Aaron as well, that in Russia the Cossacks had come time and again to ask questions and to take boys away: he would have liked to explain how he had felt when he had been confronted by the policeman. "Noah. Your grandfather, your *Zeyda*, is old. He hasn't got many years left. He . . ."

"That's not true either, Mr. Panofsky. There's no great love between you and my grandfather. You . . ."

"He didn't say it was Shloime because Shloime is a Jew."

Aaron's wheelchair blocked the doorway again.

"All right. All right. Now let me sleep already. I'm tired."

"You're not only tired, Paw. You're old. I gave up my legs and you couldn't even hand in that little thug. You should have told the old bigot when he came. Probably, though, he knows, anyway."

Aaron looked hard at him and then backed out of the door.

"If he had hit me a bit harder I would have been dead. But I would have died somebody useful. A man who had spent his life for an idea. So look at me now. He's right. I'm old. A storekeeper with a crippled boy and a pusher boy. What'll be, Noah? I can't die like this, my life for nothing. I should have turned him in no matter what."

"There is not one boy in the neighbourhood who doesn't remember you, Mr. Panofsky. Whenever we were in trouble we came to you."

"Do you think I should have told the police? Or your grandfather?"

"No," Noah lied. "I think you did right."

"If I could only have his legs back for him. He's a good boy. From the best. He . . ."

"He'll be all right. He's got the legs he gave up."

"Are you a communist, Noah?"

"I don't think so."

"This is no answer."

"Nothing is absolute any longer, Mr. Panofsky. There is a choice of beliefs and a choice of truths to go with them. If you choose not to choose then there is no truth at all. There are only points of view. . . ."

"Still, that is no answer."

"What if there are no answers? Or if the answers offered are not suitable – what then? Perhaps there are only more questions."

VIII

Going over the breakfront with a dust rag Leah remembered her father's last illness like a tale that had been told to her by a stranger.

"Leah – Leah, did you . . . If – if there is a light . . ."

Oh yes. Years, years, years. An unending road of years, each one harder than the last. I had hopes for Wolf at first. Yes, hopes. But do you think that man would even take me to a concert? Or a speaker? *Vos fur a Gan Eden!* The endless noises of the street, the children shouting at their games, came up to her vaguely, heard but unabsorbed. Leah lay down on the bed. Presently, *Noah approached her dimly out of the dark, dark fog into which she wandered, a fog swirling beneath many, heavy seas; and approaching, stroked her not-yet-grey hair and said:* There will be a light. A magnificent light. Everything will be all right.

(Jacob Goldenberg came from Karlin. In those days, and earlier, cities derived their reputation among the Jews, not for their size or industry or politicians, but for the rabbis who presided over them.

Karlin, a small community just outside Pinsk, was celebrated for Rabbi Aaron, and later for Rabbi Yitzhok. Jacob Goldenberg was born a poet and, having lived too long in another country, died a character. He immigrated to Montreal in 1902 with his wife, Esther, and settled down in a cold-water flat on St. Urbain Street. There, two children were born to them. Leah and Harry. Jacob taught the children of the other immigrants Talmud, and, on Friday evenings, the other chassidim gathered in his parlour where they studied and sang and sipped lemon tea.)

Remember that time, remember, when Noah had pneumonia? And how, I ask, did my Noah catch pneumonia? Fighting a whole class of boys yet. Why? Because they were throwing snowballs at Felder the rag pedlar. . . .

(Man is the crown of creation. And when the Messiah comes all souls will flow together and return to be united with the Universal Soul, which is God. For the Evil One will be conquered and a New World will be established. Israel Baal Shem Tob, who was the founder of the Chassidic movement, taught that it is man's highest idea to become the clear manifestation of God on earth. So he created the ideal of the Zaddik, of which he was the first. The Zaddik, or Chassidic saint, fuses his soul with the Oversoul. He contains the largest number of sparks of divinity, and God, who is forever with him, illuminates not only his spiritual life but even his most trivial conversation.)

Was there a Jew in Montreal who didn't know – who didn't have a good word for – Jacob Goldenberg the Zaddik? I can still see him plain as a picture. That nice beard and such deep brown eyes as you never saw and a sort of missingness about his mouth. Oh, father. All right, he gave away most of the small sums he earned. Harry, had he not won a scholarship, would have been unable to go to McGill. But didn't I adore him? Didn't I take charge of the household when Maw died in 1918? Who used to save stale bread for him so that on winter mornings he could spread crumbs in the snow for visiting sparrows? Noah, listen, on our long walks through the ghetto people always pointed us out on the streets, and Paw often stopped to give advice or a blessing.

"Leah – Leah . . . if you see – if there is a light."

Coming home bloody, my boyele, shivering, soaked to the skin. "It's in His hands," Dr. Holtzman said. A fine man, Holtzman. Paw taught him the Aleph Beth. So what happened when I had him up one evening with his awful *yentah* of a wife so that we could talk about old times? Wolf sat in the corner – bored! I remember Lou Holtzman, Wolf said. I remember him when he was a *pisher* with a running nose delivering milk for his father on St. Dominic Street. So . . . So he's the doctor. I should put up a show for him? I am what I am. No shows. Left with a grey oxygen tent, and, inside, a grey-faced boy. Coughing, rasping. *Lord, Lord, take me instead.* He is only a boy. . . .

My father, may he rest in peace, saw beauty in every man.

"Garbor works on the sabbath," Herscovitch told him.

"Poor Garbor. He is so good to his children. So in order to earn a living he must work on the sabbath."

"Rosenberg is an atheist," Felder said.

"Rosenberg? He who gives so much to the poor? Imagine how much he must suffer being without God. . . ."

Remember, Noah? Remember the stories he used to tell: "One Yom Kippur eve when the pious Jews of Berditchev assembled in the synagogue for *Kol Nidre*, Rabbi Levi Yitzhok did not appear. It was late. The sun had almost set. Can you imagine the state of the congregation? The fear, the anxiety. It grew darker, the time for *Kol Nidre* had passed, and still no rabbi! Messengers sent off to his home reported back that Rabbi Levi Yitzhok had long since left for the synagogue. Had the soldiers fallen upon him? The Jews scattered through the streets of Berditchev frantically searching for their beloved rabbi. The worst was feared. But, finally, suddenly, he was discovered in a poor man's hovel bending over the cradle of a howling infant. The infant had been left alone in the house when the parents had gone off to the synagogue."

All right, what happened, happened. Around 1925 Paw's leadership, his popularity, began to slip. But who was the first to notice that there were fewer pupils and a dwindling of disciples in the parlour on Friday evenings? Who? The men – some friends! (I should have a nickel – a penny – for each one of them that he helped.) Fancier rabbis they got themselves. Politer ones. *Noah beckoned wildly from within the fog.* "A light, Maw. A magnificent light. I see it." Sure, sure, sure. *You think I don't know he isn't there – that I'm dreaming?*

Why did he resent me taking him to school, and picking him up afterwards? *Do you know how many accidents there are every day?* Leah coughed softly, and sought a cooler spot on the pillow. 1925. Yes, that was the year. A stranger began to appear in our house. A dark, broad-shouldered man with bushy eyebrows. After having introduced himself as the son of a scribe – him, the son of a scribe! – he sat in the corner there like the cat's meow on Friday evenings never asking questions – no, not him – or joining in the readings. You should have seen Melech in these days, Noah. Sitting there with his shoes unshined and – pheh – his fly unbuttoned. Paw only allowed him in the house *out of pity*, Noah. Melech sent his sons to study with Paw – but that had nothing to do with it. Paw *wasn't* flattered by Melech's attentions. Times were hard, Paw needed pupils. But Melech knew what kind of – Paw was welcomed as a great man in Melech's home. Why not? But Paw wasn't fooled. You know what he said to me? "Who did Rabbi Levi Yitzhok love more than the peasants?" Oi, I laughed.

Listen, Noah, when Paw visited Melech he always brought me with him, and when Melech visited Paw he always brought that man – his eldest son – with him.

"This match was made in heaven," Paw said.

"To marry my son into such a family," Melech said, "is the greatest dowry that I could wish."

Leah twisted in her sleep and sobbed quietly. Remember your first quarrel with Melech, Noah? Only a boy, yes, but you told that old – that old – that – who-knows-what . . . More brains than all of them put together, all of them, lying around like I don't know what on Saturday afternoons with their shoes off and picking their noses and snoring and their feet smelling and telling each other filthy jokes they heard in the Gaiety probably and all frightened to death of their father; well my Noah isn't!

Noah, in the months before the wedding I wrote him long poetical letters about love and the beauty of the soul. It's like a burn remembering those letters. You can't imagine. . . . The boys in Panofsky's teased him.

"Well, Wolfy, it's like any other bit of machinery. Comes the day in every man's life when he's got to put it into operation."

Noah, Noah. He couldn't understand why – the two of us living only four blocks apart – I wrote him those letters. When we were together I read to him from the novels of Sir Walter Scott and the poems of Lord Byron. Every night I cried myself to sleep. . . . Every night. Our marriage wasn't consummated for several months. I . . . When Melech found out he spoke to Paw and Paw spoke to me and within a short time I was pregnant with you, *boyele*.

A wild outburst of sobbing followed, her heart thumped very quickly. My confinement was so hard: Night after night I sat alone here in this cold drab flat taking novels like pills while that man played cards around the corner at Panofsky's. Who heard my weeping? Who? But as I got bigger I knew that I was going to have you, *tzatzgele*, and that you would be a rabbi or a great surgeon or a poet. A Byron.

The night you were born, Noah, that man was at the movies. He didn't like hospitals. Leah seized the pillow and crushed her red and swollen face into it with a passion that surprised even her. Later Paw

– who was old and ailing and no longer with disciples – came to stay with us. That was during the depression, Noah. I had to use all my wits in order to make ends meet. Do you think that man would cancel the subscriptions to his magazines? "I'd buy them on the news-stands, anyway. This way it's cheaper." So I walked twenty blocks in the freezing cold rather than spend a rotten nickel on a streetcar ticket. I begged money from Harry. Greenbaum gave me piecework to do at home. Other old friends contributed a dollar here and a grocery order there. Max – who had just gone into business – gave me his books to do. Listen, Noah, I swore up and down that you would have everything. Somehow I managed to take out that small insurance policy for you. Remember when Friedman said: "If you find fifty cents a week too difficult you can switch to a smaller policy." Oh no. Such mothers come a dime a dozen – not that I'm asking for thanks. Aren't you thanks enough? Listen, I sometimes went without food rather than let the insurance payments lapse. The only person who I wouldn't accept help from was Melech.

Nu, if Paw had a stroke soon after he moved in with us and had to stay in bed after that was it *his* fault? Who passed the following few nights on a cot in Paw's room, me or that man? All right, so I didn't go back to that man's bed for a few weeks. Paw was sick.

"Why is it Harry doesn't come for a visit?"

"I don't know, Paw. I guess he's got exams or something."

"Yes. Exams. Felder still comes. He came to ask me for advice yesterday. But the others . . ."

"It's a depression, Paw. Everybody's got troubles. . . ."

"Money – no money – is not troubles."

"Yes, Paw."

"A word from me, Leah, used to be something for them. For all of them. But in the last years – you know what? – the children laughed in the street when I passed."

"People stop me in the street every day, Paw. They all want to know how you're doing."

"Lie to an old man."

Melech – don't you worry – came often, Noah. But Paw saw that he was ignorant and he was disgusted by him.

"Remember, Melech. Your children must come to God out of love. Otherwise, their prayers are dead prayers. And are not heard in heaven."

Melech listened, but he said nothing. He didn't agree. But he had a tremendous respect for Paw, I'll tell you. Paw was a Zaddik. *Years, years, years*. Listen, Noah, in his last days Paw wasted away and turned grey and was delirious almost always. He saw things. He talked with the Baal Shem Tob and Rabbi Levi Yitzhok and Sheneir Zalman and Rabbi Dob Baer. Between you and Paw – *boyele* – I hardly slept a wink.

"When the Baal Shem Tob – well, when he died – there was a light . . . a kind of light. If – I'm not saying – but if you should see anything, would you . . . I mean don't be ashamed to say. . . ."

And for six long days, oh God, he watched me, his eyes full of expectations.

"Do you think . . . I mean will many come to the funeral?"

"You're not going to die, Paw. You'll get well. But not a Jew in Montreal would stay away from your funeral."

Harry said that I was killing myself. Paw, he said, should be sent to a hospital. But I wouldn't hear of it.

"Leah – Leah, did you . . . if – if there is a light . . ."

"Yes, Paw, there is a light."

"You see it?"

"I see it."

"Can you . . . I mean . . . *Describe it*. Quick!"

Years. An unending road of years, each one harder than the last.

"Maw? Are you sleeping? Maw . . ."

Leah struggled with the many, heavy seas. She was borne upwards, conscious, unwillingly. "Noah, it's really you. How lovely! Let me look at you, *boyele*."

He was astonished to see how she had altered. Her hair was greying, her cheeks were hollow. Her eyes were red and swollen and lacked their former vitality. He noticed that her bed had been moved into the living-room. "Maw, you've been crying," he said. He kissed her forehead. "Your father used to say do not make a woman weep. God counts her tears. Come, get dressed. I'll take you for a walk."

"No, Noah." She smiled. "You should have warned me that you were coming. I would have fixed my hair. I bet you think your mother is old and ugly."

"Not at all, Maw. You look fine." He took her hands in his. "You . . ."

"Go on. I can see from the way you look at me."

Leah had a long, melancholy face with yearning eyes and a severe mouth. In this room, among her possessions, her manner was subdued. But Noah remembered that when he had used to take her out or when she had sat in the chair at meetings she had been quickly transformed into an eager, vital woman. Once, when Noah had taken her to a movie, she had said to him: "I feel so young. I'll bet if we met any of your friends on the street they'd take me for your sister or something."

"How are things with the Ladies' Auxiliary, Maw?"

"I don't go any more."

"And Mizrachi?"

"I've given up enough of my energy to them already."

Noah felt like weeping. He pressed her hand. It was rough and cracked and warm. She is no longer Jacob the Zaddik's daughter, he thought sadly. Jacob is dead. He looked at her tenderly – but could think of nothing appropriate to say.

"Come closer," Leah said.

She kissed him hungrily and he felt poor in that he could only return the gesture feebly and with fear. "Maw, I didn't even bring you anything. Flowers or . . ."

"You came yourself. That's a present."

"Are you sick, Maw?"

"Nothing. Harry says I'll be up and around before you know it. I have to lie down for a couple of hours every afternoon, that's all. I get headaches and it hurts me – I think it's my blood-pressure. Look, as long as you're all right. My life is finished. I . . ." She laughed emptily. "There I go again. You've got your own life to lead. I'm not going to make myself a weight on your back. So, how do you like college?"

"Not very much, Maw. I'm thinking of leaving."

"Leaving. Why?"

"I'm pretty restless."

"Restless, he's telling me. Don't I remember? You were in such a hurry to be born." She smiled wanly. You're no Adler, she thought. When I look at you I can feel what my father, may he rest in peace, was like as a young man. "You think that man – your father, I mean – cared if you went to school? You could have been a truck driver like him." She laughed. "Never mind. But you look thin, *boyele*. Do you eat enough? Where do you stay?"

Her voice came to him dimly, like weeping from another room. Yet she was strong, clever, too. He knew that. Why didn't she reproach him?

"I'm staying with my English professor. I'm not driving a cab any longer. I correct papers and things."

"With a professor? Did you tell him that your grandfather, may he rest in peace, was a teacher and a poet? Maybe I'll come and visit you one day? Couldn't I come for tea?"

The Japanese gardens were not thriving in the sun. The rubber plants, shrivelled, had been bleached brown. The soil had turned to dust. After the plants have died, he thought, she will put the tiny porcelain figures in the breakfront and throw the earth out and use the green pots as fruit bowls. There seemed to be a lot of safety in that.

"Of course you can come for tea, Maw," he said ineptly.

"You can be a professor, too, Noah. Or a surgeon. Anything. As long as you put your mind to it."

Colour had come back to her face. She seemed livelier.

"How's Daddy?"

"Noah" – she sat up in bed propping up her pillows behind her – "something's come over him. One day he fainted at work and Paquette brought him home. He stayed two weeks in bed. You know what he says? I wanted him to kill his father. Have you heard such a story? He sits in the den nearly every night. He's there right now. You should go in and talk to him later. I know you don't want to. But I'd be the last to stop you. You shouldn't take sides." She squeezed his hand. "Just looking at my boy is better than any medicine. Have you got a girlfriend, Noah?"

He avoided her eyes. He wished that – with him, anyway – she would not talk artfully. She has sacrificed so much for me, he thought. He bent over and kissed her on the forehead. "No," he said. "I haven't got a girlfriend." She smiled. Alternately, he felt strong attraction then revulsion for her.

"Listen, *boyele*, many a girl would be happy to catch the likes of you. But you've got plenty of time yet." She coughed. "Max comes to visit me sometimes. He always asks about you, Noah. He's sure to be elected alderman. And after that, who knows? The others tell stories about him. Jealousy, that's what. Don't they talk about you? Here, Noah, one minute. Get me my purse."

He handed her the purse. She opened it and took out an envelope and pressed it into his hand. "Your birthday present. You were twenty-one last month. Remember?"

There were five twenty-dollar bills in the envelope.

"Now give me a hug and a big kiss."

"I can't take it, Maw."

"Why not? Every week I put away five dollars for my *boyele*. Take it. Don't refuse your mother one of the few pleasures she has left."

Suddenly, he wished her dead. That horrified him. He shivered. He leaned over and kissed her and crushed the money into his pocket. "Maw. Maw, I – I'm going to see Daddy. . . ."

"Sure. Go ahead." She patted his cheek with her hand. "And Noah, be nice to him. That's the best way."

"Who said I wouldn't. . . ." He flushed angrily. "What right have you . . . All right. I'll be nice."

"That's a good boy."

She watched him go.

Not all the Jews had come to Jacob Goldenberg's funeral: but Melech, and others, had paid the expenses, and on his way to the cemetery, the synagogue doors had been opened and a special prayer had been read. He had been a Zaddik. He had been born a poet and, having lived too long in another country, had died a character. *A gathering yellow fog of exploding yellower lights, and Leah reached up wearily but in vain for a fading retreating Noah before she was washed back down under many heavy seas.* I've suffered so much, Noah. I must have you back. I can't go on . . . I'm not going to be used all my life. I've made too many sacrifices already.

IX

The following few days were hard for Noah and hard for Miriam and hard for Theo too. Noah, ignoring her adoring looks and his hopeful talk, stayed longer in bed staring at the ceiling. He was haunted by the image of his mother weeping on an unkempt bed in a room that was crowded with dying plants. That man, her husband, dreaming in his den. His mother had waited, month after month, for his home-comings from school, a face in the window: "Well, *boyele*, did you come rank-one?" He remembered old Moore, who had been cheated by his grandfather. The way I'm cheating Theo, he thought. Honest Theo who took me in and said meet my wife and read my books and sleep in my study. Theo, who, when he goes to heaven, will say: "I didn't believe in God. I didn't kill. I didn't join the Book-of-the-Month Club." So what?

I'm still trying to walk off with his wife. . . .

He began to avoid Theo. Once, he was tempted to flee. He wrote a long farewell letter to Miriam saying that what he was asking her to do was without honour, that . . . He tore up the letter. Honour, hell. *We love each other, Theo*. He went for long walks in the snow and after that in the slush. Always pausing before the window, hoping that she would sense him, that she would make some secret signs to him. But she didn't. She passed – passed often – but fleetingly: a shadow behind a blind. Oh, Miriam, Miriam. He saw men and women making love on public benches and whores standing in the rain, and his heart was breaking. *Miriam*. Often he walked over to the ghetto and tramped down the streets of his past, looking into poolrooms and fruit stores. . . . He wanted, all at once, to squeeze Melech, Wolf and Leah, Panofsky, Max, to his breast and consume them with his love. . . . But he saw little hope of a reconciliation. Before him always, wringing his heart, was a picture of Melech – an old man crumpled up in a chair: Leah – safe only with the dead: Wolf – wiggling his ears and raising his eyebrows. *Oh, God, I love them all.* Listen, I'm *not* a Goy. Sometimes, he wept. He was young and he did not know that men wept, so that made him ashamed. *Miriam, oh, Miriam*. He thought frequently of that new and unfamiliar world in which he moved and, no longer proud to have been accepted by the *Goyim*, he saw himself as a stranger among them. Only with Miriam did he feel relaxed.

And all that time Miriam watched and waited and was short-tempered: they had no time together, he seemed to be moving away from her, and she knew that she would soon have to choose between Noah and Theo. Theo, who was her husband. Who wanted a child. Who was willing to try any quack remedy for this marriage sick-room. She began to find flaws in Theo without reason or because she hungered for reasons and when he returned to her tender she was dismayed. I don't want an Ideal Husband, she thought. *I want to love and be loved.* But she could never say that to him. Never. Instead she said that she had a headache or that he was un-understanding or too understanding, that he took her for granted or not for granted. Her head swam. She did not know what to do.

Theo did not understand, so he worked harder and wrote longer letters to his mother. Deception never entered his head. He was sure that if anything was wrong the fault was his only. Perhaps I'm not paying enough attention to her, he thought. But when he offered to take her to the theatre she said, not tonight. When he tried to be loving, she said, maybe tomorrow. Then, remembering that her father had died around that time of the year, he laid her depression down to that. Miriam, he knew, had never got over her father's death. . . .

Louis Peltier, Miriam's father, had never been quite the same since that turgid afternoon in the summer of 1917 when, working on a ship, a faulty cable had snapped and twenty crates of Sunkist oranges had come crashing down on him. He had never been quite the same and never worked at anything but odd jobs again – the most perma-nent one being that of night watchman for John McFadden & Sons, Steel. Hidden away there in his small clapboard shack in the corner of the yard he built model ships and guzzled Molson's Ale under the swaying light of his watchman's lamp. When he finished one ship he burnt it and built another. Or sometimes when he was halfway through a model he crushed it to bits in his hands. Another thing that Louis Peltier could not understand was why his wife had died and that child had been born to him in 1923. April 1923, in fact. That night when he had come home from the wrestling match at the Stade-Exchange and had found his wife, Yvette Peltier *née* Roland, prostrate on the kitchen floor, all the pots on the stove steaming, and

Leo coming out of the bedroom with the baby swaddled in many towels. Madame Brault had been with him.

"She dead?"

"Yes," Leo had said.

"And the baby?"

"A girl."

"Not dead?"

"No."

"I wouldn't have gone to the wrestling, but, of course, how could I know?"

"You couldn't have known," Madame Brault had said.

"Cyr win?"

"He is champion again. What's all that stuff on the floor?"

"It comes after the baby."

"It's a fake," Leo had said.

"After the . . . What's a fake?"

"The wrestling."

"Oh. The wrestling. I'm going for a walk, I think. Keep the baby away from me. I – you mean all that stuff came out of her?"

"I'll clean it up," Madame Brault had said.

And that baby, the one that had been born that night in 1923, had gone unnamed until Paul had returned from a long, long trip four years later and had settled down and called the girl Miriam after a girl whom he had read about in a novel.

Paul was a tall and resolute man who had run away to sea at fourteen and had saved his money and had returned with his face cut by the wind and his heart past ambition and anger but not past longing for something which he could not define, but which was probably beauty, and which fastened on the child Miriam. Paul settled down. He married Brault's daughter, Louise, and opened up the *Chez-Nous* on the corner of Queen and Common Street. He adored Miriam. He always kept her clean and freshly dressed and it was rumoured that

Miriam had a room of her own and was taking piano lessons from Mademoiselle Trudeau and slept in until ten every morning. Nobody resented that. They were, in fact, proud of it. For Miriam was tall and without pimples or rickets and the people of Queen Street pampered her as though to compensate for the things that they hadn't had, and that their children weren't going to get. They liked to brag about her piano lessons and her school marks. And when Miriam came walking down the street, men adjusted their ties and women stroked their hair sadly: everybody was reverent.

Yes, Theo thought, it must be that she is brooding about her father.

That week the Kennedys invited them up to their cottage in the Laurentians for the weekend. Miriam said that she had a cold coming on but she insisted that it would not do to disappoint the Kennedys, who were nice people and subscribed one hundred dollars annually to *Direction*. Theo said that he could put them off for another week, but he was finally persuaded to go.

He left Friday night.

That night Noah read and Miriam sewed. For several days they had been counting on that night, that weekend, all to themselves, but now that they had it they both felt criminal. Noah went to bed early. Soon afterwards she also went to bed. But around one in the morning she came into his room and got into bed with him. He held her in his arms tenderly. Finally, she said: "Noah, love, say something kind."

"This apartment is intimidating both of us. We've got to get out, Miriam. Unless you've changed your mind. . . ."

"Changed my mind?"

He moved, and sat up on the edge of the bed with his back turned to her. The room was dark, but when he puffed on his cigarette he could make out many things in the brief light. He noticed that he had forgotten to hang up his trousers. At home his mother had used to do that for him. He hoped that *she* would never do that. "I visited my family last week," he said.

"And?"

He felt her cheek cool against his back, her hands a restraining thing on his shoulders, and he turned around and kissed her gently. Then he took her face in his hands and kissed her again. She clung to him urgently, her head hard to his chest. He stroked her hair. "When I am not with you," he said, "when there are others around, it is as though that time was wasted or of no account. I keep thinking up the most romantic things. I would like there to be tests that you could put me to."

She touched his ear with her mouth and said a poignant thing. "If there were a war, and we were separated, I could write you love letters. I keep thinking about things like that. . . .

"I'll tell you something stupider," she said. "Is that right? Stupider?"

"It doesn't matter."

"When I was a child I used to save up funny things that I would not tell anyone except my lover. Like" – and she laughed – "I like the smell of gasoline. Do you?" He didn't reply. "You don't have to," she said. "But you mustn't laugh." She kissed his chest. "I was told that when you love a man there is nothing that you wouldn't do for him. I used to be sceptical. But now I know differently."

"I should hope so," he said.

"Oh, aren't you tough?"

He kissed her lightly and laughed and bit her ear. "I'm as hard as nails," he said. "You watch out. Sleeping dogs should be taken with a grain of salt. I feel like standing on my head. Can you stand on your head?"

"I can sing all of *God Save the King* with my head under water."

"Hot or cold?"

"Take your pick."

"With choruses?"

"I'll even throw in a stanza or two in French."

"Well, I'm impressed. I really am. But can you stand on your head?"

"I can whistle with two fingers in my mouth and I can cross my eyes and burp at will and . . ."

"Big talker, you. But can you . . ."

"I can do anything you want me to. I can . . ."

"Look, this is serious. We may go through life without ever having stood on our heads. Gym teachers do it every day. They seem a cheerful lot too, don't they? Maybe standing on your head gives you a new outlook on life. Perhaps . . ."

She rolled over onto his chest and, suddenly serious, kissed him strongly. "You are the only peace that I have known," she said.

"Have you known many men?" he said, stroking her hair.

"Yes."

"Many?"

"Many."

He propped himself up on his elbows and looked at her solemnly. "I . . . There are things that I've read about in books," he said shyly. "I don't know how to do them. If I can do . . ."

"Noah. Noah, I love *you*."

"Yes, but . . ."

She pressed her hand to his mouth and kissed him again.

They did not talk for some time and then she told him about Queen Street.

Queen Street is in Griffintown, near the waterfront. In that maze of streets – Queen Street among them – between the waterfront and Wellington Street many tall brick chimneys poke skywards and all day long there is the banging and clanging of machinery and blast from the furnaces. Interlaced between the factories and workshops, like putty between bricks, are the tenements where the longshore-men, the welders, and machinists live. Many of them are Irish, others are French Canadian. On a summer's day grubby children, many of them with tuberculosis, play, cough blood, and pummel each other with rocks, moving between the machines and trucks and junk piles like frantic lice. At night the heat drives the people out into the streets where they gossip loudly, being used to yelling over the racket of the machines.

"I didn't know that you had been poor," he said.

"My father was afraid of me but beer changed him. Sober, he stooped and his eyes were dead. But when he was drunk he seemed to feel himself taller and a kind of yearning came into his eyes. He fixed up an adorable little garden in the corner of the junk yard, just beside his shack. There was a chair for him and I used to sit on an empty beer case. He used to make things for me. A doll's house out of old orange crates. Rag dolls. Holding my hand he used to tell me stories. Shut your eyes, he'd say. We are sailing down the Yellow River in China. We've already been down the Amazon, remember? We got caught in a blizzard on the Bug and the Nile had too much sun for the likes of us. But the Yellow River is perfect. Look! Flowers are floating downstream with us. Listen to the men singing on the banks! What is that lovely child doing with a broken old man? a Chinaman asked. You tell him, child. He's your father. Say that. . . . Sometimes, when he had too much to drink, we used to sneak off to the harbour together. But we had to watch out for Paul. He didn't like Papa to come near me when he was drunk. Papa would cry, you know. He would wring his hands and look at me imploringly and weep. Oh, if only I had been older," she said, "I would have understood. But I was only twelve at the most. From time to time he would point at the foundries or at the ships in the canal. 'Machines,' he would say, 'ships. . . . Everywhere there are machines.' Then he would imitate the noises of the various hoists and presses. Oh, Noah, when I think that I told Paul about it." She held her hand to her cheek. "But he frightened me so badly when he did that. Anyway,

Paul gave him hell. Papa never came near me again when he was drunk. He spent most of his time in that horrid shack. . . ."

Noah kissed her throat and, undoing her pyjama-top, rested his head on her breasts. Her hand was in his hair. A kind of lethargy came over him. That world, which was turbulent and chaotic; outside, where strangers had ambitions, needs, contests; there, where there was dying – no longer existed. All that remained was him, the woman in his bed. The darkness around us, he thought, belongs to others. We will be a light burning in the city. Let the others gather round and be amazed. Or let them stay away.

"My grandfather, the poet, used to say love the rich. All they have is money. The poor have injustice and the future and . . ."

"Being poor *is* awful, Noah. I don't want it again."

They lit cigarettes.

"The day he died was a hot, bright day in summer," she said. "He must have been planning it for months in his shack. It was a Wednesday, and for no apparent reason he had put on his good suit. But by that time nobody cared or noticed what Papa did. He was a kind of joke on the street. The men, when they saw him all dressed up, teased him mercilessly. 'Going to meet your girl, Louis?' I looked out of the window and they stopped. I remember – funny – I remember that leaning out of the window I was afraid that I might soil my dress. I waited for my father to pass down the street so that I could shut the window again. But he took his time and I was so annoyed. He tottered off the pavement. Then he postured defiantly in the middle of the street, his hands on his hips and his legs spread apart. Everybody laughed. I laughed myself. Then Claire screamed. She saw the truck coming and she understood. I, the others, didn't. . . ." Miriam brushed her hair back nervously and swallowed hard. "Noah, he ran towards that truck waving his fists in the air as though to break it. The yell that came from his lips. . . . It all happened so quickly – I honestly think that he meant to smash that truck. I didn't even have courage to look. I turned away and collapsed on my bed. When I looked again he – it – was covered with a blanket. There was a crowd. Paul came upstairs with his wife and she took me away to the nuns. I wanted to stay. He was my father. I had betrayed him. But Paul wouldn't let me. That's when I began to hate him."

"He sounds like an awful bastard. He . . ."

"The next day I saw the inside of that shack for the first time. He had made landscapes on the walls. They were made out of an arrangement of different-coloured beer-bottle tops – each one nailed into the wood. . . . There were several pictures of me on the ceiling. There was one of us together in his 'garden'. . . . The shack was torn down long ago. God, when I think of all the loving work that went into that arrangement of bottle tops . . ."

Her passion surprised him that night. His eyes adjusting to the darkness, he had been able to watch the swift changes that her face had undergone as desire, then urgency, finally gave way to a splendid languor. Afterwards she insisted on rubbing down the fierce scratches on his back with iodine. Then she snuggled up tight to him, and they dozed for a bit. Miriam, who had run and run and run, and who had found most men as satisfactory, as expendable, as cosmetics, felt, now that she had arrived, a tremendous need to rest.

"I'll quit college on Monday," he said, "and look for an apartment."

"Noah, you mustn't quit. I'll work. What would you do if you quit?"

"I'll drive a cab again. I was thinking that if we both worked for about six months we'd have enough money to go to Europe. Would you like to come to Europe? Would you like to come to Europe with me?"

"Yes, of course, but . . ."

"But what?"

"We should make plans. What do you want to do? We can't just . . ."

"Drift?"

"Yes, drift."

"Let it be said of us that we made no plans. That the others schemed, got money and position, honours, futures, but that we – who dissented – ruined ourselves with loving."

She giggled. "Aren't you being just *slightly* pompous?" she said. "However, let's leave it for now. I've got some money saved. We can go up to Ste. Adele for the summer. We'll take a cottage."

"Ste. Adele is restricted."

"I'll tell them you're an Arab."

Noah's anxiety passed quickly. He laughed. "We'll fart when we have visitors and drop rocks on passing cars." He turned to her suddenly. "Let's get a shack that's really beat up. Early every morning you can rush out on to the moors in your nightgown. We'll fix up your hair with seaweed and order a god from Eaton's. I'll hang out of the upstairs window with a bottle of Javel in my hands and then you yell up to me – very distant-like though – 'Heathcliffe. Heathcliffe.' There'll be a catch or two in your voice and my hair is streaked with head. 'Get thee to a nunnery,' I yell, 'or this too, too solid flesh may resolve itself into a Jew.' Then . . ." He pulled her to him and kissed her and she responded gladly. "I was thinking the same thing myself," she said.

When they awakened again around noon they heard voices in the living-room. For that's when Theo arrived with the Kennedys.

Unfortunately the door to Noah's room was open. Marg turned away discreetly. "Oh," she said.

John took her arm firmly. "We'll wait in the car," he said.

But before they had left to wait in the car they had looked at Theo reassuringly, as though they had meant to be good enough to rub out what they had seen – unless (there had been something practical in Marg's look) he required witnesses.

Theo turned away from the open bedroom door and collapsed in an armchair and shut his eyes and held his head in his hands. Miriam leaped out of bed swiftly and flung Noah's trousers at him. "Your pants," she said thickly.

Noah got into his trousers calmly, but his head throbbed.

Theo looked up at them blankly. His first sexual experience had been shameful to him. His mother had discovered a set of lewd photographs underneath the shelving paper in the toilet medicine cabinet. She had asked him point-blank how often he masturbated. And Theo had burst into tears. Recalling that incident, facing his adulterous wife and her lover, Theo felt partially gratified. "John suggested that we drive into town to see if you felt better."

"This is dreadful," Miriam said.

But from the way she had said that Theo couldn't understand what had been dreadful – her having been in bed with Noah or his having discovered them.

"I don't believe this. Why, we're so happy together. Everybody says so. . . . You can explain it. I'm sure you can. I'm not going to lose my temper. You were drunk, that's it. Isn't it?"

Noah looked at Theo. Their eyes met briefly, and Theo looked away first. But there had been no anger in his eyes. Shock, and something deeper than that.

"We weren't drunk," Noah said ruefully.

The room swayed around Miriam. She believed that universal love – an ointment properly applied – would heal all worldly ills. She had arrived at that conclusion not only out of mental laziness but also because she was afraid and ointments obviously conceal more surely than they heal. Such loves, such remedies, are without truth. So, as she found her present circumstances sordid, Miriam suddenly turned against both Noah and Theo. They were ugly, unlovable. She wished them both away. She wrung her hands and wandered into the bedroom and back into the living-room. *Why doesn't Paul come to take me away?*

"Please button your pyjamas," Theo said.

Obediently, she buttoned her pyjamas.

"Haven't either of you anything to say? Don't you think that you owe me an explanation?"

"I'm sorry that it had to happen this way," Noah said, "but . . ."

Theo turned to Miriam.

"We had a lot to drink," Miriam began falteringly, "and we . . ."

Noah was shocked. He looked at Miriam severely and then turned to Theo. "This is terrible for you, Theo. But it is for her too. Probably more so. But we weren't drunk. We . . ."

"Noah. Please, Noah. You go. Later . . ."

Theo got up and confronted Noah more confidently.

"I took you in off the streets, Noah, and – and – you made her do it. You had to get her drunk first, though. Not that it matters. Except that now my wife and I know exactly what kind of person you . . ."

"You don't understand, Theo." Noah faced Theo firmly, refusing, beforehand, to play the role that was being offered to him so blatantly. To apologize, agree that they had been drunk, and then, afterwards, to go ahead with a surreptitious affair. "You may make love to my wife as long as I don't see and you don't tell." He sensed that Miriam and Theo were united against him in the same way as Melech and Wolf had joined forces much earlier. Wolf had said: "You can go without a hat. Eat ham. But not in front of *Zeyda*." Perhaps, Noah thought, eating ham was not so unimportant after all. Surely this society has as little veracity, if more novelty, than the one that I have sprung from. Noah was exhilarated. He felt that he was no longer merely a rebel. An iconoclast. He was beginning to develop a morality of his own. Still embryonic, he thought, but . . . "You don't understand, Theo."

"Noah. . . . If you feel anything for me, if . . ."

"The Kennedys, darling. I just remembered. . . ."

"F— the Kennedys," Noah said.

"Nobody seems to be asking *you* to worry about anything," Theo said. "But *we've* got a reputation. You're moving out, Noah. Right away. I refuse to allow Miriam to see you again."

"We're not having a dirty little affair, Theo. You've got a reputation, but Miriam and I are in love. I'm going, but she comes with me."

"You're mad!"

Theo tried to turn away from him but Noah blocked his path.

"Ask her."

They both turned to Miriam.

Miriam stared back at them with terror. Noah's ruthless manner alarmed her and yet she felt more disgust than compassion for Theo. Oh, if only she were dead. Would they wait? She looked first at Theo and then at Noah. No, *he* wouldn't. Noah reached for his jacket. He had been slighted once before. "No," Miriam said, surprised at her own voice. "Don't. I – Theo, I'm sorry, I – I'm in love with him. . . ."

Theo stifled a sob. He swung back as though to hit Noah, shut his eyes, tottered, and collapsed on the floor.

"He's fainted," Noah said.

"You were so cruel, Noah. I never . . ."

"He's fainted," Noah said stupidly. "He . . . I did – Miriam," he said, pulling her to him desperately, "we *must* love each other truly. We . . . He's fainted."

Miriam stared at him disconsolately. She held her hand to her cheek. She was frightened.

3

Spring 1953

To understand what a fine place Montreal is when spring is coming you must know the winters that come first. Chill grey mornings; sun bright in the cold noon sky but giving off no heat to speak of; skies darkening again early in the afternoon; long frosty nights with that window-banging wind whipping in burning hard from the north, pushing people before it like paper, making dunes and ridges that hurt the eye to look at on the mountain snows, burning children's cheeks red and cutting like a knife across flat frozen ponds. Old men blowing on their wrinkled hands, boys with blue lips, and women with running noses all huddled up and knocking their feet together in the bitter cold waiting for liquor commissions to open and banks to shut, late dates, streetcars. . . .

So when the first rumours of thaw reach the city everybody is glad. That first rumour, coming towards the end of February, is usually hidden away in the back pages of the newspapers. It says that two government icebreakers, the *Iberville* and the *Ernest Lapointe*, have started poking their way up the frozen St. Lawrence towards Montreal. That's a while before the NHL hockey play-offs, and most people on the streetcars are talking about how the players are moving slow because of the heat. The resorts up north stop advertising themselves as the St. Moritz or Davos of Canada: they begin to talk of the sun, their pamphlets saying how so many happily married couples first fell on their beaches. That first thaw is a glory. The big snow heaps on Fletcher's Field and a whole winter's caboodle of snowmen begin to shrivel and shrink away. Giant sweepers roar up and down the streets wiping a winter's precautionary sands off the pavement. You can make out chunks of yellow grass here and there like exposed flesh under the shrinking slush that still sticks to the flanks of Mount Royal. Occasionally, it snows: but noon comes and all the gutters are gurgling again. There is a green, impolite smell to the streets.

With the first thaw the change takes hold: there is a difference to everything, the difference between a clenched fist and an open hand. The kids get out on their roller-skates and make most side-streets a hazard. Belmont Park opens, so do the race tracks. Ships steam into port from Belfast and Le Havre and Hamburg and Liverpool and Archangel and Port-of-Spain. NDG organizes softball teams, the ladies of Westmount plan their flower-shows, and the Jr. Chamber of Commerce sets aside one week as Traffic Safety Week. The man who reviews books for the *Star* will say that spring is here but J. P. Sartre is without that traditional Gallic charm, and young writers aren't cheerful enough. But best of all is St. Catherine Street on an April evening. Watch the girls, eh, their hair full of wind, as they go strolling past in their cotton print dresses. Men, sporting smart suits and spiffy ties, waving enticingly at them. See the American tourists having a whale of a time frantically, a Kodak strapped to one arm and a lulu of a wife to the other. . . . Kids wandering in and out of the crowds yelling rude things at girls older than themselves. . . . Sport fans clustering at corners waiting for the *Gazette* to appear. . . .

In parks, playgrounds, and on Mount Royal, tattered men with leather faces loll on benches, their faces upturned to the sun. Maiden aunts hopeful again after a long winter's withering knit near to baby carriages which hold the children of others. Come noon, lovers freed from the factory sprawl on the green mountainside while the children tease and the tattered men watch laconically and the maiden aunts knit near to baby carriages that hold the children of others.

Everybody is full.

Now that Melech Adler was without work he did not know what to do with all his days. He still started off his morning by reading the obituary column in the *Jewish Star*, but the death of old friends no longer made him sad. He still attended services in the synagogue every evening but the other old men avoided him. Melech Adler made many crude jokes about death, and they thought him morbid. He had begun to read the illustrated magazines and daily papers. Here he read of a strange and unlikely world, *their* world, wherein crimes were committed for the sake of passion and men had mistresses and were not afraid of being judged. Then, likely as not, he would turn to Jenny. Their old men had young women. They hadn't devoted all their lives to their families. He recalled the stories that he had heard about Greenbaum and the young French Canadian girls who did piece-work in his factory. What if Greenbaum outlives me, he thought. He prayed harder. He remembered those beautiful evenings, long ago, in the home of Jacob Goldenberg the Zaddik, and cursed himself for having been so shy then, for having been too overawed by the other man's holiness to ask questions. Jacob, may he rest in peace, had used to tell of the trials of the Baal Shem Tob so wonderfully well. Oh, to be a man of God. He remembered his pious father, the scribe, who had written many Torahs by hand. I could have been a scribe too, he thought nostalgically. *I didn't go against him. I renounced Helga, who clapped her hands together when she sang.*

Every afternoon Melech Adler locked himself up in his office for two hours and Wolf sat outside and wondered.

"*Nu*, Jenny, you know what they call their children? Byron, Cecil. Are these Yiddish names? Do dey come to visit us any more on Sundays? They go to Plattsburg. Nurses they get for the children.

My missus wishes to kiss her own grandchildren so it ain't sanitary. I should retire, Max says. What . . ."

"Max means everything good," Jenny said gently.

"Max. We got him for a prime minister in the family. I should retire, yeah? Go to Plattsburg? Go to the beach to look at naked women? Me, I work. I worked hard. So what do I get for a thank you? Leah is ashamed for the coal yard. Who paid – I'm not saying nothink, he was a fine man – but who paid her fodder's funeral? Ida hangs the walls with movie stars. And Shloime? Shloimi is a . . ." Mr. Adler began to cough. He no longer visited Panofsky because he was ashamed of what had happened. He cleared his throat and took another sip of tea.

"Shloime will learn," Jenny said. "He's young yet. He . . ."

"He'll learn is right." Melech got up. "Right now – for a fact – I'm going to teach him his first lesson."

"Melech. Please, Melech. . . ."

But he had already loosened his trouser belt and started up the stairs.

"If you ask me," Wolf Adler said, putting his Coke down on the counter and wiping the crumbs off his lips, "if you ask me, Karl, doctors don't know from their ass to their elbows. Look, your paw got hit over the head so they sew him up and say, goodbye, good luck, I'll send you a bill in the mail. But he's not the man he was, is he? Just between you me and the lamp-post, he's not the same guy. Take my wife now. They tap her chest and take samples of this and X-rays of that but so what – *so what*? You're as good as gold, Mrs. Adler. That's what they say. Honest. But she says she's sick and she oughta know. So if you ask me – and I've had experience let me tell you – if you ask me, doctors should be taken with a grain of salt. Certain diseases are still a mish-mash to them."

Karl unscrewed the top of the biscuit jar, took out a chocolate biscuit and offered one to Wolf. Then, overturning his Coke bottle,

he downed his drink in three quick gulps. "Poison," he said, popping
a mushy chocolate biscuit into his wet, wide-open mouth. His jaw
clamped shut and the biscuit crumbled, bits of brown fluid trickling
down the sides of his fat pink lips. He wiped his lips clean on the
sleeve of his soiled white shirt, and burped loudly.

Wolf grinned. He gobbled down his biscuit, then slipped his
thumb into his mouth and picked a sliver of crust free of a tooth.

The boy came in with Karl's *Gazette*, and the two friends split the
paper wordlessly. Karl took the sports section.

Panofsky's was buzzing. Men crowded around the two bridge
tables which had been set up near the Coca-Cola freezer. Gin rummy
was being played at one table and pinochle at the other. Most of
the men were jacketless and two of them, who lived right around the
corner, were wearing their slippers. Their talk was easy and their
jokes were familiar. They had known each other for years, and most
of them were related in one way or another. They, the sons, were still
orthodox. The synagogue was a habit and a meeting place for them.
The *Goyim*, a mystery. Something to talk about. They were substan-
tial men. Extremely good to their wives and enormously fond of
their children. They worked hard all week. Sunday was their night.

Kravitz, the grocer, grinned broadly. "Gin," he said.

It was a warm, spring night. The door was kept open.

"Hey," Karl said. "This column. Liss'n, Wolf. 'City Councillor
Max Adler and an unnamed blonde made a cosy twosome at the
Chez Paree last night. Canvassing votes, Max? . . .' *Unnamed blonde*
yet. I should have such troubles. Your brudder Maxie is some b.t.o."

"Look, Karl, those kind of dames mean trouble with a capital T.
Here, listen what I just read. Bing Crosby's wife has died. According
to the laws of California that means he has to pay taxes on her share
of his property. In other words, a cool million. So what happens? He
hasn't got it. He's got to mortgage his horses and his yacht and his
farm. I'll bet you tonight Bing Crosby wishes that he was just a little

guy again. Money means troubles. Max is growing too fast. He owns who knows how many cottages up in Ste. Agathe now. But five'll get you one that he couldn't raise a G overnight. Everything's tied up. Comes a depression and first thing you know no more la-de-da in the mountains at four hundred uckbays a cottage. Bango! No more unnamed blondes. And what, tell me, if the blonde has clap? Max isn't so happy as people think. More than anything he'd like to have a kid. Always he's asking me where's Noah. Me, I'd rather stay with my father. I told you what happened with the derrick last winter? So. What if I hadn't been around to save him? Plunk would have gone three tons of scrap on his head." Wolf paused. Again he stood by the open door of the inner office, the strong-box almost within reach. "And as far as Noah goes – this is just between us, you know – but . . . what I hear, he's in deep with the dames too."

"Give, give. What do you hear?"

"I hear."

All talk stopped suddenly.

Wolf looked at the card-players and then followed their gaze to the open door. His eyes met Shloime's. Shloime grinned.

Karl picked up an empty Coke bottle. "Out," he said.

"I wanna speak wid my brudder." Shloime twirled his key chain. "You got a law against that, Mr. Soda Jerker?"

Kravitz got up and began to walk towards the door. He was a big man.

"No, wait," Wolf said. "I'll speak to him outside."

"Listen, boychik," Kravitz said, "you keep away from this store if you know what's good for you. Capish?"

"You a communist too, Kravitz? I don't know what happened to Panofsky. But I hear stories. Maybe us young guys don't like commies so good? Who knows?"

Kravitz came closer and Shloime backed away. Wolf pulled Shloime outside.

Wolf was sweating. "All right. What do you want?"

"Liss'n. Paw is crazy or sumptin. He's having a fit. He just kicked me out of the house – for good. He says it was me yet who robbed Panofsky. He's gone mad. I tell you. You should see him. He ripped up all my pictures and magazines because they're full of naked women he says."

"All right. What do you want from me?"

"Look, Wolf. Let's make it short and sweet. I'm broke and I want fifty bucks."

"Liss'n, Shloime – man to man – I am a guy who doesn't take sides. Fifty bucks is nothing. But I give it to you – well, that's like giving it against Paw. As far as I'm concerned you can do what you like, but I don't want to get involved."

"That's all I wanted to know. Goodbye, sucker. But I'll fix you too. I'll fix the whole bunch. I hate them. You included."

Wolf watched bewildered as Shloime walked away into the warm, spring night. I would never steal, he thought. I'm a Jew. But he almost admired Shloime for stealing. That's something *they* do. He passed his hand through his hair, and then stared at his hand. Leah was really sick now. Wolf could not understand why he had such awful luck. Everybody likes me too, he thought. I mind my own business. I never say a bad word against a person. I go to the syna-gogue. Why can't people let me alone, he thought. What did I ever do wrong?

A car whirled around the corner, but Wolf didn't notice. It was Ida and Stanley. Stanley, who worked as a cutter in the Knit-to-Fit, owned a '38 Buick. He parked a short way down from Ida's house, away from the lamp-post light. He tried to slip his hand under her skirt, but she stopped him quickly.

"A girl's gotta think of what people say," she said. "You'll give me a rep for being hot."

"Everybody does it but."

"Look, mister. We're not going the limit until after we're married. I'm no Ettie Firstein. Be good, Stan, *please*. I want you to respect me."

"But we're going steady, kiddo. Ask anybody but."

"Stan. Pul-eeze. People can see us."

"I'm so horny, kiddo. I'm crazy about you but."

"That makes me the rabbi of a French glue factory in Japan."

"Let's go inside."

"You crazy!"

So they sprawled out on the sofa in the living-room.

"Stan, when are we going to get married?"

"Soon, soon. But do you think Max'll gimme a job? Christ. I'd like to be an operator like him. Why don't you introduce me, eh?"

"Stan. Don't, Stan. I'm scared stiff."

"It's just your sweater but. C'mon, everybody does it."

After he had gone Ida sat down on the sofa and lit a cigarette – the first that she had ever smoked. The cigarette made her feel sweetly remorseful. She began to suspect that there were many more pleasures and many fewer punishments than those catalogued in the law according to Melech Adler. She stepped outside and sat down on a chair on the balcony. There was still that pain in her stomach. The night had already begun to fade and there was a rumour of dawn in the sky. Dizzy but calm, she was aware of smoke fumes forming sensual around her. When the cigarette was finished she suffered from a poignant sense of loss, almost as if a death had occurred, and she soon longed for another.

II

Soon after St. Jerome, a prosperous French Canadian mill town with a tall grey church, the horizon widens and the highway begins to rise, rise and dip, rise again from the valley and into higher hills. Sloping easily on all sides are the slow, pine-rumpled hills. Old and shrivelled cliffs appear like bruised bones here and there, and in the valleys below, the fertile fields are yellow and green and brown. There is the occasional unpainted barn or silo – blackened by the wind and the rain – rising out of the landscape as natural as rocks. Billboards, more modern, stick out of the earth incongruously. The slim and muddy river, sheltered from the sun by birch and bush, winds northwards drowsily but insistent between the still hills. Cottages – a mess strewn on a hilltop or a pile of them spilled sloppily into a valley – appear every ten miles or so. From time to time, as the highway climbs higher north, some ambitious cliff or hill pokes into the soft underbelly of a low grey cloud. These higher hills, sometimes called mountains, are often ribbed by ski-tows, trails, and the occasional derelict jump. Bears, the stray deer or two, are often rumoured in these parts, but, like the pretty girls who beckon from the travel brochures, they are seldom seen.

About forty-five miles north of Montreal a side-road turns up off into Ste. Adele en-haut. It's about three miles to the lake. Ste. Adele is the retreat of Montreal's aspiring middle-class, and, as a resort town, is prone to all the faults and virtues of that group. The cottages are clean but prosaic: no Jews are wanted, but, on the other hand, they are dealt with diplomatically. The French Canadians tolerate the Presbyterians from the city because they have brought prosperity to their village, and the Presbyterians find that the French Canadians add spice to their holiday: they accept their haughtiness as philosophically as rain on Sundays. Few on either side are bilingual.

The pinewood cottage they had rented was about five miles off the highway, pretty high in the hills and by the side of a mountain stream. It had three bedrooms and an open fireplace in the living-room. There was a rock-garden of sorts around by the front and a fine breeze by the stream. The old, musty furniture had been picked up at auction sales many years ago and was bruised in a warming, familiar way.

Noah and Miriam had had a busy week before coming up to the cottage.

They had moved, temporarily, into Mrs. Mahoney's and they bought a '41 Ford for three hundred and fifty dollars. Marg Kennedy phoned on Wednesday and asked Miriam to meet her for a drink. Marg was a quick attractive woman who earned more money than her husband and was interested in child psychology. She wrote commercials for a soap company. John, who had got over being a socialist, worked in an advertising agency. The Kennedys were buying a duplex on the instalment plan and planned to have three children, spaced over six years. Miriam met Marg at the Ritz on Sherbrooke Street. That quiet bar is one of the most fashionable in Montreal. Entering the bar, which she had accepted as something nice long ago, Miriam suddenly remembered that first afternoon when Noah had called and she had known instinctively that he would find her sophistication hard. She gazed at Marg, who sipped the correct drink and wore the right dress. This is how I must have appeared to Noah at first, she thought. She was afraid. Marg waved, Miriam smiled. Smiled, and realized with a certain sadness, that this friendship of so many years had lapsed.

Afterwards Miriam joined Noah in the Yacht Club. She had a lot to drink. "Sweet Marg says that I'm thirty. She says that you, Mr. Adler, are a dirty little boy who needs a haircut. She says that she used to like having a bit of fun herself but that – let's face it – we're getting on and the time has come to settle down. Theo, sweet Marg says, wouldn't mind if I had an affair or two, but why humiliate him? She also says that John's lousy in bed. That John is not as bright as she is, and that that makes it tough."

They drove up to Ste. Adele on Friday night.

Those first two weeks were the happiest of their lives. Not that there had been any especial afternoon or evening that was so very memorable, but everything, even the most commonplace incident, seemed quite beautiful in retrospect. They got up early every morning and walked hand-in-hand in the woods. They ate lunch on the screened porch and afterwards took a blanket out and slept or read in the sun. Noah felt freer than he ever had previously: there was no past and no future. He did not worry about his family. She watched him jealously. For the first few days she had missed Theo. Earlier, when she had been shopping in Montreal, she had been able to stifle her thoughts with work, but those first few days in the mountains he had intruded on her joy like a recurring bad dream. For several years she had lived narrowly but within certain conventions, everything being habitual. Secure, also. Alone, they had had very little to say to each other, but that, in retrospect, had been more reassuring than boring. She worried about Theo. Had he remembered to thank Aunt Clara for the lamp she had sent for Christmas? Would he pay the butcher bill? Remember not to be so belligerent about his politics when the dean was around?

Theo and Miriam had met at McGill. That had been a time of baffled men and evening and paper souls and loving like fast handshakes. Writers, famous and forgotten since, who had been crackerjacks with French-kiss symbols. Indolent, imitation Rimbauds. With John Kennedy, Marg Bradshaw, Herb Shields, Chuck Adams, Mary Walsh, Pip McLeod, and others, they had formed a group of vigorous and politically conscious rebels. Nobody had thought of Theo and Miriam as being anything more than a part of a group. As a matter of fact, Miriam seemed to be seeing a lot of Chuck Adams. Chuck, however, was one of the first to go. He joined the RCAF. The others followed quickly. Theo, through no fault of his own, was the last to go. That's how the two of them had been thrown together.

Second-Lieutenant Hall searched for his friends on his last night in Montreal but all of them, except Miriam, had dispersed. So Theo and Miriam set out into the night intent on drinking their way through every bar in town. But without the rest of the crowd – without Chuck in particular – they had surprisingly little to say to each other. They tried, however. Miriam evoked a few forced laughs by reminding him of that night when Mary had disrupted all of Windsor Station – outraging the flag-carriers and scandalizing the teary-eyed – by coming down to see off Pip McLeod dressed in widow's black and sweeping down the platform on roller-skates. Some girl, Theo said, and then told the story of how Chuck had damn near got himself thrown out of McGill. Chuck was mad, Miriam said. And so they drifted from bar to bar, determined to have a night that could be committed to memory, embellished upon and written of to the others, who were in Alexandria or London or Hong Kong or Toronto. But they soon ran out of anecdotes and they did not know how to talk to each other. Miriam felt that she had failed the others. Theo remembered that when Chuck had gone off there had been a hell of a party. Everybody had had fun.

But they couldn't call it quits. They watched the clock in one anonymous bar after another, until Miriam frantically suggested that they go up to her apartment. That had been his thought, too, but only as a last resort. Miriam, he thought, was Chuck's girl. Chuck was away fighting. So they failed at making love, too, lonely for the others even in bed. Afterwards they were still left with time. Theo started off on another Chuck Adams anecdote and Miriam, suddenly conscious of the pathos of their situation, took him into her arms and wept bitterly. Theo did not understand. Miriam sobbed. Theo fled. He waited around for more than an hour in that chill station which was as vast as his melancholy, until his train left at 7:15 a.m. Miriam didn't see him.

He wrote her from England, France, Germany, and from England again. At first she answered his letters as a kindness. His early letters were cautionary. Hers were factual. Then one day she wrote him a long and gloomy letter. Chuck was missing over Germany. "When will this madness end? What if Stalingrad falls?" And he wrote back: "Remember that night in Montreal, the night of my departure . . ."

Memory swindled them. That wretched night took on glamour in retrospect. They recalled that there had been drinks and love-making, and not the desperation that had been inherent in both. Wave after wave of yearning letters broke on her, each one more full than the last. Soon she found herself thinking, why shouldn't I be loved too? I'm tired of running, tired of searching. He's so solid. . . .

Their parting had been clumsy. She had expected that there would be a sadness shared, or a kind exchange for the sake of memory. Instead she had said that the alarm clock was hers and he had said that the radio was his – when it wasn't. What was to be done with the dishes? Wedding gifts? Which records were hers and which books were his? Finally and between sobs she had said that she would take nothing. But he had said no, he wasn't in need of her charity. So they had quarrelled again. She had fled the apartment, leaving everything behind. But she had returned the next day when he was away at lectures and had taken her things away. She had left the alarm clock and the radio behind.

She watched Noah anxiously. Everything he did was new. Unexpected. What if he left her? What if . . .

But after a few days she felt that even her anxiety had passed. She surrendered herself gladly and without motives to her lover and the sun and living without habit or security.

After dinner they would sprawl out on the rug before the open fire.

"I feel so utterly dependent on you now. Does that frighten you, Noah?"

"No."

"I'm sometimes afraid that you'll meet a younger woman. Somebody prettier. Or more intelligent."

"If I do, we'll send her away. We'll . . . Funny, I would like everybody to be in love now." He laughed. "You're so neat. Did you know that? You're always cleaning or mopping up or sweeping. I noticed that this afternoon."

"Marg wouldn't mind us. Neither would the others. If they thought that we weren't serious."

"I'll bet. I guess she'd make you a member of the club. I guess she'd issue you with a badge and a book of secret signals and a douche bag. Christ."

"I love you, Noah. I've never been so happy. Something's always spoiling things. Don't let that happen. Please don't."

One rainy afternoon he wandered off by himself down the dirt road. The sky swept down darkening the day and hiding the hills. People on all sides ran for cover. Horses disturbed in their stables whinnied and kicked. His hair adhering to his head, water running down his neck, Noah felt more sympathy for the horses. He was suddenly filled with a sense of his own small condition. If I were a horse, he thought, I would gallop up to the top of the highest hill and bray louder than any thunder. Then he sat down under a tree and watched the rain peck small holes in the dirt. He stared pleadingly at the people who were huddled in doorways under awnings. *Come, come out and dance. Shout. Sing.* Even as a boy he had been disturbed by the fact that people stopped talking during a storm or, if they did talk, talked too loud.

The hills greyed and black clouds swirled, lightning cracked and then the rumbling distant, closer, and the rushing in the trees. Down, down, swoosh after swoosh of rain. Eventually he kicked off his shoes and, up again, wandered into the woods singing the prayers of his boyhood boldly. At last the rain stopped. Clouds broke up and softened until the sun – magnanimous beyond compare – condescended to shine down in the woods and on the reappearing hills, as if nothing, nothing at all, had ever happened.

Waiting for him, huddled up on the screen porch, teeth chattering and chain-smoking, she saw him appear sodden and shivering out of the woods, barefoot, his eyes wild. She had been through an awful time. He's bored, she thought. He's leaving me. Miriam leaped up and led him into the bedroom. She undressed him and rubbed him down with a towel and gave him brandy. He seized her. Something in his eyes made her struggle against him. They grappled briefly. She bit him and he yelled. Then responding to a current that raced madly through her loins she submitted to him eagerly. His love-making that afternoon often verged on violence, even if it never quite broke out that way. That last climatic groan that usually broke from her lips seemed, that afternoon, to infuriate him. He muttered imprecations. His caresses could have been blows. Each time she thought that he was exhausted he managed to summon up energy again from the darkest places. Finally, however, he grimaced as though in great pain and rolled away into a corner of the bed and fell into a deep sleep.

"How long can this go on, Noah? Don't you want to do anything?"

"Are you afraid, Miriam?"

"Of you, mostly. I'm living with you yet I don't know you. You seem to go only so far and then . . . There is a part of you that I can't reach or understand."

"Miriam, how far do you think two people can really go?"

III

Back in Montreal, Theo was worried and angry but he was going to face the whole problem intelligently, without emotion. She'll be back, he thought. That kind of thing never lasts. At Oxford she had had an affair with Chris Taylor, who had emended the most recent edition of the poems of George Herbert. But that had been a thing of the spring. This thing with Noah, Theo thought, is different.

And it was. Noah wasn't a member in the sense that those in the group in Montreal, and afterwards in the other group at Oxford, had been members, with a sort of option on the extra-curricular lapses of other members. Not only that. But Noah was a Jew as well. Now Theo, if anything, was not an anti-Semite. As a student he had refused to join anti-Semitic fraternities and still later he had boycotted restricted hotels and restaurants. That's why he felt cheated. Why should a Jew take away *his* wife? There were other complications, too. Miriam aside, Theo had not slept with any other women save whores. Whores in France and Germany, when the need had been great or when the fear of being branded a queer had demanded such behaviour. He hadn't enjoyed that kind of thing much. He was against such transactions in principle and he had had to get drunk first. But all the same his experience with women had been paltry. Most of his sexual experiences had been characterized by anxiety rather than pleasure. He hadn't guessed that the others in the officers' mess – those who spoke crudely and with lust – had been even more panicky than he was.

Among the superstitions of his boyhood, and later of the officers' mess, had been one that said Jews and negroes were without equal in bed. If that were so, and if that accounted for her attraction to Noah, then Theo was both glad and sorry. Glad, because then the affair was only a thing of the body. Sorry, because then the affair was an affront to his own virility. Theo would have liked, just once, to have made a woman grateful to him in the way that hot bitch from the CWACS had been grateful to Major Fournier.

At first he had been delighted and spiteful to a certain extent about his new-found freedom. Now I can write that book on Landor, he thought. Then he had been depressed by the empty apartment for several weeks. He wrote a sentence or a paragraph and then found some excuse to abandon his work. What if the book turns out bad? Who says that I have to write it?

Three weeks after Miriam had left him Theo wrote to his mother asking her to come and stay with him. That was just about when he began to play a new role in the lecture rooms.

English 102, one of his summer classes, was a survey course in English literature. Beginning with Chaucer, G., and ending with Eliot, T. S., it included a poem or a thought or a few pages of satire by almost everybody and was, like good table manners, designed to make for full Jr. Executives. Theo was accustomed to the groan that rose like a puff of smoke from the class when he first handed out the reading list. But that summer when a Miss Collins stood up and asked the perennial question – Sir, which of these writers are *really* important? – he was not his usual kind, reassuring self. Instead he stared back into that haze of similar faces and said: "None of them is important, Miss Collins. Not one of them ever won the V.C. or had as many readers as Mickey Spillane. Several were homosexuals and most of them drank too much." Not very witty, he knew. But it impressed them. They laughed.

Mrs. Hall arrived on a Wednesday. She was tall and grey-haired with a mouth like a small drying cut, and obviously voted intelligently. Seated in the armchair she leaned forward fanatically absorbed, much as if she sat on a public platform weighing the speaker's every word. Theo, like a Liberal candidate who had just sat down after a rather glib but empty speech, submitted uneasily to her tattoo of penetrating questions. Waiting with some suspense for the unseen audience of socialists to burst into applause after her attack had completely shattered him.

"Theo dear, naturally you would tell me that you satisfied her. But let's be completely objective. How many times a week did you have sexual intercourse?"

"Mother . . ."

"Did she have an orgasm each time?"

"Mother, I . . ."

"Theo, this *is* important. I'm not pursuing this for the sake of vulgar curiosity."

Friends, women in particular, were sympathetic. Joan, Paula, and Betty competed with each other to have him as their guest. Theo refused to allow any of them to say a cruel word against Miriam. All of them agreed – considering that she had left him for a mere boy – that that was pretty noble of him. But wasn't that just like Theo? Sort of Christian. How come we hadn't noticed him – not really – in all this time?

So Theo, who had never really been considered interesting by his friends, enjoyed a new popularity. He did not question it. But he also did not know what to do about Marg, who was particularly friendly. Forward, rather. He guessed that he might be able to have an affair with her, but he was going to stay faithful to Miriam. That would be his triumph.

IV

Noah and Miriam had a month together that was full of loving and sun and idleness. Together, they were complete and had felicity, separated or with others there was a kind of tension.

The second month, however, was different.

Noah drove into Montreal every Wednesday to visit his mother. Miriam usually went with him and spent the day shopping and visiting friends.

Leah was not well. Vindictiveness had sipped the colour from her long, melancholy face. "I guess I should be grateful that you visit once a week. *She* probably doesn't like it." Leah referred to Miriam only as "she" or "her" or "Mrs. Hall." "I understand things for the first time, Noah. My father – let me tell you – had a good daughter in me. But great man that he was, he was also shrewd. That's why he . . . As long as I was married to him my father was still the only man in the house.

A terrible thing to say? Maybe? But what have I got from you with all my struggles? I can assure you, Noah, that you wouldn't take care of me the way I took care of my sick father. You've got your Mrs. Hall. A lot of good she'll do you! Do you study? You might as well have been a truck driver, like they wanted. Look at you. . . ."

Noah saw Wolf only once that month. He found him sitting at his desk in the den. Wolf nodded and wiggled his ears and made his glasses go up and down on his nose. I'm your son, Noah thought. Do you count me among your tormentors too?

"Maybe you can tell me what she wants, Noah? Everything I do she finds fault with. But one thing, eh? At least *I* can look into mirror nights. Max may be richer – a b.t.o. from the b.t.o.'s – but I've got no regrets. Maybe I didn't get to the top but I haven't broken anybody to get where I am. Isn't that right?"

"Yes, Daddy. That's right."

"She's trying to make a split between Paw and me. Paw may be this and Paw may be that but he's still my father. And you listen here, my boy, but you'll never have a friend like your dad. You think I don't know you think I'm a dumb-bell? All right, go ahead. Think what you want. But I watch everything like a regular hawk, I tell you. Max is the King of Siam for her. So what? A guy named Louis was once the King of France. Did you know that Max has started up a new company? Ajax Trading. All right. But in that business he doesn't call himself Adler. *Allen*, if you please. *Mr. Allen.* Max is getting a bit too big for his ootbays."

They went to Panofsky's for Cokes. In those surroundings Wolf became friendly and more expansive. "Noah, listen, she's very sick. The finest doctors don't know exactly what it is. One of them, a real expert, said it's in the think-box. She'd be all right, he said, if she wanted to. Go talk to the *Goyim*. What's the difference if it's in the mind or the legs or the plumbing or the heart or the you-know-what? Sick is sick and that's the fact we gotta face . . ." Wolf spoke of her disease with pride. He seemed to feel stronger, the man of the house, for the first time. "Thank God there's nothing wrong with my ticker," he said, pounding his chest with his fist. "Paw ain't exactly ship-shape, you know. Listen, we're all gonna catch that last bus one day. Rich and poor alike. Knack!" He made a sweeping cut with his hand and many imaginary heads rolled. "But it's a good thing that I'm okay because somebody's gotta bring in a few pennies into the house. . . . Listen, Noah, Max likes you. No itshay. If you caught him in the right mood – if you told Max that he should tell Paw that I should be a partner, I think your mother would brighten up a bit. I'm not asking for myself. . . ."

Noah remembered how long ago the two of them had used to go to the synagogue every Saturday morning. When the rabbi got up to speak Wolf and others had used to retire to the back room where they had gossiped about business and sports. "Speechs," Wolf had used to say. Noah didn't want to speak to Max. It wouldn't help, he thought. But the pathos of his father's demands unnerved him. "I'll speak to him," he said lamely.

Wolf slapped him on the back timidly. They ordered more chocolate biscuits. "What's it like with them?" Wolf asked. "You know . . ."

"What do you mean?"

"Do they really go for the bottle that much?"

"Some do, some don't."

"Is it the real McCoy what they say about their wives? That you can – well, you know – play tiddlywinks with them?"

Noah flushed. "No," he said.

"I've heard that some of them – now I'm not saying it's true – I'm just telling you what I heard. That some of them are men who like men. Now you wouldn't for the life of you find a Jew doing that. Hell, it's no fun, anyway. What do you think?"

"You're right about it not being much fun, I guess. At least not for you or me, but . . ."

"All right. Look at it from this angle. On New Year's they drink to beat the band. We fast. It's healthy to fast. It cleans out the system. Hey, you know why our dames wear two-piece bathing suits?"

"No. Why?"

"To separate the meat from the milk. . . ."

Noah laughed. "Hey, what did the chief rabbi say when he went to visit the pope?"

"*Vus is neis*, Pius?"

"*Gut Yontiv*, pontiff."

They both laughed richly. Wolf nearly upset his Coke bottle. Noah coughed up his chocolate biscuit.

"Sometimes everything is good, eh?" Wolf said quickly. "It would be good all the time if only people were nice to each other. . . ."

Noah averted his eyes. A vast sadness overwhelmed him.

"Anyway, it *tuchos* a long time. But as I was saying. I'm not against them. Paw, now, spits when one of their funerals pass. Me, I'm for every guy having an even break. They don't like Paw, you know, but I'm well liked. Moore says I'm a good Jew."

"The hell with Moore," Noah said sharply.

Wolf hardened. He hadn't understood.

"How's the *Zeyda*?" Noah asked desperately.

But it was too late. Wolf's suspicions had been aroused. He doesn't like Moore because he's a plain man, Wolf thought. Me, too. He has no respect for guys like us. If I were a partner in the business, if I had the money in that box, he would respect me. You bet he would. "You should visit *Zeyda*, you know. He's got plenty of ashcay stored away. He keeps it in a box. He . . ." But Noah wasn't listening. He was trying to think of a way to correct the sudden and unfortunate misunderstanding between them. He stared at Karl, who sat on the kitchen chair next to the Coca-Cola freezer, grinning absently.

"Hey, you listening? You . . ."

"Yes, Daddy."

"You're too smart, Noah. You should have respect. You and Shloime. Do you know Paw threw Shloime out of the house? Shloime says he hates us. Me, too, he hates. He says he'll get even. You – you think I don't know about you and that femme? You think . . ."

"Please let's not quarrel, Daddy."

"Sure, sure. You run around all you want. Who gets blamed? Me, I get blamed. Ever since you've been a small *pisher* I've spent my time apologizing for you to others. You care? I could go to hell tomorrow as far as you're concerned. Look at you. You're no longer a Jew and you'll never become one of them. So what are you? A nothing. . . ."

Added to the guilt that he felt about his parents' troubles was a slow creeping shift in his relationship with Miriam. He was restless, having been without any occupation for too long, and he began to resent her dependency on him. He had been amused, earlier, by the fetish that she had made of tidiness, but now that kind of thing increasingly got on his nerves. She was forever cleaning up after him – replacing books on shelves and wiping up ashes and collecting glasses and folding his trousers and sweeping under his chair – as if, in order to compensate for what outsiders thought an illicit relation-ship, she was going to keep the interior as clean and as well-ordered as she could. However, he didn't consider the matter worth fighting about. So he let it go. But he was alarmed because his relationship with her – the petty anxieties and the duties – was beginning to duplicate his relationship with his mother.

On that first Wednesday that he drove into Montreal to visit his mother Noah bought a French grammar and a dictionary and on his return to Ste. Adele he began to spend his mornings studying. He fixed up one of the bedrooms as his study. She was not allowed to sweep or tidy up in that room, but unfortunately he felt himself without privacy even there. He was always conscious of her waiting in the next room. Bored.

He felt intimidated in bed at night. He knew that eventually she was going to turn to him and say: "What are you thinking about?" And in chill anticipation of that question he found himself thinking what he could say that he was thinking about. Then he was ashamed. It's all in my head, he thought. He turned to her tenderly, but for the first time since they had met that tenderness was simulated. Loving was becoming his responsibility.

"I was snubbed again in the village today. Somebody must have told Mrs. Callahan that we aren't married. I think her daughter is one of Theo's students."

"Surely you don't let things like that worry you?"

"Noah, I'm a woman. Whenever I go into a store I keep my left hand in my pocket. That's where my ring should be. . . ."

"But Miriam, love, I'll marry you gladly."

"Would you? Do you realize that when I'm forty you'll still be in your twenties?"

"Twenty-nine. Perhaps we should leave Ste. Adele. I could get a job in Montreal."

"Driving a cab? Noah, you're a child. Besides, don't think it would be that easy for *us* to get an apartment."

"Divorce Theo and we'll get married."

"Before I divorce him I'd like to know if you have any ambitions beyond driving a taxi."

"Yes. I'd like to be a partner in my father's business."

Miriam felt isolated.

On that first Wednesday when she had driven to Montreal with Noah she had phoned friend after friend, only to be snubbed by some and reproved by others. So that she had been forced to realize, with a suddenness that was jarring, that she was no longer Mrs. Hall, the professor's attractive wife, who was welcomed at faculty teas, garden parties, and in the homes of Montreal's bright young people. All those trappings that had become her identity had been washed away with Theo and for the sake of love. Pop! Her security, all that she had striven for, had burst like a balloon. Miriam was terrified.

Her first love affair had been with Chuck Adams. She remembered that the bedroom had been full of books. He was brilliant. She had been told that. His unfinished manuscript had been piled neatly on the table, beside the liqueur cabinet. She had undressed with her back towards him.

"Would you like a drink first?" he had asked drunkenly.

"No. But you go ahead." Then she had touched his chest with her hand. "Men are so warm," she had said. And Chuck had laughed an abrupt, affable laugh and had put down his drink. "Please try not to hurt me," she had said. "I . . ."

"I'll be easy."

"Would you like another drink first?" she had asked quickly.

"After, maybe."

He had been the first to awaken. Big and muscular, he had jumped out of bed and grinned into the mirror. "What a stud! Look into that mirror. They should make me a YWCA secretary. God, think of all the women I'll never lay! I'm weak, Miriam. The easiest make in Montreal. Be a good girl and scratch my back, eh?"

"If you show me where you keep your things in the kitchen I'll make breakfast."

He had noticed the chill in her voice, and they had gotten through breakfast with some embarrassment.

"C'mon, Miriam. Be a sport. Hell," he had said. "This is 1940. All we did was have a turn in the sack."

She had given him her phone number and the name of the place where she had been employed for the summer. She had waited five days. A week had passed. Two weeks. But Chuck hadn't phoned. She had known all about him. That he had had affairs with the others, for instance. Marg had pretended not to like him. "Son of the rich, you know. Bit of a snob." But Miriam had been drawn to him. Why didn't he call? Wasn't she attractive enough?

He had finally called, and they had spent a fine long weekend together in the Laurentians. But after that he hadn't called again.

She had not yet been twenty. But there had been something hopeful and wild, a kind of craving in her eyes, that had drawn men to her easily.

Beauty, like male ballet dancers, makes some men afraid.

"Round heels. Any fool can see that that kid could never get enough," Collins had said at lunch one day in Mother Martin's, popping a meat ball into his mouth. "Some priest's probably going into her."

And in reply Jerry Selby had winked.

Jerry Selby was the senior partner of Selby & Clark, an advertising firm that was going places. A week after he had hired Miriam, Jerry's wife had passed through the office and frowned. "Don't be silly, honey," Jerry had said. "Even if I wanted to, I wouldn't. Never pays to monkey around in your own back yard. But that girl's a selling point. Take old Collins, now . . ."

Jerry had disgusted her. But he had paid her more than she had been worth. He was insistent. I'm weak, she had thought. I would like to drive down Queen Street in his Buick. Still, she had repelled his advances. She had been waiting for Chuck.

Miriam had seen Chuck in the Cafe André that night.

"I'm leaving the day after tomorrow. If it lasts, I'll join the RCAF. I'm thinking of . . ."

"Why haven't you called?"

"I've been busy. Hell. Be a sport, Miriam. Don't . . ."

"Will you write?"

"Sure I'll write."

"No you won't."

"Miriam. Hell . . ."

"Be a sport. Hell. Be a . . . Would you like my phone number for your friends? I'm a very good sport, Chuck. You tell your friends that."

"Look at Theo, there. He's crazy about you. Why . . ."

"I would like to take this beer bottle," she had said. "Break it. And twist it into . . ."

"Let's go up to my place," he had said thickly.

"I was surprised you remembered my name that first night. I was scared, you know. I thought you would turn to me in bed and ask me my name."

"Listen, I didn't make any promises. All we did was . . ."

". . . was have a turn in the sack."

"Yes. That's all."

"You get up now, you scram, or I'll break this beer bottle and do what I said."

She had not seen him again until after the war when she had visited him in the St. Mary's Veteran's Hospital. He had been very bitter about his crash and – once out in the hospital corridor – she had cried.

She did see Jerry, though. "There's nothing like it, baby," Jerry had said. Many other men had followed, and she had acquired a reputation for being that kind of girl. Nobody had understood that all those men were being used in anger. That all that time she had been looking for the one man who could destroy her. Word had got back to Queen Street. She was wild. There had been some despair, and some gratification also, in that. They had been brought up on lines. They had been told, for instance, that there was God, but not that He was dead. They had been told that Canada was a free country but not that although only the leisured could afford freedom all men were free to die for it. They had accepted the lies that had been offered them like the wiser natives must have accepted shiny beads and bits of broken glass from the white traders, not because they had believed but because they had chosen not to quarrel.

Pausing in the heat, Miriam remembered how the people of Queen Street had turned against her. A wild woman. Paul had said:

"Of course you're welcome. You're my sister. Come around when-ever you like. But phone first. I don't want the kids to know." Looking down a sweltering St. Catherine Street she saw only the tenements of Griffintown and heard nothing but the banging and clanging of machinery. A landscape made out of an arrangement of different-coloured beer-bottle tops loomed up before her. Her father dressed in his best suit and waving his fists and yelling, rushed towards the oncoming truck. All her nerves tingled. Noah, her lover, had led her out onto the sands and into the water, until, having gone so far that it was no longer possible to wade but necessary to swim, she turned around and saw that the shore was far, far away. What if Noah swam away from her?

What about Theo? Was he having an affair? Being unfaithful? She was almost tempted to phone him. Perhaps he could help her?

St. Catherine Street shook. Damp streaks poured down grey bank buildings. Cellophane ice decorated a hundred similar AIR CONDITIONED signs. She slipped in the nearest door. Fans whirred after her, waitresses swept past with wet patches under their armpits, and the stout ladies who sat in Murray's Restaurant, fanning them-selves with menus, paused to stare at her. All of them. Hold it, Miriam thought. Hold it. She concentrated on the window but St. Catherine Street, that had plenty of twitching neon and screech-ing horns and lots of people passing quickly and too much heat, had no help and offered no answers.

From that day on each morning's awakening was another ordeal. Another muffled shriek. She began to search for omens. If the milkman arrived before nine then the day would be good; if Noah didn't finish his coffee at breakfast then the day would be foul. She seldom left the cottage without returning to see whether the door had been bolted, or prepared coffee without checking twice on whether the gas jets had been turned off. Everybody is talking about us, she thought. Noah, perhaps, doesn't realize it. He doesn't care about such things. But – why do I hound him? What am I trying to do to us? Isn't this what I wanted? When he read at night Miriam watched him with hatred and love and envy. He was her world now. The time of beauty and the wild years too, Chuck and Theo, Paul, were all stale memories. She dipped into these memories the way other women dip into their knitting-bags, dropping a few stitches here and embroidering a bit there, but the suspicion that she had no identity of her own, no inner strength, frightened her. He has that quality, she thought, but he doesn't know it yet. She recalled that her first impression had been that he was a ruthless man. He seemed to move from one experience to another assuredly, leaving what was no longer useful behind him without regret or sentiment. She suddenly realized that for as long as she had known him he had never lost his temper. Social injustice outraged Theo, not him. He had once told her that he wept occasionally. But she would have to see that to believe it.

He began to play a part with her. But Miriam was astute. When he first began to bring her flowers and other gifts she started to suspect his feelings. She knew that Noah liked most things to be understood. She was torn between a fear of losing him and another fear, just as real, that warned her that she had better let go before it was too late. Once or twice she prayed. She went for long walks on the hills and got into the habit of sitting absently by the stream behind the cottage, her feet dangling in the water. She remembered that day she had gone to meet Marg at the Ritz, for that had been the first time that she had seen things through Noah's eyes. Gradually he had possessed her completely. She felt that she no longer had any vision of her own. She started to dip more critically into her memories. Theo had obviously needed her, and that had given her a kind of dignity. She began to understand that there was a dichotomy in her approach to living. A part of her wanted the security that was Theo and another part of her – that had not been acquired – wanted love. She remembered that Noah had once said that the decision that she had come to had been no decision at all. She had not chosen. She wanted love, but on the terms of security. I have ruined myself, she thought.

One morning Noah found a letter on the dining-room table.

"Dear Marg,

Why don't you come to visit us?

Aren't we old friends?

You know that I've left Theo and am living with Noah up in Ste. Adele. I would like so much for you two to meet. Noah is younger than I am and a bit vague about his plans, but we love each other terribly much. I don't know if and when we'll get married. Getting a divorce is such a mess in Quebec. But he is the finest man that I have ever met and I'd be simply lost without him. I almost think that I'd commit suicide if he left me or . . ."

He dropped the letter.

It had been left on the table – casually – but opened and on the book that he was reading. He had no doubt that the letter, addressed to Marg, had been written for him and left there for him to read. Beating her, he thought, would have been kinder. He walked over to the window and saw her sitting – a bent and solitary figure – by the stream. A shudder ran through him. He wanted to rush out and embrace her, but he didn't. He was too ashamed. He had stripped her, another and lovelier human being, and the sun was so fine in her hair. He slipped out of the back door and wandered down the dirt road.

If he left her, the Adlers would be triumphant. They would say that an affair or marriage between a Jew and a Gentile was doomed from the beginning. But, on the other hand, he wasn't going to marry Miriam to spite the Adlers. He did not want to hurt her, but neither did he wish to marry her for the sake of pity. What do I say now? he thought. What do you do with used people? Send them to the laundry like soiled shirts?

One evening the tension that had been gathering for so long broke out savagely between them.

"I saw Whitelaw this afternoon. He asked me point-blank if we were married. No, I said. We weren't. He wanted to know why. I tried to explain it to him, but he didn't understand. He's quite sad, you know. He wanted me to return to his place with him. He said that if I left you he would . . ."

In the last few days men were always propositioning her; others, less bright than him, were always settling into fine jobs, getting on in the world; and numerous others were always talking about them behind her back.

He suddenly realized that she bored him.

"Miriam, you're becoming a gossip. Let's return to Montreal. I'll get a job."

"Are you going to drive a cab again?"

"I've told you several times that I can see no difference between driving a cab or lecturing in England or . . ."

"Why bring Theo into this?"

Her voice was near the breaking-point.

"I didn't."

"Remember, Noah, *you* asked me to leave him."

"Don't be calculating, Miriam. It's not like you."

"Calculating!" She leaped up and flung her hair back and laughed brutally. "Calculating! If you want to leave me will you please, please, please go ahead. I can join Whitelaw. He knows what kind of woman I am. Or there's always my sleeping pills or . . ."

"Sleeping pills! What are you talking about?"

She turned away from him and began to pick ruthlessly at the screen.

"Why, that's ridiculous. Suicide. Did you read that in one of your *Ladies' Home Journal* stories?"

"I don't see what's wrong with my reading the *Ladies' Home Journal* or *Good Housekeeping*, if I want to. You read what you want and I read . . ."

"This is awful."

"*I* started it, I suppose."

"No. I did."

She whipped a package of cigarettes off the table and lit one, exhaling smoke furiously. Her face was scarlet beneath her tan. He got up and stepped towards her but she pushed him away.

"Perhaps you're trying to back out of this because I'm not a Jewess? Maybe all you wanted was a couple of months with a fast woman? Maybe you're scared and . . ."

"I won't bother answering that," he said, but as soon as she had said that he realized that she had been anticipating the quarrel for a long time.

"Don't come on with that Jesus Holy Christ act with me, Noah. Save it for the sorority girls."

"That's not what I mean. I . . ." He was suddenly struck by the vulgarity of their predicament. As long as they had been truly lovers there had been nothing immoral about their relationship, but now that they had begun to bicker, they had become simply another sordid adulterous couple. "Never mind."

"I get them for the recipes. So that I can bake you your goddam cakes and roasts."

"What? You get what?"

"The *Ladies' Home Journal*." She stamped her foot on the floor. "Scalloped fish en cocotte! Liver and bacon hot-pot! Cod à la Bercy! Understand?" She dropped her butt to the floor and stamped on it.

"I'm sorry. I . . ."

"Can you tell me just once what you want, Noah? What you really want?"

He hung back defensively. That's unfair, he thought. *What do you really want?* He stared at her.

"You're an opportunist, Noah. I realized that the first day . . . I realized. You're a ruthless man. As soon as you've used something you . . ."

He jumped up angrily. "I'm not ruthless."

"You don't treat your mother or your father decently. You . . ."

The phone rang.

"Answer it," he shouted.

"Don't order me around."

And rang again.

"Christ."

Again. And again.

"Even when you quarrel," she said, "you've got to be superior to that quarrel at the same time. I'll bet you even watch yourself in bed. Don't you *ever* let yourself go?"

Noah swept the receiver off the hook swiftly. "Hello," he said belligerently. "Yes, speaking." He turned to Miriam and shrugged his shoulders. "My mother," he said. "Hello, Maw." His face went suddenly white. "Oh no," he said. "When?" Miriam watched him fearfully, and her anger passed. Noah was perspiring freely. "What," he said. "What?" His shoulders sagged. "I'll leave right away," he said, "but . . . Yes. I understand. But . . . Yes. *Yes.*" She lit a cigarette and slipped it into his mouth. "But why did he rush into the flames?" There was a pause. "Please, Maw. Please try not to cry. I can't understand what you're . . . Yes. Yes, Maw. All right. I'm coming." Another pause. "Yes. Good night."

The receiver flopped back on to the hook almost of its own volition, and Noah turned to her. "My father's dead," he said.

"Oh, Noah."

"I hardly knew him, Miriam. I . . ."

She took him into her arms. "How did it happen?"

"I don't understand. Somebody called to tell him that the office was on fire. When he got there the whole works was blazing. The – the damn fool rushed into the flames." Noah moved away from her and sat down. "It was an old building. A shack. It collapsed on him. He . . . Oh, Christ." He held his head in his hands. She poured him a stiff drink. "He . . ."

"Drink this."

"'Drink this.' God. He . . ."

"Drink."

"He . . ."

Noah drank. He didn't say anything for several minutes. He stared.

"Would you like another?"

"I really haven't the right to mourn him, poor . . ."

She poured him another drink.

"He's buried there. They're still pouring water on the ruins."

"I'll drive you into town."

"Somebody phoned him. Just before he left he turned to my mother and said, 'The crazy fool. So that's what he meant.' I don't understand."

V

Shortly after seven o'clock the next morning Noah took a taxi down to the coal yard on St. Dominique Street. A mist still lingered on the streets. The sky was soupy and full but, although it might rain, it was going to be hot. That much was clear. A fireman in a rubber coat still kept watch over the dusty twisted heap that had been the office. There was a charred, bitter sting to the air. The yard was a black muddy sea. Sodden sacks floundered in puddles and even the street outside was dark with wet coal dust. An ambulance was parked across the street. The previous night Noah had arrived to find all his aunts and uncles seated around his mother like cats around a bird-cage. Noah had noticed with alarm that Nat had been using the Japanese garden for an ashtray. But Leah hadn't seen. She had been crumpled up in her chair, a dazed figure newly conscious of her widow's role but not yet of the death that had occurred. She had looked up and gasped briefly when Noah had entered the room. "My *boyele*," she had said. Noah had nodded, as though to confirm that. Max hadn't been there. Later he had remembered that Shloime had been absent too. "Your father is dead," Leah had said. "Yes. I know." Noah had been conscious of the others watching him. At first he had not been able to understand their hostility but then he had remembered Miriam.

"You're not supposed to shave," Itzik had said contemptuously.

"Have they recovered the body?"

The men had looked away from him.

"Some son you were to him."

That had been Goldie.

"Have they . . ."

"No," Leah said.

Noah had turned to Melech. "How are you, *Zeyda*?"

Melech hadn't answered. But Noah had noticed that his grandfather's skin had yellowed. He was wizened and shrunken and his filmy eyes were rich with the rancour of the old. His skull was prominent.

"Couldn't you even wear a hat on the day your father died?"

That had been Itzik again.

"I think you'd all better go now. My mother looks worn out."

"Are *you* throwing us out?"

"It's one o'clock. Nothing can be done until tomorrow."

"I repeat. Are *you* throwing . . ."

"Yes. I am. I think my mother should rest."

After they had left Noah prepared tea for his mother.

"He's dead, Noah."

"I know."

"He was my husband after all. He's dead."

"I know."

"You don't remember when my father died?"

"Not very well."

"You're all I've got left, *boyele*."

Noah nodded to the fireman, and remembered that his mother had made that sound like a threat. Hell, he thought. Max's Cadillac pulled up across the street. Hell. Three of his uncles climbed out. Nat and Itzik and Lou. Noah walked across the yard and met them on the pavement. "G'morning," he said.

"You're not supposed to exchange greetings," Itzik said sternly.

"Where's Max?" Noah asked.

"D'roit. He's flying in. He should be here before noon."

"The cops found an empty tin of kerosene," Lou said softly. Then he pressed Noah's arm and shrugged his shoulders. For he liked the boy, and he liked Wolf, too, but he couldn't put his feelings into words.

"Do you know how to say *kaddish* at least?" Itzik asked.

Kaddish is the prayer for the dead. Itzik, who was the most orthodox of the boys, was a lean man with wobbly blue eyes and a sour mouth. The secretary of Max's company, he was fond of saying: "Everybody says I'm too honest. But that's the way I like to do business."

"Yes, I do." Noah turned to Lou. "Is that *Zeyda* in the car?"

"Yup."

"Do you think it wise for him to be here?"

"You stop him. Me, I'm gonna stay healthy."

The crane moved into position about a half-hour later, and that's when the crowds began to form. Only a few of the curious at first. Noah's eyes fastened on the shovel. Jagged teeth glittered hungrily in the sun. Paquette arrived and climbed into the cab. So the shovel would soon begin to probe into that heap of twisted timber and rags and scrap for his father's body. Noah noted absently that the scale that had been used to weigh Moore's scrap so long ago had not been badly burnt. Nat and Lou were both wearing rubber boots. Fishing-boots. They posted themselves in the mud. That's where the loads and ultimately his father's body would be dumped. Itzik gave Paquette his instructions. An elderly woman pointed at Noah. "That's the son," she said.

The crowd thickened. There was a girl with long swift black hair and hollow eyes who sucked urgently on her thumb and obviously wanted to flee – but couldn't. The promise of un-boredom was too big. She was a fine-looking girl though, with breasts that were just starting and lots of impatience in her manner. Clouds parted and dissolved and very soon the yellower sun was surer in the emptying sky. Noah smiled at the girl, but his smile was cut off suddenly when he heard the crane engine cough and start. His heart leaped. The shovel creaked agonizingly and broke clean of the earth. "How did the fire start?" a man asked him.

"I don't know."

"He doesn't know. If you don't wanna tell me so say so. Me, I know plenty. I was just checking. I been living on dis here street for you know how many years?"

"What do you know about the fire?"

"I know what I know. Plain enough?"

A swarthy man with dense eyes, he plucked his nose each time he made a point.

"Why won't you . . ."

"I tell you, you don't believe. You do believe, I'm a witness. I'm a witness, I go to court. I go to court, no work. No work, no food. No food, no . . ."

Noah walked away. Another day, he thought. He joined Lou and Nat. "How long do you think it'll take?" he asked.

Nat stared at the wet mushy stump of his cigar and then shoved it into his mouth. When he spoke, the cigar shifted from side to side. "Until noon at least. They've got to go through years of scrap before they get to him."

Noah watched the shovel dig into the grey rubbish for the first time. A puff of dust rose from the shifting heap like a protest. The shovel swung towards them slowly and dumped a first burnt-offering at their feet. Then, back towards the heap again. In order to get a better view quite a few people had climbed up on the adjoining piles of coal. Many were still reticent, for although the sun offered gladness and assured them of a long repetition of days, a contradiction, death, made many shadows among them. There were lots of children about. "Is there a dead guy in there for real?" one of them asked.

"Yes," Noah said.

"Hey, Art! ART!"

Noah walked away and felt the sun fiercer on him. He rubbed his eyes. Itzik appeared and handed him a skull-cap. "It's not nice," he said, "people should see you without a hat today . . ." There was a slow, sucking quality to his voice. A leech on your back.

"Itzik, listen, we've got a long day ahead of us so . . ."

The Ford pulled up across the street and Noah brushed Itzik aside and walked over to it.

"I thought you were back in Ste. Adele," Noah said.

Miriam and Noah watched as the shovel opened like a mouth, dumped another load into the mud, and then clamped shut again.

"When do they expect to . . ."

"Not until noon, anyway," Noah said.

They watched the shovel dig into the rubbish again.

"You look tired," she said.

"I haven't slept yet."

She stared at his hand. "What's that?" she asked.

"A skull-cap," he said. "You're supposed to . . ."

Melech was watching them from the Cadillac.

"Darling," she said.

He was staring at the shovel.

"I'm sorry about last night, Noah. I didn't mean what I said."

"Last night? Was it last night? Christ." He smiled briefly. "I . . . Of course, darling."

"I'll be back in a couple of hours. All right?"

"Bring me a small flask of rye."

He turned away from her and rejoined Lou and Nat.

"Listen," Nat said. "Why look for trouble?" He plucked the cigar from his mouth. Noah stared. "Me, I'm Dorothy Dix with a ceegar, eh? Look . . . Tell her to stay away."

"She's got feelings, too."

"Me, I'm Nehru. Neutral-shmootral. But Itzik, you know, he . . ."

"I know that."

A lachrymose man wearing white linen leaned against the ambulance and chatted with that girl who had the long swift black hair. More and more children began to appear. Several of them must have had it in for Art. They chanted:

> *Gene, Gene, built a machine,*
> *Joe, Joe, made it go,*
> *Art, Art, let a fart,*
> *And blew the whole machine apart.*

The grocery store across the street ran out of Cokes around 11:30. As the heat became more intense the older people in the crowd faltered and retreated to shadier spots. Of all, they alone seemed reconciled to what had happened. "Lucky it wasn't two. Or three. A whole family even." Others were also suffering from the heat, but stayed more enthusiastic. "If they should find him, call me – call quick." Many women and sometimes whole families leaned bulkily out of windows that looked out on to the coal yard. From time to time a banana peel or an apple core fell to the pavement. Soot-soiled curtains occasionally flapped against their faces and were brushed away impatiently. A few babies bawled. A sing-song of comment rolled to and fro from window to window. Passing cars slowed down. Somebody, usually Mort Shub, would walk up to the driver and explain the proceedings importantly. "I knew him. Used to see him every day. A prince of a fellow." Sometimes the car passed on, but more often the driver parked around the corner and returned to join the crowd. Several of the drivers were from Outremont and were in the district on a rent-collecting tour. They carried important briefcases. One of them engaged Mort in an earnest conversation. "Haven't these people any decency? Why don't they go home? Think of the children." He looked like the kind of man who did not take his employer's name in vain and who had honoured his father and his mother ever since they had died. Mort made a feverish rebuttal. "We're all neighbours. Wolf and me were like this. We . . ."

The crane shovel continued to dig into the rubbish, swing right, and drop a load at the feet of Nat and Lou. Then back into the heap again. There was a brief outburst of anxious laughter when a pair of bloomers got caught in the teeth of the shovel. Itzik rushed up to the shovel pink-faced, and Paquette waited while he freed the offending bloomers. Three cops arrived around noon and the crowd was bullied back a reasonable distance from the heap of rubbish. Noah was red-eyed and dizzy. Sweltering faces swirled before him. A pit of sorts had been dug into the rubbish, and Noah climbed up on to the rim and searched the wreckage intently. Dust clogged his nostrils. Noon came, and Paquette was allowed to break off for a half-hour.

A sign went up in the window of the grocery store.

COKES IN STOCK AGAIN. SANDWICHES. COLD SNACKS.

A bushy-haired man in a rumpled suit addressed a group of sceptical, jacketless men. "You see what I mean? Accidents like this happen every day. A man with a family," he said, smacking the wet palm of his open hand once for every word, "should have a policy. You've got to . . ."

"How many commas in a bottle of ink?"

"Yeah, sure. But listen, you've got to . . ."

"Moishe, hold on to your calories on such a hot day. Me, I got an agreement wid Prudential. They don't deal in kosher meat and I don't sell policies by me in the shop."

". . . got to protect. PROTECT."

A stooping man with dust on his boots stopped Noah. He patted his hand tenderly. "I'm sorry," he said. "I knew your grandfather, the Zaddik. Say a word to your Maw."

Noah walked over to the Ford and Miriam handed him a towel. He wiped his face and neck. She poured him a drink and he gulped it down wordlessly.

"You're covered with dirt," she said.

He held out the paper cup again and she refilled it.

"Do you want me to get you anything to eat?"

"No. I'm not hungry. Did you bring the flask?"

"Darling. Oh, Darling."

Noah noticed that Nat and Itzik were quarrelling. Itzik, pink-faced, was pointing at them. Noah lit a cigarette. She handed him the flask and he slipped it into his pocket. "Would you wait around the corner?" he asked. "Part of the desk has been uncovered. It won't be long now."

"There's no place to park."

"I know. We could charge half a buck a head. But they don't mean bad. They . . . Go to the Bar Vendôme. I'll be around later."

"I think you should eat. I . . ."

"I'm going to phone my mother."

She watched him walk away. Itzik started towards her and Miriam, who wanted to avoid a scene, put the car into gear quickly.

Voices were lowered when Noah entered the grocery store. There was a dark, damp smell to the place. Noah stared at a sweating hunk of cottage cheese. The sign over the cash said: "MEXICAN MONEY IS

ACCEPTED IN MEXICO. HERE, CASH WILL DO FINE." The phone
was on the counter.

"Hello, Maw?" A pause. "No. Not yet." Another pause. "I know.
Yes. I know. But . . ." Noah put his hand over the mouthpiece and
turned to the crowd. "You tell me if I'm not talking loud enough for
the people in the back." Several men turned away, embarrassed.
Noah turned away too. Also embarrassed. "This is a public place," a
woman said. Noah uncovered the mouthpiece. "Quiet for once in
your life," a man said. "He's the son." "No," Noah said. "*No.* You stay
home. I'll phone as soon as I have news."

Outside, Panofsky stood in the sun. He gripped Noah's hand
firmly. "It's terrible," he said. "I just got here and I ain't staying. I . . ."

"I understand."

"If you need anything. If there's anything I . . ."

"The women are with my mother. They must be driving her
crazy. Why don't you go up there and talk to her?"

"I'll take a taxi."

Paquette climbed back into the cab. The boom creaked.

"Art! HEY, ART! They're starting again."

Nat and Lou resumed their positions. Nat pulled a framed picture
of Weizmann out of the heap. The glass had been shattered.

Noah walked over to the cab and motioned for Paquette to stop
the motor. He handed Paquette the flask of rye and Paquette slipped
it into his pocket surreptitiously. "Itzik is watching," he said.

Noah nodded. "When I wave," he said, "please stop digging. That
means I've seen him. I don't want the shovel – the teeth to . . ."

"Sure. I understand. Your father and me were good friends.
Remember? I used to come to make the fire in your house on
Saturday mornings. You were so high then. . . ."

"I remember."

"That Itzik, he was always full of . . . If you like I'll bash him in
the teeth."

"I would like. You don't know how much. But you need your job."

Noah climbed back on to the rim of the rubbish heap. Paquette waved and started up the motor again. The shovel moved towards the pile.

Itzik yanked at Noah's trouser leg. "What did you say to him?" he asked.

"Nothing."

"Nothing! Listen, be reasonable, you must have said *something*."

"He told me that he used to light the fire for us on *shabus*."

"You handed him something."

Suddenly Noah realized that Itzik's jaw was level with his foot. That was tempting, but he turned away. Itzik tugged at his trouser leg again. Noah ignored him.

Around two in the afternoon the weather turned again and the sun was reduced to a widening yellow stain in a swirl of grey cloud; but the heat, if anything, got worse. Everything you touched was burning or wet or blistering. Noah tasted the salt on his lips. He kept staring down into that pit that was getting bigger and bigger, but from time to time things started to spin and he had to look away and walk around for a bit. All his nerves sparked like exposed wires. Max's plane had been delayed. The crowd slimmed out. The kids started up a game of kick-the-can down the street, but kept a spotter watching the crane. Several rumours made the rounds. One said that they had caught the man who had set fire to the office, and another that Wolf had not plunged into the fire but had walked away from it, obviously suffering from amnesia. But Moore, who had seen Wolf rush into the flames, had already been questioned by the police, and as far as Noah knew there was still no proof that the fire had not been an accident.

Those who still remained on the scene around four o'clock began to grumble quite openly. Several of the windows that looked out on the yard were banged shut like a reproach. Would they continue to dig if they didn't find the body before dark? Why couldn't the crane work quicker? A few women brought chairs down from their kitchens and began to gossip and knit in the shade. Discussion groups formed. Louis Berger the bookie said that it was always ten degrees hotter in the ghetto than it was anywhere else in the city. "The weather observatory," he said, "is on a ritzy lake ten miles out of Montreal. And the building – air-conditioned! Why? Because the *Goy* who runs the joint – a third cousin eighteen times removed of the Mayor – can't stand the heat."

Rimstein the rag pedlar, three soiled moth-eaten suits slung over his narrow shoulders, his sorry face worn from the heat and his beard protruding from his chin like a tangle of rusting cord, shook his head sadly. "In such a heat," he said, "Our People wandered forty years over a desert."

"And there was no *shmaltz* herring and wine waiting for them in the synagogue after, eh?"

Melech Adler stared inscrutably out of the window of the Cadillac. Itzik came up to him.

"If when you find him," Melech said, "and there should be a box, I want it. Nobody should look in the box."

"A box?"

"Listen what I tell you and no questions. Noah shouldn't . . . I want the box. Nobody should see."

A stillness prevailed. "Not even a leaf is moving," an elderly woman said.

Rimstein turned to Louis. "We are short one man for the evening service," he said. "So you come to the synagogue tonight. Maybe it'll bring you luck with the horses."

"What does God know about Daily Doubles?"

"It is written: 'I would rather be called a fool all my days than sin one hour before God.'"

"Written! Everything's gotta be written for us Jewboys! When Rabbi Herman comes around trying to scare up some *gelt* for his holy shakers everything's gotta be signed in three million carbon copies. Still, he doesn't do so bad for himself, the old *goniff*."

A few minutes after four Noah saw his father's feet protruding from under a slab of charred wood. The toes pointed inwards. He waved and Paquette stopped the shovel in mid-air. Noah scrambled down into the pit.

"Art! ART! Hey, guys! Quick!"

A roar went up from the crowd.

Windows banged open one after another like shots being fired into the heat. Black policemen made a circle around the heap of rubbish and held back the surging crowd with threats. Several men cursed. The two men who were dressed in white linen opened up the doors to the ambulance and got the stretcher out. About twenty people detached themselves from the crowd and assembled at the back of the ambulance. A few of them had cameras.

"Art! HEY, ART!"

Noah crouched in the pit and cleared slab after slab of charred wood off his father's body. He looked up and saw Nat and Lou and Itzik standing on the rim of the pit. They spun around him like figures on a top. Noah stared at the body. Wolf was huddled up and held an iron box to his stomach. A charred wooden beam pressed against his back. His face was distorted. The eyes were opened, the mouth was slack. The clothes were burned but his body was intact. One hand was in the box. The other held on to it grimly. Noah swayed and bit his lips and opened the box. There were several rolls of parchment. Hebrew letters had been meticulously drawn on all of them.

"Paw says you let that stuff alone," Itzik yelled hoarsely.

Noah didn't even look up. He found a yellow stack of letters that were written in Russian or Polish. There were also several faded snapshots of a plump girl that had been frayed by too much handling. One of the snapshots, probably taken at a village fair, showed a strong young man with his arms around the girl. Melech had had no beard then. Noah discovered other letters on fresher paper. He slipped the snapshots and several receipts and a bundle of letters into his pocket and examined one of the scrolls again.

> "*In the beginning God created the heaven and the earth. And the earth was without form and void; and darkness was upon the face of the deep. And the spirit of . . .*"

Each letter had been laboriously formed. But the hand that had created them had been shaky. Itzik scrambled down into the pit. Behind him came the two men with the stretcher. Noah dumped the scrolls back into the box and climbed up the other side. His head was whirling. He had not yet grasped the significance of his find. Clearing the pit, he felt Itzik tugging at his trouser leg again. Noah pushed through the crowd and across the street to the Cadillac. He handed Melech the box. "That's why he ran into the flames," he said.

Melech looked at him – his mouth opened and his hand pressed to his throat suppressing a scream.

"*Zeyda*, I . . ."

That swarthy man with the dense eyes grabbed the box and yanked out one of the scrolls. A crowd gathered around him. The swarthy man plucked his nose and held up the scroll and yelled: "Wolf Adler died for the Torah."

Melech seized the box.

Noah stared stupidly and began to sway.

"WOLF ADLER DIED FOR THE TORAH."

A woman fainted. She was seated on a kitchen chair and a man was fanning her with a newspaper.

A face swam out of the sun to Noah. Itzik's finger shook under his eyes. "You're a tramp," he said. Then, for he must have caught a whiff of Noah's breath, "and a drunkard too." Noah tried to break away but Itzik held on to him. "Your father died for God but you're a . . ."

"Itzik, please. . . ."

An incensed crowd pressed around them.

"You may come to the funeral but after that don't you dare . . ."

Noah turned away but his path was blocked by the stretcher-bearers. His father's body was covered with a blanket. Noah let them pass. Itzik grabbed him again. "God will . . ."

"I should hit you," Noah said. "I'm angry and I should hit you. But that would be my short temper against your short mind."

"ADLER DIED FOR THE TORAH. WOLF ADLER . . ."

The swarthy man held the scroll aloft before a throng of admirers.

"Go ahead," Itzik said. "Hit me. You're rotten!"

"EVERYBODY LISTEN. WOLF . . ."

Noah stared at the swarthy man. "Please tell him to stop, Lou. I know he died for the scrolls but . . ."

". . . ADLER DIED FOR THE TORAH. LISTEN!"

The doors banged shut and Noah saw the ambulance pull away just before Itzik – holding him very tight – began to shake him and shake him.

Somebody took a picture.

Lou separated them. He pressed Noah's arm and shrugged his shoulders. His eyes were moist.

4

Summer 1953

That was a bright morning – the morning of Wolf Adler's funeral. The shrill blue sky was without clouds or depth. Those birds that had anticipated the oncoming winter filled and fluttered in the blue blackly; lots of twittering, swooping arrows, bound south. Trees postured limply, their leaves yellowing, on both sides of the street. An angering, ubiquitous sun ricocheted off black sedans and sweltering faces and mushy asphalt. Many a frazzled flower yearned for the shade of red-brick walls or balconies in the occasional parched garden of City Hall Street. The crowd of mourners gathered there that morning was estimated at "more than a thousand" in the afternoon edition of the *Star*. The *Gazette*, however, claimed 1,500 mourners several hours later, and the *Herald*, appearing the following morning, began its story with "Nearly two thousand Jews . . ." Anyway, there was quite a crowd. Lots of the hoi-polloi but a few important people too. Take – for instance – Buddy Gross of 20th Century Promotions, who had been responsible for the splash of full-page memorial advertisements in all the newspapers. A black-boarded picture of Wolf and a poem. (Max had objected to the ads at first. But Buddy had told him: one, the reporters would get the story anyway; two, Max had a bastard of a

campaign coming up; and three, it was an honour to the community.)
Now David Lerner, who was also there, was a horse of a different
colour. Formerly a communist and still a poet, Lerner was famous for
his lyrics throughout Outremont. Possessor of a real rhetorical gift,
he wrote speeches that were read by philanthropic millionaires at
Zionist banquets. He had gotten two hundred dollars for his ode
celebrating Wolf Adler. That, and a total readership reckoned at
800,000 by the Audit Bureau of Circulation. (A considerable jump
over the three dollars and less than two hundred readers his *Ode to
Sacco and Vanzetti* had earned him some years back.) Take Rimstein
the rag pedlar. He had ruptured himself long ago and in an even
colder country to keep out of the Czar's army, and had come not to
mourn a friend but to size up the coffin and to keep in the sun and
with the crowd. The swarthy man with dense eyes, Yosel Wiserman,
hoped to see another family squabble. Also present: Louis Berger the
Bookie and Hoppie Drazen. Twersky, landlord. Yidel Stein. Pinky's
Squealer. Many elderly women with wizened faces and yellow shawls
wept copiously. Professionals, they seldom missed a wedding and
never a funeral. Simcha Rabinovitch – now there's a better Jewish
joke than most. Born in a tailor shop on a dark tenement street,
Simcha had walked across Latvia and through Russia and down into
China – where another tailor had forged papers for him – and across
to Japan and San Francisco and over the American continent to
Montreal, Canada, where his Uncle Herschel had given him another
stool in another tailor shop on another dark tenement street. There
he stooped, the marathoner arrived, robbed of the dream that had
sustained him through all his hiking. There was no parking space
available for blocks around and all the windows of City Hall Street
were stuffed with howling, disputatious spectators. Estelle Geiger,
who had been up in Ste. Agathe with the children – wasn't it better
to spend money on enjoyment than on doctor's bills? – and who had
been elected Queen Esther by a landslide at the YMHA Purim Ball of
1949, was there with six other wives. Seven ripe peaches with black

hair. After the funeral they were going to see *The Robe* at the Palace and then Normie had promised to take them out to dinner at Ruby Foo's. Black policemen in magnificent goggles patrolled the route between the house on City Hall Street and the synagogue on silver motor-cycles. One of them, Omer Desjardins, had used to be on the anti-Red squad and knew the constituency of Cartier intimately. When he had last raided Panofsky's he had allowed him to keep *Left-Wing Communism: An Infantile Disorder* because he had known that it was a medical book. Art Gold turned up with the kids, Gloria Anne and Sheldon. President of the Committee for Better Relations Between Gentiles and Jews – "There are three sides to every argument. Yours. The other guy's. And the right side." – he hoped to organize a Wolf Adler Memorial Fund. Youngsters shinned up lamp-posts whilst many of their elders, who had movie cameras, stood on the rooftops of cars. Benjy Tulch, whose father had been killed in a running gun-battle with the RCMP when his family had still been bootleggers, twisted in the seat of his M.G. Ah, it was a fine day. You can have your slap-dash of an autumn day with insanely bright leaves falling at your feet, you can have the dreams of your loose spring evenings that end up being just dreams, you can even have all the snows of winter, but give me a white day with a blue sky and a dazzling yellow sun. Rosy women and brown children and pink-faced men. Hey, remember that day Moishe the Idiot farted during the Kol Nidre service? Or that time they raided Chaim Shub's shop for printing phony raffles? Hell. Hey, remember Bloom? "MAKE BLOOM YOUR BROOM, CLEAN UP CARTIER." The crowd surged to and fro before the door to the house. Moishe Garber, who was a recent arrival from Lodz, wanted to know if the house was for rent. He had a family of five, he said. Press photographers leaned against cars. Aaron Panofsky watched from his wheelchair. The Hook, and a few nimble-fingered others, moved stealthily among the crowd. Inside, prayers were being read:

The Rock, his work is perfect, for all his ways are judgement: a God of faithfulness and without iniquity, just and right is he.

Brothers and sisters, father, mother, wife and son of Wolf Adler, who had died a hero, stood around the pinewood coffin like hesitant swimmers standing back from a deepening pool. Leah wept dryly and Melech glowered and Jenny squeezed a handkerchief to her swollen eyes. Noah had a tendency to stare blankly.

Gusts made up of hundreds of hot, festering voices banged like rain against the shut windows.

If a man live a year or a thousand years, what profiteth it him? He shall be as though he has not been . . . He awardeth unto man his reckoning and his sentence, and all must render acknowledgement unto him.

Goldie gulped and reached out and crumpled up on the mute coffin. Knocking fiercely on the pinewood, she yelled: "Wolf. Wolf. Forgive me! Have mercy on us, Wolf!" Max pulled her away gently. "Easy," he whispered. She broke away and turned wildly on Noah. "He shouldn't be here. He's a . . ." Her voice trailed off. Leah began to moan softly and her brother, Harry, patted her shoulder. "There," he said. "There, there."

The Lord gave, and the Lord hath taken away; blessed be the name of the Lord.

Max and Itzik and Nat, Karl Panofsky, Harry Goldenberg, and Noah were the pall-bearers. Leah whimpered incoherently, the other women watched with horror, as the men grappled with the coffin and finally heaved it onto their shoulders rockily. A dreadful moment followed when the pall-bearers got twisted in a swirl of relatives in the hall. The coffin, slipping treacherously, almost toppled to the floor. Ida dug her nails into Stanley's arm. "I don't want to look," she said. "They open it at the cemetery and you're supposed to. I can't. . . ."

Outside, the crowd quietened. Identities were consumed one after the other until it became one taut, expectant face. Truly, this was the crowd that had waited at the foot of Sinai on the third day.

A swarthy man with dense eyes yelled: "Wolf Adler died for the Torah. WOLF ADLER IS A HERO."

The coffin was borne like a ship among them. Six men toiling under a shifting weight, thinking separate thoughts and leaving individual curses left unsaid. The elderly and the superstitious rushed towards them hoping to touch the coffin before it was swung into the waiting hearse. A red, blotchy face rubbed against Noah's cheek. The sun beat down without pity. Cameras turned.

"May the Almighty comfort you together with all the mourners of Zion and Jerusalem," a man yelled. "Amen," yelled many others. Silver motor-cycles mounted by goggled policemen began to cough and splutter. Melech Adler glowered back at the sun and shed no tears and clenched his yellowed fists in his pockets. Buddy Gross cornered the reporters. "Here's a copy of the rabbi's speech," he said. "He was Max Adler's brother. Remember that." He pressed envelopes into their pockets. "The rabbi's name is Fishman. F-I-S-H-M-A-N. From here we go to the synagogue. We . . ."

"How do you spell Max?" one of the reporters asked.

Gross stared and then grinned widely. "That's funny," he said. "That's pretty good."

Samuel Panofsky wheeled Aaron towards a waiting car. "Don't start anything," he pleaded. Aaron smiled bitterly. "I don't go to the circus to tease the lions. I go to watch."

"WOLF ADLER DIED A HERO."

Noah felt the coffin cutting into his shoulder and remembered that the last time he had met his father had been in Panofsky's. Wolf had wiggled his ears and raised his eyebrows – a gesture that had defined their relationship pretty neatly. Goldie was right. Wolf Adler hadn't had much of a son. Much of anything, you might say. Noah stared at Itzik's tense narrow back. Had Wolf rushed into the flames to save the scrolls? Noah doubted that. Who was the girl in the faded snapshot? Tomorrow, after I've slept. Thank God Miriam's back in Ste. Adele, he thought.

Max poked Lou. "Where's Shloime?" he asked.

"Turrono. We sen' a wire."

"He didn't get it?"

"How in the hell would I know?"

The wide-open doors of the black hearse beckoned.

Estelle Geiger stood on her toes. "Is that the one who lives with a *shiksa* in Ste. Adele?"

Leah was helped into the dark Cadillac and immediately sank back into heaps of cool pillows. Oh, the crowd. All of Montreal. A mass of flushed faces flattened against the car window.

The silver motor-cycles swung around in front of the hearse and spun in circles like bewildered, injured birds. A lost boy wailed. The coffin was eased into the hearse and a platoon of mourners fell into step behind the shut doors. Members of the crowd began to reclaim their lost identities again. Groups broke up, shifted, and formed in other combinations. Many people rushed for their cars and started for the synagogue, others fell into rows on either side of the pavement and followed after the slow, black hearse.

When the funeral procession finally reached the synagogue the doors to the hearse were flung open and Rabbi Milton Fishman, a pink-faced eagle, his prayer shawl flapping in the breeze, his beak dipped into his black prayer book, read a special prayer on the synagogue steps. Wolf Adler had not been a Zaddik, but he had died a hero.

After that the hearse, followed by nearly one hundred cars, drove more quickly to the Jewish cemetery in Cartierville. Noah stared absently out of the window of the first car. His mother moaned. He watched as the city slipped away and vacant lots and buildings under construction became more frequent. He noticed the Ajax Trading sign on many of the construction shacks. Max had sold them the land. They finally turned up the gravel road that led to the cemetery. There was lots of grass that had been yellowed by the sun between the endless rows of tombstones. In Everlasting Memory of My Beloved Wife. Lest We Forget Harold, Peace to His Dust. Smaller stones for the children, bigger ones for the rich. Lean ones, fat ones. Tall, small. White ones, grey ones, brown and decrepit ones. Noah remembered overhearing that several wealthy Jews had recently been buried in coffins that were waterproof and air-tight. Not so Wolf Adler, who was being buried in cheap pinewood according to the orthodox laws. Noah gazed at the affluent trees and was struck by the incongruity of their maturing on so obvious a fertilizer. A green iron fence separated the synagogue lot from the lots of other congregations and societies. The Workman's Circle lot was located on lower land. Marshland. Distinctions did not end at the grave after all.

Three husky labourers with muddy shovels waited beside a pile of rich brown earth. Beggars shook tin cans like threats under the faces of the mourners. A tattered man with a bronzed face sold Haggadahs. Birds chirped in the trees. A woman with damp eyes sold black books of mourners' prayers. Away, far away, the city was a grey pulpy mass looming incoherently out of the hot brown earth.

The pall-bearers assumed their burden again and, praying, passed between the two rows of mourners.

> *He that dwelleth in the secret place of the Most High shall abide under the shadow of the Almighty. I will say of the Lord, He is my refuge and my fortress: my God; in him will I trust.*

MAX

Me, I put my trust in Dow Jones. I don't go for all that hocus-pocus about God being such a big deal and being shipped downstairs – COD, I'll bet – just for laying somebody else's goods on the q.t. Anyway, it's kind of nice for the family. Publicity for me, too. Hey, I wonder how much I'm gonna have to fork out for Milty's speech? Aw, chicken-feed. But a guy croaks and he's out of business – no comebacks. Me, they're gonna burn. Religion here, religion there, I don't want any worms chewing on my *kishkas*. Wolfie didn't have enough brains for a quarter of a headache but he never short-changed a guy in his life and offhand I can think of two hundred other bastards who I'd rather see cashing in this morning. Take Ratner, for instance. You know how he got that order for the bridge and terminus away from me? I may *shmear* a commissioner occasionally but at least *I* don't lick a *Goy's* ass for a deal or kick in with ten Gs for some goddam convent up north. Aw, chicken-feed. Noah must feel pretty bad right now, but he's got class and a head on his shoulders. My Miss Holmes would go for him, too. Listen, if he wants he can keep that broad of his, but why bring a cow when you can get milk out of the bottle? Noah's a hundred per cent. I need him. Who in the hell have I got for a manager in that office when I'm away? Itzik's so busy counting the bars of soap in the johns and having fits over the bank credit that he wouldn't know a million-dollar deal if he was hit over the head with it. Nat? Lou? Meet Mr. Mayo Clinic of Montreal. I take care of all the cripples in this family. Aw, chicken-feed. Poor Leah. What a life she had with Wolf! A woman of her upbringing. That's not nice, I guess. Wolfie's dead. Hell. Facts are facts. I'll take care of you, Leah. Don't you worry. Noah, too. *Nu*, let's go. We can't stand here until Christmas.

Surely he shall deliver thee from the snare of the fowler, and from the noisome pestilence . . . Thou shalt not be afraid for the

*terror by night; nor for the arrow that flieth by day; nor for
the destruction that wasteth at noonday . . . Only with thine
eyes shalt thou behold and see the reward of the wicked.*

ITZIK

Wicked is right. What Wolf did will go down in the history of our
people but Max with all his talk and money will be forgotten just like
that. I wonder if it's true about him and Miss Holmes? Paw says that
when he dies Max will keep the offices open on the sabbath. Not as
long as I'm with him. Oh no. He thinks I'm stingy or stupid but if I
didn't hold him back on the overdraft the business would have failed
long ago. Ask Nat. I know more about the laws than any of the boys.
Ask Paw. A Jew who doesn't keep the sabbath isn't worth two cents
even. Let my brother, the hero, be a lesson to them. If there's another
flood, if . . . Noah deserves to be dead. Ask Paw.

*Because thou hast made the Lord, which is my refuge, even the
most high, thy habitation; There shall no evil befall thee,
neither shall any plague come nigh thy dwelling.*

HARRY GOLDENBERG

I'll obviously have to give her another shot after the funeral. That
girl. First she fell for Father's fantastic delusions about his own saint-
hood – thank God the Jews have turned away from Chassidism – and
now she must try to reconcile the Wolf she knew with the man who
died for the Torah. She's a difficult woman, but Wolf was a fool.
Anyway, I hope the electrocardiograph proves me wrong. But if I'm
right, will Noah help? I hardly know him. He seems a bit like Father,
but with Leah's stubbornness. He should have been able to turn to
me for guidance. What could he expect from *his* father? Or from that

vulgar, superstitious family? He's just about my boy's age. But Harvey's a go-getter. Perhaps we can help him? Sheila should be able to introduce him to some decent girls. That mistress of his won't do his career any good. Shameful business. Can he be a communist? We go forward two steps, then along come . . . Thank God Alger Hiss was a Gentile. When will the Jews learn to behave themselves?

> *Thou shalt tread upon the lion and the adder: the young lion and the dragon shalt thou trample under feet. Because he hath set his love upon thee, therefore will I deliver him: I will set him on high, because he hath known my name.*

NAT

I'm a fatalist. What's a fatalist? A fatalist is a *shnook* who marries a woman like Goldie. Elementary, my dear Watson. Ah, well. Here today, gone tomorrow. We'll have us a pinochle when we meet up there in the big beyond, Wolf. Put in a good word for me, eh?

> *He shall call upon me, and I will answer him: I will be with him in trouble; I will deliver him, and honour him. With long life will I satisfy him, and shew him my salvation.*

NOAH

I am thankful, Daddy, that if you were here you would have had the good sense to have turned your back on it. Speeches, you would have said. Prayers. You would have walked away. But I can't. Ironic that you who suffered so much all your life for what people said should not be capable of hearing when they, the people, are at last saying fine things about you. Because you have died I will learn in time to remember you for the warming things you have said and for giving me life. Time, too, is a liar. "He died well." Or did you die foolishly, Daddy? Scrolls? What about the kerosene tin? Who phoned you that night? I'll remember you, Daddy. That much I can say honestly.

As the higher sun made dry patches in the heap of rich brown earth beside the grave, Melech Adler inched back from the open pit. There was the ache of wood and the grinding of pulleys as the coffin was lowered into the grave. Outside of that the only distinct sound was Leah's low, animal moaning.

"May he come to his resting-place in peace," another man hoarsely.

People looked at the man with surprise.

Jenny shrieked. "Have mercy. God. God."

"May he come to his resting-place in peace," another man mumbled.

Rabbi Milton Fishman, his prayer shawl flapping around him, assumed his perch at the head of the grave and dipped into his black prayer book.

LEAH

So many people. All of Montreal. Wolf, Wolf. I'm sorry, I . . . *Look at the old dog.* I'll bet he's suffering. His time is coming soon all right. Look at him! He won't have a funeral like this! Would you like to make him a partner now, Melech? Wolf, I . . . Paw said this match was made in heaven. *Was he a prophet after all?* My husband may have been only a coal merchant, but . . . Oh, God. How much can a woman suffer?

> *God, full of mercy, who dwelleth on high, cause the soul of*
> *Wolf, the son of Melech, which has gone to its rest to find repose*
> *in the wings of Shechinah; among the souls of the holy, and pure*
> *as the firmament of the skies, for they have offered charity for*
> *the memory of his soul; for the sake of this conceal him in the*
> *mystery of thy wings for ever, and bind up his soul in the bond*

of life; may the Lord be his inheritance, and may he repose in
his resting-place in peace, and let us say, Amen.

A jumble of "Amens" followed.

Rabbi Milton "Pinky" Fishman was sincere out of necessity. He
believed in God as an insurance salesman believes in Prudential.
"Our hearts are heavy today," he began, facing the hot and restless
crowd. "Some of you here are mourning the nearest and dearest of
your kin. Others are mourning a friend. The simple fact is Wolf
Adler has been called to his Eternal Reward. Why? It would not surprise me if many of you are looking into your hearts and asking
yourselves that question of questions right now.

"Wolf Adler died for the Torah.

"Wolf walked fearlessly into his flaming office to rescue a few
pages of holy parchment – and today he lies dead before us. Why?
Why are the dear hearts and gentle people that we love taken away
from us? How can the Almighty, blessed be He, whose attributes are
justice and righteousness, deprive us of our loved ones? Many are the
trials and tribulations that you face in a lifetime. First of all, there are
the day-to-day problems. A quarrel with your husband or wife. Your
son wants to know who made the grass green. Your daughter has
come of the age when she is to be initiated into the mysteries of
womanhood. These problems – however small they may seem at first
glance – are salt to the meat of our daily lives. But as sure as two and
two make four we are eventually brought face to face with the
problem of death. Why? The patriarch Abraham asked: 'Wilt Thou
indeed sweep away the righteous with the wicked? . . . Shall not the
judge of all the earth do justly?' Your manners are different from
those of your forebears, but let me assure you here and now that
there is nothing new under the sun. Moses, too, pleaded with the
Almighty, blessed be He, to make Himself fully known to him when
he said: 'Show me Thy ways that I may know Thee.' Job complained

about God's ways with men and was answered thusly: 'Hearken unto this, O Job, stand still, and consider the wondrous works of God. Dost thou know how God enjoineth them and how he causeth the lightning of his cloud to shine? Who is this that darkenth our counsel by words without knowledge?'

"Yes, my friends, how many of you caught up in the hurly-burly of modern materialism have paused to wonder at the beauty of Creation? Did you know that there are not two snowflakes exactly alike in the whole wide world? I'll tell you something else, too. There is enough food for thought in one snowflake to last you a lifetime.

"The Almighty, blessed be He, is a Master Painter indeed!

> *"So God created man in his own image, in the image of God created he him; male and female created he them.*

"So don't come to me and say some of you are poor, others rich. Some handsome, others ugly. One lucky, another unlucky. In the words of Shakespeare – the greatest poet of all time – 'What a noble piece of work is man.'

"Yes, my friends. I would like to think that Wolf Adler will be a shining example to you and your children. He was a noble piece of work, indeed. A little man, one of many. He didn't build the Empire State Building or invent the aeroplane. *Time* magazine never made him Man of the Year. But without Wolf Adler, and countless others like him, life on earth would be barren. A meal without salt. A week without the sabbath.

"Wolf Adler, a simple man, died for the Torah. My heart and your hearts go out to his nearest and dearest – a loved one has been taken away from them. Today we are seeing him off on his last journey.

"Wolf's passing has glory, my friends. Honour. He died a Jew. His family has reason to be proud as well as sad." The rabbi lowered his voice. "We are living in very historic times, my friends. Never before has it been of such vital importance to remember that ancient covenant that we made with the Almighty, blessed be He. Never before has the Almighty, blessed be He, been in such dire need of defenders. Today the freedom-loving nations of the world are locked in a life-and-death struggle with the octopus monster communism. . . . There is a conspiracy against God. The tentacles of the Kremlin reach into the darkest corners. . . . How many of our brethren behind the Iron Curtain have been imprisoned, their only crime being that of having worshipped the God of their fathers . . .?

"Rabbi Eliezer said, 'Repent one day before thy death.' His disciples asked him, 'Does anyone know on what day he will die?' He replied, 'All the more reason to repent today, lest tomorrow he die. Let his whole life therefore be spent in repentance.'

"There is one here among us – I will not name names – who has turned away from God and his people. He is a secret sorrow to his family. And to him I would say, remember the Jews of Germany. They too were assimilationists. But they learnt their lesson too late. I hope – I hope from the bottom of my heart – that you to whom I am speaking will learn from the shining example of Wolf Adler.

"To him to whom I am speaking I would say no man is too big to pray.

"The President of the United States, Mr. Eisenhower, prays every Sunday. A great man, and a great friend of our people. Is anyone too big to humble himself before his Maker? Atheism leads to disrespect for our parents and to treason. Weren't our people sufficiently shamed by the Rosenbergs?

"The father of the departed, Melech Adler, is well aware of the need of God. A devout Jew, Mr. Adler has been a pillar of our community for many years. This is a sad day for him, but a proud one too. He has brought up his children in the tradition of the Torah and one of them, the oldest, has died for the Torah.

"The Jews of Montreal will remember and honour Wolf Adler for many generations. There are those who gain eternity in a lifetime, and others who gain it in a brief hour."

Rabbi Milton "Pinky" Fishman cleared his throat and stepped back out of the sun and away from the grave. Noah looked up at him and Fishman averted his eyes. People stared at Noah from all sides.

MELECH

Who burned down by me the office? A *Goy's* office the police protect. But a Jew's . . . Maybe Wolf after all knew what was in de box? Didn't he come in that day? Couldn't he have seen it with his eyes? There are letters missing. Receipts. I don't want by us no scandals, I . . . Wolf a hero! If Noah finds out what Wolf thought was in the box he'll . . . They're all waiting for me to die. Wait. You wait.

Max nudged Noah. "That speech'll cost me five hundred bucks."

"Oh. Maybe you were the him to whom he was speaking."

"Not on your life," Max said.

Man and bottle form a unity. The bottle, upturned, clutched to a toothless mouth: the man, head bent backwards, trembling. *I've seen life, plenty of it, but they don't care a goddam. Think me a lush. Served my seven years I did and seen the sun drowned in the China Sea. Had my tail, too, you bet.* Old Moore, born unasked-for to a Paddington barmaid and a commercial traveller fresh out of Dublin, James Dermot Moore, a scavenger now, yes, sure, but in the old days all a gal could ask for in his sailor pants, Moore leans against the green iron fence of the burial lot. *Them kikes are all alike.* His burning eyes are fixed on the mourners. Wood alcohol dribbles down his chin. *How many of 'em, all got up to jesus and thinking they own this f—world just because they're burying old Wolf, seen what I seen? Oh, I could tell 'em lots about their fire.* The man, coughing, dumps the empty bottle to the gravel path. Glass splashes. He staggers away blindly. *I'm not what they think and Mavis'd take me back any old time I want and be glad of it. I'm Moore, damn it. I could tell Melech stuff that'd burn his ears. Bloody big hero. I'm Moore, got more pals than you can shake your finger at. Ask anybody. Moore, that's me. Six times round the Cape. Moore's the name. Anybody wanna fight?*

Noah stared at Max. Max grinned, and Noah turned away.

SAMUEL PANOFSKY

Slaves we were in Egypt until Moishe got us organized and poking us with useful lies led us over that blazing desert to a fertile land that he never got to see himself the way Lenin got to. So there were kings and quarrels and hullabaloo and before you looked around there we were in chains again, but being led out this time. They spread us out, so help me God, over a fortune of countries like a fistful of dirt flung into a fast wind. So go tear your heart out. Here we stand listening to the biggest fool of all blabbing to us about eternal rewards and what a shame were the Rosenbergs. . . . We discovered cures and it didn't help and we made for them philosophies and they chased us away and we invented so they'd take the invention and deport the inventor and we made beautiful pictures and books and they weren't ours and even money – which is the cheapest of things – they wouldn't let us keep. Always tenants, never landlords. Anyway, now newer ones are already back there in that fertile land making believe that history goes backwards. Not that I don't wish them from the best with their tourists from Outremont and their bourgeois politicians. But you go talk to the *Goyim*. You go if you want and tell them Marx and Spinoza, tell them Trotsky too, tell them Einstein and Freud, tell them, tell them that a small man died for nothing in a fire

in a time from big, big bombs and made for us a smaller hero than
we usually put up.

Itzik poked Noah. "*Kaddish*," he said. So Noah began falteringly,
"May His great name be magnified and sanctified in the world that
is to be created anew, where He will quicken the dead and raise them
up unto life eternal. . . . O may the Holy One, blessed be He, reign
in His sovereignty and glory during your life and your days and
during the life of all the house of Israel . . . and say ye, Amen."

The others replied: "Let His great name be blessed for ever and
to all eternity."

"Blessed," Noah said, "praised and glorified . . . yea, beyond all
blessings and hymns, praises and consolations, which are uttered in
the world; and say ye, Amen."

A grave-digger dug his shovel impatiently into the heap of rich
brown earth. Noah watched. "He – He who maketh . . . He who
maketh peace in – in high places, may He make peace for us and for
all Israel; and say ye, Amen."

II

A huge basket of fruit sent by the executive of the synagogue decayed
slowly but with miasmic certainty on the living-room table. First the
bananas, then the grapes, pears, apples, and plums, were burned
brown and pulpy by the sun. All week long the curious and the bored
and several of the truly concerned filed in out of the hot night and,
mopping their foreheads and shifting damply in their chairs, ladled
out their slop of regrets in which platitudes floated like indigestible
dumplings. The honest were mostly silent. But the others, those who
were dedicated to all that was uplifting, juggled with conversation,
not daring to drop a truth.

During *Shivah*, a Hebrew term that means seven days of mourning, a light is kept burning in the house in memory of the soul of

the departed. It is customary for the mourners – parents, brothers and sisters, wife and children – to wear dark, preferably black garments. Marital relations are forbidden. They sit on low stools or chairs and wear cloth slippers or sandals. All the mirrors in the house are covered and the men don't shave.

Early every morning Harry Goldenberg arrived and gave Leah an injection. The two of them held mysterious conferences in the kitchen. Lou consumed cigars laconically. Nat, who was not allowed to tell jokes, sulked in the corner. Each morning the milkman left three quarts of milk for Max's ulcers. On the afternoon of the second day Moore staggered drunkenly into the living-room. He wanted to speak to Melech. Max took him firmly by the arm before he had a chance to speak and led him into the bedroom. They were together for about an hour.

For the first three days Noah sat silently on his stool smoking one cigarette after another. Some thought that he was angry, others thought that he was ashamed. He showed some flicker of interest when Rabbi Fishman showed up on the evening of the second day: but the anticipated outburst didn't develop. The next morning Melech trapped Noah in the kitchen. "You have stolen some of my papers from the box," he said.

"Yes," Noah said.

Melech seized Noah's arm fiercely. "When I die," he said, "you shouldn't come to the funeral. That'll be put in my will."

Noah walked away, but not quickly enough.

Melech shouted after him: "I would not be surprised if he committed suicide because of all the shame you brought him."

"So you don't think he died for those scrolls either?"

Melech didn't reply.

Responsibility, Noah thought. Nights he sat up with his mother, who wasn't sleeping, and read to her from the poems of Lord Byron and Sir Walter Scott. "The stag at eve had drunk its fill/As danced the moon on Monan's Rill." Getting up each morning was a choice that was not made without a long, tortuous struggle. He held on to sleep the way a drowning man must cling to his share of driftwood. But this particular share of wood – sleep – was waterlogged. The short, drifting spread between sleeping and full consciousness made for many dilatory journeys. Finally, each morning, there was the febrile feeling of his ship being pulled back into a whirlpool. Noah rowed madly with both oars. But the oars were broken. Always, just prior to awakening, he was with his father again in Panofsky's. Chocolate biscuits crumbled in their mouths and insipid jokes were made and his father, having misunderstood a remark of Noah's, accused him of having been an embarrassment to him ever since he had been a small boy. Then, just as Noah seemed on the brink of truth, of something half-heard, he was startled – rescued – by a fuller awakening. That's when his other difficulties began. Walking, for instance, was an odd sensation. You first put one foot, then another, on the floor – there appeared to be only two – and pushing your body upwards, lifting one foot after the other cautiously, you seemed to move forward over space. Thirty-two steps were required to the toilet. Eighteen big ones were sufficient to get him to that stool in the living-room. There, people talked.

Mrs. Edelman: Wolfie dead? I still can't believe it. I tell you I was in Ste. Agat' when I got the news. You know Kirstein's Hotel, Goldie? Pheh! Don't ask. They serve you there what they call a steak and a rock would go down easier. Every day, gas pains. I got here by me on the heart a fire I walk around with all day. You know how much it cost my Moey – my Malcolm, I mean – to keep me in the hotel? *Rooms.* I got a room, I tell you, overlooking the loveliest garbage pails in Canada. You could die from the heat. After my mattress sleeping on the floor would be like floating on air. Ask me what's next door? The Gentlemen's Room. Listen, Abe Myerson's father – God bless him – should live another hundred years. But how can a man with a bladder condition come to a hotel? Every fifteen minutes he's in there flushing. Why did he rent a room? A lease on the toilet – you should pardon the expression – would have suited him better. Anyway, Leah, time is a healer. You got a fine boy. You're still young. . . .

Pincus Weintraub: City Hall Street ain't what it used to be when Wolfie and I were young. Take a look at the greenhorns all around. They speak with accents two miles long and they never wash behind the . . . Aw, if they were so broke like they say you tell me how come they got the fares to go from Poland to Montreal? Another question. Do you know that some of them are moving into Outremont? Wives who still wear wigs! After all we did here to improve conditions they'd like to put us back into the middle ages. . . .

On the afternoon of the third day Noah wandered into the hall and heard his mother on the telephone. "For the last time," she said, "he doesn't want to speak to you. Besides, he's not in." She hung up.

"Was that for me?" Noah asked.

"No, *boyele*, of course not."

That evening Noah locked himself up in his bedroom and drank lots of coffee. A vigour returned to his body. Looking out of the window, he realized that he hadn't been out for three days. Miriam, he thought. Miriam. He looked into the mirror. His eyes were red. He was badly in need of a shave. Hell, he thought, *I'm* not dead. He slipped out of the house. Panofsky was delighted to see him. He hung around grinning happily while Noah shaved in the kitchen. "You're welcome like a son here," he said.

"What did you think of him, Mr. Panofsky?"

"Not a bad man. Scared stiff of your *Zeyda*. Of your Maw, too. But . . ."

"In Kirstein's Hotel they serve you a steak and a rock would go down easier," Noah said. "Can you lend me ten bucks?"

"I can lend you a hundred."

"Moscow gold," Noah said.

Outside, the heat persisted. Noah did not want to call Miriam yet. There were too many things that he wanted to think about first. He

turned up Fairmount Street whistling an air from *The Seasons* of
Vivaldi. The Café Minuit, on Park Avenue corner of Mount Royal
Boulevard, was not very crowded. Noah ordered a bottle of Molson's
beer and grinned broadly for no reason at all. The tall blonde who
sat at the bar was quite drunk. "You can't come up to the apartment,
Harry," she said thickly. "How do I know when he'll turn up?" "He
eats out of your hand," Harry said grudgingly. Noah turned away
from them discreetly. "He eats out of my hand, honey, as long as I
keep sugar in it," she said.

Noah drank. He laid out the photographs and letters and receipts
on the table and considered them thoughtfully. The blonde girl in
the photographs was plump with small eyes and a silly smile. In that
yellowed picture, probably taken at a village fair, Melech held her in
his arms with some embarrassment. Noah could almost hear the
girl's giggling echoing through the years. Who is she? A mistress?
The photographs had been smudged by excessive handling. What
does Melech think of when he looks at her? Noah was suddenly
struck by his own obscene manners in meddling with Melech's past.
Hell, he thought. My father died for the contents of this box. But he
immediately recognized the falseness of his rage and it was some
time before he could bring himself to go through the letters and
receipts. The receipts, from the post office, were for monthly money
orders to Miss Helga Kubalski, Sadowa Ulica, Lodz, Poland. The
first receipt was dated June 18, 1911, and was for twelve dollars.
Payments increased through the years. Thirty dollars, eighteen
dollars, twenty-five dollars. The last receipt was dated July 12, 1939.
Imagine keeping this to himself all these years, Noah thought. But
how does my father come into this? *Did he know?* The letters were in
Polish. That's merciful, Noah thought. I wouldn't have been able to
resist reading them. There were photographs enclosed in many of
the letters. The blond boy with curly locks did not resemble Melech.
The last picture showed him in an army uniform. He was smiling. It
was the kind of picture a man sent to his sweetheart. That last letter

that had come from Poland was dated August 22, 1939. Melech's letters continued through the war years and after. But, of course, none of them had been posted. The last one was dated August 25, 1953. That had been three days before the fire. It was difficult to see the relationship between the righteous and God-fearing Jew and the young lover embracing a giggling girl at a village fair. Oh, Melech, Noah thought. My poor, suffering *Zeyda*. Still, he thought, you did wrong to punish us.

The other blonde, the one at the bar, staggered towards the door with Harry. "I never did learn how to say no to you," she said. Harry squeezed her arm.

Noah wandered back absently. He was shocked out of his reveries when he noticed the Ford parked opposite the house on City Hall Street. *Miriam*. He bounded up the stairs, taking them two at a time. The living-room was dark, but the light was on in his bedroom. He absorbed the scene instantaneously and with horror. His mother, his mistress. Leah was crumpled up in her chair, a soggy handkerchief clenched in her fist. Miriam sat tensely on the edge of Noah's bed. Her quick, red-tipped hands flipped through the pages of an old copy of *Life* magazine. She puffed swiftly on the cigarette that dangled from her scarlet mouth. She was wearing that green silk scarf that he had last seen when she had come to stay with him at Mrs. Mahoney's. I love you best when you are angry, he had said. The scarf still accentuated the vulnerability of her throat.

Noah grinned. He couldn't help it. "Hello, Miriam."

"Hullo."

"You two have a nice chat?"

"*Mrs.* Hall and I . . ."

"Noah, did you know that I phoned *eight* times in the last three days?"

"No. I had no idea. Honest."

Noah turned to his mother. She fumbled with her handkerchief.

"Max wouldn't let, *boyele*. He said that after the *Shivah*, but . . ."

"Max doesn't run my life, Maw. You know better than that."

"She answered the phone. Not Max. She said that you didn't want to speak to me, darling."

"Maw, did you . . ."

"I hardly know what I'm doing these days, I . . ." Leah's fist tightened around her handkerchief. She seemed to have difficulty in breathing. "I made a mistake? I was trying to protect you, *boyele*. Wouldn't I do anything for you? I . . ."

"All right, Maw. Take it easy."

Miriam leaped up and squashed her cigarette on the floor. "I came to get you, Noah. I'm all alone in Ste. Adele. I want you to . . ."

"Miriam, I . . ."

"I want you to come back with me – now – tonight."

Noah smacked his hands together and rubbed his jaw anxiously.

"When a Jew dies," Leah began softly, "the son is supposed to sit *Shivah* for a week. My *boyele*'s father died a . . . We Jews, you know . . . When . . ."

"Noah is not a Jew that way, Mrs. Adler. He's broken with the – the dark ages. He told me that himself. Besides, I understand that you and your husband didn't exactly . . ."

"Christ, Miriam."

"Will you please stop Christ-ing and Miriam-ing me. Will you . . ."

"And you, Maw," Noah said, "have no right to say 'we Jews' to her."

"Are you coming, Noah?"

"Now?"

"Yes."

"Can't we wait a few days. Isn't this rather . . ."

"When I'm not with you, when there are others around, it is as though that time was wasted or of no account. I would like there to be tests that you could put me to."

Noah flushed. The darkness around us, he remembered, belongs to others. We will be a light burning in the city. Let the others gather round and be amazed. Or let them stay away. Noah turned and faced his mother remorsefully. He remembered the insurance salesman coming every week and the rusty cocoa tin on the top shelf of the pantry in which the pennies had been hoarded. "Miriam, this *is* cruel. Couldn't you – couldn't we – wait another few days?"

"Don't worry about me, *boyele*. Go. Take your happiness . . ."

"Are you going to be taken in by that, Noah? Are you? You were much crueller to Theo when you asked me to choose between you."

Noah felt that blow physically. "I was," he said. "Maw," Noah began, "it's true that I don't believe in sitting *Shivah* and praying. I'll come in to visit . . ."

Leah seemed to heighten herself in her chair. Her breath came awfully short and her face turned grey. She gasped. Perspiration poured down her face. She clutched her chest feebly. It seemed to be held in a vice. Tightening, and pressed down under a huge weight. A pain darted down her left arm and another – even swifter pain – up her neck and jaw. Her eyes were lit with agony. Noah reached out and she collapsed in his arms. He lifted her gently onto his bed.

Miriam paused at the door. She saw that he was trembling.

"I'll phone you tomorrow morning," he said softly. "I'll drive up for the afternoon."

She had hoped that he was going to ask her to stay.

Harry stayed with Leah for about an hour. Noah waited in the living-room. Smoking in the dark.

"She'll sleep now," Harry said, rolling down his shirt sleeves.

"Heart?"

"Yes." Harry sat down beside Noah. "I think we should have a talk."

"Is it all right if I go out for a walk now? Can we talk in the morning?"

"Certainly. She'll sleep now. Let's have breakfast together."

"Thanks, Harry." Noah paused. "You're sure it's okay if I go out?"

"You go ahead. I'm staying the night anyway."

"You're kind, Harry."

Noah went in to look at her before he left. She was sleeping. He kissed her hands.

The night sky was deep black and littered with stars. Slim, resolute buildings loomed tall against the hot sky. Neon twitched. Stragglers loitered on corners. St. Catherine Street, deserted, spun out before him like an unanswered question. The occasional homebound whore or baffled drunk walked past quick and unassured, stripped of funds and paid for rumpusing, without commotion and no longer accompanied. Wanting people, unused, headed unwillingly for the longer and more asking night of their rented rooms. Nobody crowded for streetcars: nobody waited under clocks. The lying day was done for. Theatre marquee lights had gone out. Nightclub neon spluttered, then failed. Only the stars stayed on. That, and the quiet. But the stars were too high and the quiet sought them out rudely.

Noah, however, knew where he could still get a drink. He went to Gino's on Dorchester Street. Here the neon, the chromium women and the tinsel men, were all unneeded. Most of the regulars were drunk on arrival. Hope had expired and glamour was defunct. The whores did without ruses and the men drank solemnly without too much talk. Noah strained to adjust his eyes to the smoke-filled room. Stumbling between tables he finally found a vacant stool at the bar. He ordered a whisky, and searched in vain among the many stunned faces for a hint of vitality. He would have liked somebody sympathetic to talk to. Perhaps, he thought, I too will end up looking at my watch. Pretending that I'm waiting for a friend. Or that the stranger I might talk to is the oldest of my friends. Or absorb myself in a job. "I'm a busy man, you know." He felt the photographs and receipts in his pocket. Nobody will mourn for you, Melech. This is Montreal, and we serve many Gods. We believe in minding our own business and the freedom to agree with us. When we go to heaven one will say, I did not cheat on my income tax, and another, I used to give up my seat on streetcars for old ladies.

Miriam. Miriam, he thought. Miriam.

Many pillows were propped up behind her. Leah still pale, but she was also very agitated. "I may live for only a few months. . . ."

Noah remained by the window with his back turned to her. He clenched his fists and felt something yield deep inside him. Heart, he thought. But I would have gone, anyway – had I still loved her. His hands slipped into his jacket pockets and recoiled swiftly when they touched the letters and receipts. "Miriam," Noah called out softly. "Miriam." Then his hands fell limply back into his pockets again and he crushed the letters viciously. What if I *do* love her, Noah thought, and have turned against her out of fear?

"*Boyele*, you won't have to take care of me so long. I probably won't last. . . ."

"Please, Maw, don't talk like that."

"Your father left an insurance policy of five thousand . . ."

"Please don't go on. Please. . . ."

"We can get a small apartment in Outremont. . . . We . . ."

The broken oars burst free of their locks. The boat itself broke up underneath him. And Noah, who did not call out for help, felt the waters close over him.

"Yes, Maw. Anything you say."

III

She found Miriam perched on a rock by the stream.

"Marg," Miriam said.

They embraced. Then, their hands still joined, they stood apart in the sun and studied each other like competing dancers. She's altered, Miriam thought. Marg had used to be a lean woman with a vital face and lots of quickness to her body. The woman who smiled at Miriam under that sun was nervously thin with eyes that made fast calculations and a face that was hardening.

Miriam was barefooted. Her hair, bleached by the sun, hung in swift tangles round her neck. She squeezed Marg's hand. "Come on in," she said. Marg seemed dubious. "Noah's in Montreal. His father died a few days ago. He . . ."

"Yes. I know. They ran a rather vulgar ad in the papers. Apparently his father was something of a . . ."

"Noah had nothing to do with that."

Marg peeled off her long, white gloves. "I can't get over how wonderful you look," she said. "Would you recommend him?"

Miriam faked a tiny laugh. She poured drinks.

"I've been sent here on a rather delicate mission, darling." Marg picked a sliver of tobacco off her wide, sensual lips. "You might say that I'm the poor man's Eden. I . . ."

"Theo?"

Marg moistened her index finger and ran it down her leg. "Damn these nylons." She looked up and smiled ingenuously. "Don't anticipate. I've planned my little speech."

"How is he?"

"Theo?"

"Yes."

"In a mess. You happy?"

"I think Noah is leaving me."

"Oh dear."

I mustn't break down, Miriam thought. I mustn't.

"Do you want to talk?" Marg asked invitingly.

"I – I behaved rather foolishly last night. We had a bad quarrel just before Noah got the news about his father's death. I think that my bitching was beginning to bore him. Anyway I drove in to see him last night and made a scene in front of his mother. She's dreadful, but she's got a tremendous hold on him and there was a scene and she had a heart attack. She . . . I don't know if you understand how strong Jewish family ties . . ."

"Remember David Shub?"

"The boy who sat next to you in English 107?"

"Yes. We were going to get married, but . . . We're the last word in bed, darling, but eventually they all settle down with a dreadfully respectable Jewish girl who cooks them that awful greasy food and turns out a baby a year and is paraded about in mink."

"Will you please stop." Miriam bit her lip. "Noah's different," she said.

"Aren't they *all* different?"

"Did Theo send you here to ask me for a divorce?"

"No."

"Would you like another drink?"

"Yes, but you'd better get yourself a Kleenex first."

"I'm sorry." Miriam blew her nose. Then she poured more drinks. "How's John?"

"John's John."

"Are *you* happy?"

"I'm not like you, Miriam. I don't expect to be happy. I think all men are bastards. I . . . Were you in love with Chuck?"

"Yes."

"He was laying both of us. You knew that?"

"Yes."

"That's where we differ, you see. I wasn't in love with him. I enjoyed him while he was around. You don't hurt as easily that way."

"Perhaps."

"Would you like some advice?" Marg asked.

"Go ahead."

"Noah's ten years younger than us. You're an adventure to him. He . . ."

"He's . . ."

"He's *not* different. Damn, I haven't come here to torment you. I want to help."

"I'm sorry."

"Theo's the same as any other man. Right now he'd be willing to forgive and forget. Etc. But in a month, or two months . . ."

"I'm not going back to him."

"Miriam, be sensible."

"I'm not going . . . He married me so that he could have someone to blame his failures on. We were never in love. We . . ."

"Never *in what*? Aren't you being slightly romantic?"

"I'm in love with Noah, Marg. I don't care about his family or . . . I'm going to hang around and fight it. I want him. I'm not . . ."

"*I'm* Theo's mess."

"You."

"Oh, don't look at me like that. He was lonely. I didn't think he'd take it so seriously."

"You're afraid," Miriam said.

"He's an awfully moral lover. Not to haggle about his other failures in that direction. He'd like to tell John. 'We can't go on being friends.' He's impossible!"

Miriam giggled. "I'm sorry," she said.

"If you're not going back to him, if you insist on this Noah of yours, will you at least speak to Theo and ask him not to say anything to John about – about us?"

"I'll phone him tomorrow."

"Promise?"

"Yes."

"I still think you should go back to him."

"I can't. It would kill me."

Miriam giggled after the car had driven off, but soon after that she felt terribly depressed again. She prepared dinner. She ate her bacon and eggs on the screen porch, not at all sure that she would be able to keep it down. It was almost eight o'clock. A breeze swept down from the hills and twisted in the tall grass, and Miriam put on her sweater. Pink tongues licked at the clouds, and the sun dipped lower, less hot but still brilliant, in the fading sky. The pine-stubbled hills that were sprawled on all sides turned a lusher green. Bloated frogs croaked. A swarm of crows flew past, cawing blackly and intent on some distant field. The shadows on the road grew longer. No dust stirred. Miriam got up and collected the soiled dishes.

That's when she saw Noah walking towards her. He was already on the lawn. Miriam trembled. "Noah," she said.

He hadn't heard. Not yet. He waved, but his gesture was without spirit. Immediately Miriam anticipated the worst. But she smiled anyway. "Hello," she said.

"Hello."

"Let's go swimming," she said quickly. "You can eat when we get back."

Noah started as though to say something. A protest began in his eyes. But Miriam stopped him, putting her hand gently to his mouth. He smiled feebly. Each of them suffered from a sudden, deeply felt pain. "Whatever it is," Miriam said softly, "it'll keep for a bit." He seemed doubtful of that and Miriam pressed his hand and smiled as well as she could. "Don't worry, darling," she said. "I know."

They got into the car together and drove for a mile without a word being spoken. Finally Miriam turned to him. "Can you stay the night?"

"Yes. Certainly."

Then they looked at each other. Amazed. Both of them remembered the last time that question had been asked.

"I guess our roles have been reversed," Miriam said.

The beach was deserted. They walked hand in hand out into the lake. Her inscrutable smile smacked richly of superior knowledge and he shirked from it.

"We could swim out far and not come back," she said.

Her voice had a hard, dangerous edge to it. There was still some sun left and it passed through her hair unfairly lovely. Noah touched her cheek gently. "The first time I went to a restricted beach," he said, "a guy chased me with a canoe paddle. But I got away."

"You'll always get away."

That hurt. He pushed her back into the water with the flat of his hand and then swam out after her. They swam for about half an hour and then ran back on to the beach and flopped down exhausted on their blanket. The sky darkened. The hills, a blur at first, were gradually consumed by the night. Noah smoked.

"What if I were pregnant?"

Noah jumped up and rubbed his shoulders with a towel. "Stop teasing," he said.

They didn't talk driving back. He waited on the porch steps while she went inside to prepare sandwiches. A slight wind came up from the stream. Noah got up and found her in the bedroom. Three bobbypins were held between her teeth and her wet hair adhered to her bronzed shoulders. She had one leg in her slacks. Her bra, flung hastily over her shoulders, had not yet been strapped. Noah reached out for her impetuously and held her tight to him. "No. Please, Noah. I can't." Her cheeks were salty from tears. "The toast'll burn." She wiggled out of his arms.

Noah changed and sat down on the porch steps again. From far away, up from the next valley perhaps, came the sound of people's laughter. Others were having a party.

"Are you cold? Can I get you a jacket?" Miriam asked.

She was wearing black slacks. Her hair had been combed back straight and in her eyes there was some terror, some tenderness, and a lot of the child. She set the tray down on the porch. There was a bottle of whisky and sandwiches. She sat down beside him and lit a cigarette. "Go ahead," she said.

Noah slapped his arm and killed a mosquito. "I'll have a drink," he said. "You?"

"All right."

Her needs were contradictory. She despised him for what she thought he was going to say, but, on the other hand, she was afraid that he was suffering immensely, and that made her feel tender towards him.

He told her about the scrolls that his father had supposedly died for. He said that he couldn't believe it. He told her about Melech's letters, and about the empty tin of kerosene. "There is the kind of Jew," he said, "who gets the same nourishment out of a *Goy* as the worst type of communist gets from a lynching in the south. Take the *Goy* away from him and you're pulling out the thread that holds him together." Those people in the next valley, the ones who were having a party, were playing music loud. The music came to them in gusts. "Another kind of Jew claims all the famous dead and flings them into the faces of prejudiced persons like bits of coloured paper. Einstein, he says. Anti-Semites always begin by telling you that Jesus Christ was a Jew. The Rosenberg case, if it didn't prove anything else, proved that the middle-class Jew is more middle-class than Jew. Hell, that wretched judge."

"Hold on," Miriam said. "I'm going to get more soda. I'll be right back."

Noah got up and walked over to the road and picked up a pebble and tossed it towards the stream. The pebble swooshed through the trees, bounced off a rock, and plopped into the water. . . . A frog croaked. There were plenty of fire-flies. "Hell," Noah said.

Somebody shrieked at the party in the next valley. Laughter followed, splattering into the night. A bottle crashed. More shrieks, more laughter.

"Noah?"

"Coming."

Drinks were poured, but they didn't start talking right away.

Miriam wept inwardly, certain that this was their final night and hoping against that certainty. She recalled all the devious routes, beginning with Queen Street, that had brought her to these porch steps to share a bottle with a rueful lover. "Tired?" she asked.

"No."

He's resentful, she thought, because I pushed him away from me in the bedroom.

"Funny," Noah said. "Ten years ago a man who was religious was a fool or a liar. Now the pendulum has swung back." He laughed. "The West have got God again the way the middle-aged light up on their childhood. If God weren't dead I guess he'd be editing *Time* today. Maybe he is. Who knows?"

There was a fine, cool smell to the night. The moon, red and altogether too pretty, was high and perfectly round in the pitch-black sky.

"I'm getting drunk," she said.

He grinned and brushed her hair back with his hand and momentarily felt a resurgence of his old love for her. Changing, he thought. Even two people sitting together, two people who know each other damn well, and there's always the changing back and forth.

"It's too bad," he said, "that there is no longer anything that one could wholly belong to. This is the time of buts and parentheses. All that seems to remain are one's responsibil . . . Oh, Miriam, I wish that most men – me included – were taller and all women lovely. I . . ."

Two headlights shone into their eyes, then moved sideways and away. There was the clean hard knock of pebbles being kicked up on the road – and then the car appeared. A woman leaned out and shrieked and waved a bottle at them. They couldn't make out what she had said. Then zoom and away. Tail lights, red, into the night.

"I guess they're coming from the party," she said.

"I'll bet they're back in an hour," he said. "They'll swim in the lake. Somebody will catch somebody with the wrong somebody and . . ."

"I'll be right back," she said.

Noah felt the liquor taking hold. He wanted to make love to her, but he couldn't. He wanted to tell her that he was leaving her, but he couldn't do that either. Heart, he thought. I wonder if she'll ask me when the time comes, ask me like he asked her, if there was a light. Well, he thought, my father was a hero. That calls for another drink. He emptied the bottle and then flung it into the grass. "Cheers," he said. He stared at the dark trees that wobbled just a bit before him and listened for the rushing of the water between the rocks. The stag at eve had drunk its fill/As danced the moon on Monan's Rill. Christ, he thought. I should have hit Itzik. "Miriam." She didn't answer. Noah got up. He staggered into the living-room. She was seated on the sofa. "Miriam?" She puffed hard on her cigarette and he made out her face as something chill and quite alone in the quick light.

"Noah, did you come here to tell me that we're through?"

He choked. "I came here to ask you to marry me," he said.

Again her face in the quick light. She wielded that cigarette like a star. He followed it with fascination and because he couldn't bring himself to look into her eyes. Why did I say that? he thought.

"You're drunk," she said.

"All right. I'm drunk."

"When shall we get married?"

"Whenever you like," he said, swaying.

"Do you love me?"

"I did, but . . . I – I feel a tremendous affect . . ."

"Pity?"

He felt something knot deep inside him.

"It's not good enough, Noah."

The bottom has fallen out, he thought. He turned away from her. "What'll you do?" he asked.

"That's none of your business."

He sat down beside her and tried to take her in his arms, but she moved away.

"Are you going to take care of *her*?" she asked.

"Yes."

"Is that why?"

"No."

"You're a fool."

"Perhaps."

"A coward."

"I want to rest for a bit. I'm confused. So much has . . ."

"So you're going to become a member of the community after all?"

"I didn't say that."

The room began to brighten a bit.

"I'll be able to forgive you everything in time," she said. "Except your having had to get drunk. Except your having asked me to marry you."

"I'm sorry," he said.

"Oh, go to hell."

Noah got up and began to pace the floor with the exaggerated care of the drunk. He paused by the window. The moon, a pallid thing, began to fade away. A mist settled on the woods. The sun was like a fire in the pine trees on the far hills over to their right. Creeping higher surely.

"It's morning," she said. "Would you like something to eat?"

"No."

She came up from behind and kissed his head tenderly. She hugged him fiercely for the briefest instant. "Noah," she said. Said, involuntarily, just before she let him go. "It's morning," she said. He froze by the window. A wire seemed to tighten around his heart.

"I'll never be able to forgive myself for what I've done to . . ."

"Please go," she said.

"Miriam, I . . ."

"Haven't you any consideration for me? Go. Please go."

She crumpled up on the sofa. Noah moved towards her and then turned around, having thought better of it. The screen door banged louder than her weeping.

Outside, there was a mess of cigarette butts on the porch steps. Sun glistened on the empty whisky bottle that had been flung into the grass.

It was going to be a fine day.

5

Autumn and Winter 1953–4

STE. AGATHE DES MONTS IS QUITE HIGH IN THE Laurentians, about sixty-five miles from Montreal. It is built in the foothills that finally drop into a wide blue lake called Lac des Sables. Ste. Agathe did not flourish until the Outremont Jews discovered it around 1941, and brought the boom with them. Old hotels were remodelled and enlarged, new ones went up almost over-night. Speculators, like Max Adler, outdid each other throwing up quick cottages that had Frigidaires and indoor plumbing – as opposed to the outhouses of their boyhood in Shawbridge. The quiet lake erupted in a roar of motorboats. A riding academy was opened, and summer camps – sometimes with a child-psychiatrist in attendance – were opened for the sons and daughters of the second-generation Jews.

Dr. Harry Goldenberg's cottage was located on a quieter part of the lake. Several days after *Shivah* had ended Noah and his mother came up to stay for a few weeks. Shawbridge, long ago, had been split into two camps. The orthodox and the communist. But Noah noticed that the split in Ste. Agathe was vastly different. On one side there were men like Max. Max Adler had a pinball machine in his living-room. His basement was furnished like the gaudiest of night-club bars. All his friends were quickly introduced to the wonders of his sunken bathtub, and – women in particular – to the air vent concealed in the floor of the first-floor landing that blew their skirts over their heads if the pressure was released as they passed. The flower bed on the lawn spelled ADLER when in bloom. In the other camp were doctors, lawyers, businessmen, and several of the more cultured abortionists. Harry Goldenberg was kind, but very sensible. A bookcase with a glass door protected his set of the Harvard Classics. Mrs. Goldenberg subscribed to *Commentary*. There were two children. Harvey was a law student at McGill and on the executive of the Hillel Society. Sheila, a year younger, was training to do social service work and was engaged to Larry Gould, the lawyer's son. Harvey, Sheila, and Larry were all employed at a children's camp several miles away and came into Ste. Agathe two or three nights a week. Harry Goldenberg had instructed family and friends to do their best to make Noah feel "at home." Noah, however, did not at first respond to his uncle's kindness. He avoided all of them. He took his mother for a walk every morning and the rest of the day he wandered off by himself. He didn't even visit Max. The beaches of Ste. Agathe were sandy and on a lake instead of a yellow river. There were no fat ladies in bloomers. Only the elderly spoke Yiddish. Instead of dancing to jukeboxes on the balconies of general stores the young, splendidly dressed, danced on tiled terraces to the music of hotel bands.

Noah had his problems. His father's body, the toes turned inwards, robbed him of sleep. He wrote letter after letter to Miriam, then tore them up. Evenings he sat in the bar of the Hotel St. Vincent and stared at that faded, tattered photograph of Melech with a giggling girl in his arms. He wandered over all the hills that surrounded the town and one day he climbed one from where he could see Ste. Adele. He began to spend his evenings on that hill amply supplied with cigarettes and whisky. Panofsky sent him money without Noah's having asked for it. The enclosed note said: "Now you're one of the Kremlin's agents." He began to think that he did love Miriam and had abandoned her out of fear. Drunk, he imagined that he was his father's murderer. The theft of Melech's letters represented a worse crime to him than Shloime's having robbed Panofsky. Who had phoned Wolf that night to tell him about the fire? People stopped Noah on the street to tell him that they had known his father, and that wire kept tightening around his heart. Saturday night Sheila gave a party. Noah was invited. The party, in fact, was for his benefit. He drank recklessly all afternoon and crept silently across the lawn at ten o'clock that night. He saw his mother sitting in a corner and talking to two girls. She was telling them that he was brilliant. Noah burst into the party. He knew that he was going to make a fool of himself. "Am I late?" he asked savagely.

Everybody tried to act natural.

"Noah's here," Leah said joyously.

Sheila took him in her arms and began to dance with him. "I could just kill you," she said.

Noah struggled out of her arms and began to wheel another girl across the terrace wildly. He suggested things to her that were slightly shocking and the girl left him standing alone in the middle of the dance. The terrace spun around him. Harvey seized him by the arm. "Take it easy." Harvey smiled. "Sheila's fixing some black coffee for you."

"That girl's stolen my billfold," Noah said. "Call the cops."

"Think of your mother," Harvey said urgently.

Noah squinted into a spinning confusion of faces. The moon whirled like a top. Leah confronted him. "*Boyele*," she said, squeezing all the sadness of the world into that word. Noah tottered. He patted his mother's head, and turned to Harvey. "She walks in beauty like the night," he said.

The record player started again and Noah slipped away from Harvey. He fell into the arms of two girls. Louis Armstrong held a trumpet to his ear and blew with all his might. One of the girls tittered nervously. The other said: "Your father has only been dead ten days."

"If you can't sing and you can't dansh," Noah said, "if you aren't engaged and you can't play piano, then show ush your . . ."

Harvey dragged him away. "It's the last time I come to one of your parties," Noah said truculently. Then, grinning, he added: "Las' sh one into the lake is a stinker."

Harvey tightened his grip. Sheila giggled. "It's not funny," Harvey said.

"Funny?" Noah said.

"Not you," Harvey said.

"That girl I danced with s'got trenchmouth. She tried to . . ."

"I know," Harvey said.

"If you don't lemme go," Noah said, "I'm gonna be sick all over your new jacket. . . ."

Harvey wavered. Sheila giggled again.

Noah sensed a sympathetic audience. He pulled away from Harvey in the living-room and swept a very ornate bit of bone china off the table. It was a slipper covered with many ugly china flowers. He swung it in the air and bang, splash, it came down on the floor. Harvey clenched his fists. Sheila tittered. Noah climbed up on a chair. "A spectre is haunting Outremont," he said solemnly. "It is the spectre of . . ."

He tottered. Harvey broke his fall. Noah passed out in his arms.

When he awakened the next afternoon Noah remembered enough of what had happened to feel greatly embarrassed. But before he had much time to think, there was a knock at the door.

"I brought you toast and coffee," Sheila said.

Sheila had long brown hair and bright, flashing eyes. Noah thought that her manner was too intently cheerful. Miriam's mouth had suggested much suffering. Sheila, however, obviously moved in the best of all possible worlds. There was plenty of warmth about her. There was also no doubt that she had consumed a good deal of milk as a child, but no greater suffering than the death of a pet dog was suggested.

"I'm sorry about last night," Noah said.

Sheila put down the tray and beat her chest solemnly. "A spectre is haunting Outremont." She giggled. "I could have just killed you last night but you were terribly funny in the end, Noah, and I like you a lot." She sat down on the foot of the bed. "Why do you hate us?"

"I don't hate you," Noah said.

"Is it because Daddy wants to give you Harvey's old clothes?" She cocked her head as though she meant to catch Noah's answer like a ball. "Daddy would like me to introduce you to some *decent* girls and that kind of thing, but I won't if you don't want me to. . . ."

"Are they angry about last night?"

"Mother's blazing. Daddy'll get her a new dress or a box of chocolates and everything'll be dandy. Is it true that you were living with a married woman – a Gentile – in Ste. Adele?"

"Yes, I . . ."

"Skip it. I won't pry," she said. "But isn't it awful about all the publicity they got up about your poor father?"

"Yes. It was."

"That was your Uncle Max's fault. Daddy says Max wants the Liberal nomination. He hasn't got enough education to be an M.P. He'd shame us in Ottawa. Daddy says Max is too ambitious."

"That's what my father used to say. But I like Max."

"Drink your coffee. Would you like to play tennis this afternoon? I've got the day off."

"I don't know how to play tennis."

"Would you like to go riding?"

"I'm afraid that I . . ."

"Oh, then we can just go for a walk or something."

"All right. But it'll have to be today. I owe Panof . . . a friend money. I must get back to Montreal and get a job."

Winter came swiftly that year. One day it was hot, and the next a hard wind swept in from the north and wiped the city clean of the clouds. The grey financial houses of St. James Street reached higher into the sky, as if they meant to rend holes in it. A shortage of coal was rumoured. At night the stars glittered like bolts twisted into a steel roof and a copper moon gleamed coldly. Heartier Montrealers armed with rugs and rum cheered the McGill Redmen to a few victories in Molson's Stadium. A man got up in the Recorder's Court and promised the end of the world within six days. Gus "Pell" Mell announced from Griffintown that he was planning a comeback. I'll kill Greco, he said. Palmer wrote in the *Herald* that he'd take Montreal over any city in the world. The uranium market wobbled. A twelve-year-old boy was stabbed to death on Mount Royal and the police rounded up nearly all the likely suspects. A *Gazette* editorial pleaded for protection against perversion. An M.P. got up in the House of Commons and said that the best civil defence plan for Canada was to paint big white signs on the highways saying this way to Detroit, that way to Pittsburgh. Then the snows came floating down joyfully. Day after day of it. St. Catherine Street was transformed into a white, fluffy wonderland. An early-bird of a Presbyterian minister denounced the commercialism of Montreal Christmas. A big department store came back with a full-page advertisement saying WE'RE PROUD TO SELL. EVERYBODY BENEFITS FROM MORE SALES.

Noah and his mother watched the winter coming from an apartment in Outremont.

Leah had many visitors. A lady at last, she was asked to join the Shaar Zion Synagogue. Her father had been a Zaddik, and her husband had died for the Torah. The colour returned to her skin.

Her slouch, a posture that had formerly suggested defeat, was replaced by a new animation. A hard, intense light burned in her eyes. She did not mention Miriam to him. She knew better than that. But she made febrile plans for him.

"You'll go to McGill. You've got much more brains than Harvey. You can do whatever you want."

"Maybe next year, Maw."

"Or, if you like, I'll speak to Max. He'd do anything for me."

"Don't push me with Max, Maw. I don't mind driving the cab."

"I'd like to see you married and on your way before I die. Is that too much to ask?"

"No, Maw."

"You don't need to drink so much."

"Yes, Maw."

"I'm glad you get along so well with Sheila. She's a good girl. She can introduce you to . . ."

"Maw, did he ever speak to you about the box?"

"Who? What box?"

"Daddy."

"Before you go on, *boyele*, please get me my pills. Sometimes my breath comes short. I can't . . . Thank you . . . ah . . . thanks. . . . Now what was it you were saying?"

"Nothing."

One evening soon after that Noah had a night off and decided to go through the crate that contained his father's papers. Most of the stuff had come from the bottom drawer of Wolf's desk – from the drawer with the false bottom.

Leah was entertaining Mrs. Greenspon in the living-room. Noah could hear them.

"The Ethel Gordon Chapter of Hadassah would like to send a fully equipped ambulance to Israel in memory of your husband,

Mrs. Adler. We were wondering if we could count on your help. . . ."

Wolf's diary filled an enormous ledger of the type that was used by bookkeepers. The title-page read:

THE DIARY OF WOLF ADLER
Strictly Private
Dates – Memories – Projects – Inventions & Thoughts

Each letter had its ornate share of curls and dots and wiggly lines. It was necessary to hold the next page – a sample of Wolf's signature – up to the mirror in order to read the elaborately formed letters. Following that, came several pages of dates. Births, weddings, deaths. Noah flipped through the diary impatiently. Pages and pages in code. Each letter had been printed.

V J Q W I J V U   Q   Y C N M K P I
Da Yqnh Cfngt
Y C N M K P I

There was the rattle of tea-cups in the next room.

"My husband had his faults, Mrs. Greenspon. But he never, for a minute, forgot our heritage. You remember my father, don't you? Wolf wasn't one to push himself. He was content with his small lot. He . . ."

Each page had the sub-title: "Da Yqnh Cfngt." Noah guessed that that meant "by Wolf Adler."

The code, as a matter of fact, was pathetically easy to decipher. A was represented by C, and W was represented by Y. Each letter, in fact, was represented by the second letter that came after it in the alphabet.

"Did you know that there's now a scholarship at Baron Byng in everlasting memory of my late husband?"

"No, I didn't know that, Mrs. Adler."

Noah started on a comparatively easy page and deciphered it quickly.

THOUGHTS ON WALKING
By Wolf Adler

WALKING:

How much do I walk per day?

How long does it take me to walk the equivalent of the circumference of the earth?

NOTE: All figures are approximate. All steps are maximum – e.g. big steps.

MORNING: AFTERNOON: EVENING: WEEKEND/HOLIDAYS
  statistics
  one step – one yard
  one mile – 1760 yards

MORNING:

in house, before leaving for work	70 steps
to streetcar (shortest route)	289 steps
office and yard	700 steps

NOON: (eat lunch)   000 steps

AFTERNOON:

office, yard, trips	1000 steps

EVENING:

in	100 steps
out	2 to 5000 steps

NIGHT *(sleep)*

but trips to toilet average 21 steps each

_____

AVERAGE TOTAL   5109 steps

5109 steps per day – 5109 yds – approx 3 miles

DOUBLE AVERAGE FOR WEEKENDS

Therefore, on average I walk 3 × 5 plus 2 × 6 = 27 miles or approx 4 miles per day.

4 × 365 = 1460 miles per annum

Circum. of Earth = 25000 miles

Therefore, every 20 years (approx) I walk across the earth just going back and forth in Montreal.

"My father, may he rest in peace, used to say that this match was made in heaven. Now don't think I'm old-fashioned, Mrs. Greenspon. Superstitious, but . . ."

"I'll tell you something, Mrs. Adler. You don't know how the congregations are swelling again. So many of our people are coming back to God."

Noah deciphered another page.

THOUGHTS ON TIME WASTED
By Wolf Adler

NOTE: All figures are approximate

We sleep approx 8 hrs per day – 122 days per year. I spend about a half-hour daily* in the toilet – 182 hours per year – 8 days – therefore I waste 128 days per year.

*regular day (diarrhoea, constipation, balance out)

OBSERVATIONS:

If I live until 90 I will have actually lived only (approx) 57 years – having wasted the rest of the time sleeping or in the toilet.

"You must meet my boy, Mrs. Greenspon. He's going to go to McGill. I don't know what I'd do without him, I tell you. Ever since I've been ill he takes such good care of me. He takes after my father, you know. When my father, may he rest in peace, died . . ."

Noah began to feel queasy.

There was a project to build a bridge across the Atlantic. An ideal society, with secret signals, had been planned. Another page listed Wolf's weight before and after eating, before and after defecation, for a period of two weeks. On an average day Wolf accounted for three pints of urine: but Paquette, who was a beer drinker, did much better than that. The dates of all his quarrels with Leah had been entered. Average over a twenty-year period – 2.2 quarrels per day. There was a long and recent essay titled THE INGRATITUDE OF CHILDREN.

"Noah!"

"Yes?"

"Come, *boyele*, Mrs. Greenspon is anxious to meet you."

He replaced the diary in the box.

Noah began to work overtime. He didn't cruise much, but waited for calls at the stand. That was quite peaceful and he got a lot of reading done. Then, because the garage was beginning to make sour comments about his earning capacities he began to meet the out of town trains. He spent most of his free time with the Goldenbergs and their friends. Ste. Agathe had been a revelation. A shock. The people, the laws, that he had rebelled against had been replaced by other, less conspicuously false, laws and people while he had been away. That shifting of the ghetto sands seemed terribly unfair to him. If the standard man can be defined by his possessions, then rob his house and you steal his identity. Noah had supposed himself not to be a standard man. But his house had been robbed and his identity had been lost. He was shaken. Not only because he felt a need to redefine himself, but because he realized, at last, that all this time he had only been defining himself Against. Even death was something that he did Not Want. He avoided Panofsky. That man knew what he wanted. What he wanted was positive and required a bigger reply than No.

Noah avoided Max and Melech as well as Panofsky. He wanted to have something to say when he saw them. Meanwhile he carried the letters, receipts, and photographs about with him like his sins. He often awakened in the middle of the night to reach out for Miriam. Instead there was his father's body. Toes turned inward. He was too disturbed to get much out of drinking. But he drank with the other drivers. He drank until he realized that he was doing so only because it horrified his mother. Knowing that, he drank less.

Noah wanted some knowledge of himself that was independent of others.

He envied the Goldenbergs their convivial home and he wandered among them a masked, carnivorous man. He adored Sheila and hungered for her approval. He wanted his uncle to think that he had ambition and his aunt to think that he had good manners. He wanted Harvey to think that he was an upstanding, conservative man who was speeding towards Canadian mediocrity, towards an identity that would allow him to pass unrecognized, as fast as the best of them. If they would believe all that of him then perhaps he was not diseased and perhaps some of their happiness would rub off on him. So he agreed to everything. Next year, he agreed, he would go to McGill. Harry Goldenberg felt that the St. Lawrence Street Jews should be helped, like the underdeveloped countries. A faithful husband and considerate father, he appeared to be collecting points, as though he expected his documents to be questioned at the gates of heaven. His wife, Rachel, beyond being loyal and a good mother, seemed to be no more than a part of the house, not as pretty as the Wedgwood but more useful than the Bendix. Harvey took her to ballets. The two of them were extremely devoted. Harvey was tall and dark with black curly hair and a wide, intense mouth. He alone avoided Noah. He was well-read, but he did not like to be questioned about his reading. He even denied that he owned a volume of poetry. Noah went out on double dates with Sheila and

Larry. And when it became necessary he got himself a "steady." Marsha Feldman. Noah agreed with Mr. Feldman that communism was against all the laws of human nature and with Mrs. Feldman that men, after all, were men. He discussed premarital relations with Marsha. She felt that one shouldn't give oneself prior to the ceremony unless there was going to be a ceremony, but Noah balked at the idea of an engagement.

Oh, he was a miserable flop.

Noah was so intent on conforming that he conformed too much, and was suspected as an eccentric, a non-believer, by all. He finally realized that the secret of their humanity was that each one had a tiny deviation all his and/or her own. None conformed completely. Marsha, the little bitch, had love being made to her by a McGill quarterback whilst she was trying to hook Noah. (That finally endeared her to him.) His Aunt Rachel obeyed in all things except that she secretly read the most blatantly pornographic literature, and Mrs. Feldman beat her French poodle with a whip. Terror lurked behind their happiness. In fact, they weren't happy at all: they were composed. Truth was adroitly side-stepped, like a dog's excrement on the footpath. Harvey was obviously a repressed homosexual. Everybody knew, nobody agreed to see. That lie was the strength that held the Goldenbergs together. Harvey was being helped, damned, to go through life without realizing his sexuality. That made Noah sad and inadvertently led to his estrangement with the Goldenbergs. He spoke to Harvey. He thought it important for Harvey to know that there were people who agreed to see completely, and could still love. He wanted him to know that his being a homosexual did not horrify Noah. But it did horrify Harvey. He denied everything. The family was scandalized.

"Noah, *boyele*. Why don't you go to Harry's any more?"

"That's a long story."

"It doesn't matter. Harvey's not intelligent enough for you, anyway. But you shouldn't drink, *boyele*. People are talking. I don't want you to shame your father's name. I . . ."

"My father's name! You despised him all your life, Maw."

"We had quarrels. We weren't exactly right for each other but – Noah, I want you to make something of yourself: I – it's time we discussed things. I didn't say anything when you were with Mrs. Hall because I knew that eventually you would realize that you were a Jew and . . ."

"Do you think that I left Miriam because she was a *shiksa*?"

"I know you did."

Noah stared at her. He was frightened. Her eyes gave the impression of immense strength. He realized that she did miss her husband. That after twenty-four years of wrangling . . . *I am not going to replace him for her.* I won't be another of her dead saints that she can take down off her shelves and dust like her bits of china.

"I'm not going to live so long," Leah said. "You won't have to take care of me for years the way I . . . Oh, never mind. Please get me my medicine. My head is spinning. . . ."

"Yes, Maw."

Noah spent that night in various downtown bars. He passed the Halls' apartment and stood outside in the snow again, as he had done under different conditions how many winters ago? Had she returned to him? He didn't dare ring. The screen door, he remembered, had banged louder than her tears. "You'll always get away." Noah tried the Bar Vendôme, but she wasn't there. Miriam. Oh, Miriam. He went to Gino's. Gloomy faces floated through punctures in the yellow smoke. The jukebox wailed impersonally. At the far end of the room a young soldier kissed a girl passionately. Noah took out the packet of letters and stared at them. He didn't have to look at the photographs again – he knew them. I mustn't shame my father's name, he thought. He remembered the evening of his quarrel with Miriam. His mother had said that just before Wolf had left for the office somebody had phoned. "The crazy fool," Wolf had said, "so that's what he meant." Why have I never asked her about that, Noah thought. Moore works for Max now. Why? Does Moore know who started the fire? Lou talked about a tin of kerosene that first day. Why had there been no investigation? Noah remembered that last day in Panofsky's. Fasting, Wolf had said, cleans out the system. "You should visit *Zeyda. He's got plenty of ashcay stored away. He keeps it in a box.*" Noah ordered another drink. The wire tightened around his heart again, and a hard lump of something formed in his stomach. A fat man with small loose eyes sat down beside him. His hands made a wet smack as they flopped down on the bar and then curled up in selfish balls. Noah tittered. Poor hero, he thought. The jukebox blared louder. The fat man leaned towards the bartender. "Do you think that angels can really fly?" he asked. The bartender wiped a glass intently. "Do you think . . ." The fat man exploded with laughter. His pulpy hands opened and shut greedily. Noah stared. The jagged teeth of the shovel had glittered hungrily in the sun. "WOLF ADLER DIED FOR THE TORAH." Melech had looked at him, his mouth open and his hand pressed to his throat suppressing a scream. That young soldier, floating darkly in the smoke, was watching him. Noah rubbed his hands together anxiously. Did Wolf ever discover what was in the box? Or did he die without knowing – before he could examine the contents? Noah leaned back and laughed. He slapped his lean hands on the bar, compared them with the fat man's and laughed louder. He rubbed his wet eyes with the back of his wrists. The fat man poked him. "Do *you* think that angels can really fly?" Noah poked him back. His elbow sank deeply into that enormous mass of softly obscene flesh. The fat man, who seemed to be without bones, exploded with laughter again. A whore with hollow eyes turned to watch them. The fat man slapped Noah on the back, and Noah fell into another paroxysm of laughter. The whore giggled. The fat man's cheeks quivered. "Son-of-a-bitch," the bartender said. He burst out laughing. His face wrinkled, and the laughter flowed.

That scrawny whore collapsed in Noah's arms. Her laughter was like a shriek. A small, harried man with rimless glasses grabbed the fat man's arm. "What happened?" he demanded urgently. The fat man swung his hands up above his shoulders and then, before he could speak, they dropped helplessly to his small knees. Smack. The harried man shook the other man's arm hysterically. "Tell me," he pleaded. "What's the joke?" A gusher of laughter was his reply. He turned pink. The bartender pointed at him and began to howl again. He doubled up and held his hands to his stomach as though he was in great pain. The fat man collapsed on the bar, wrapping his head in his arms. "Why are you laughing? *Please.*" The fat man erupted again. Noah giggled. The whore had pressed his hand against her breast. Her tongue licked at his ear. The young soldier approached them out of the haze and smacked Noah on the shoulder. "Join us?" he asked.

Noah stiffened. The whore looked up. She clung to him possessively.

"What are you doing in the army?" Noah asked.

The fat man's laughter chugged to a halt, ignited again briefly, and then conked out like a dying engine.

"Got a new broad, eh?"

Suddenly Noah realized that his arm was around the whore's waist. Her fingers stroked his neck. They were cold. "Yes," he said. "Her name's . . ."

"Margo."

"Margo, meet Shl . . ."

"Jack," Shloime hissed.

"Jack," Noah said lamely.

"Join us, *Jim?*"

Shloime's table was in a dim corner. There were two green beer bottles. Gold liquid in tall glasses on a drab, brown table. Shloime's girl was a plump, bleached blonde with big breasts. She was ripely drunk. Shloime sat down beside her and tightened his arm around her like a rope, his hand forming a neat knot on her breast. Her name was Mary. After the Virgin, Shloime said, winking. "You're terrible," Mary said. She wiggled. Margo wanted whisky. They ordered two glasses, and some more beer. Noah felt her hand drop to his knee like a dry biscuit.

"When did you join the army?" Noah asked.

"Last summer." Shloime turned to Margo. "Do you think sex is a fad – like night baseball? Or is it here to stay?"

"That's Jack Benny's joke," Mary said.

"What are you," Shloime asked, "one of your mother's?"

The drinks arrived. Noah noticed that the small, harried man was still arguing with the fat man. Shloime kissed Mary roughly. Noah touched Margo's knee reassuringly. He drank.

"Why weren't you at my father's funeral?" Noah asked.

"I'm sorry. Honest. But I couldn't get leave. The sarge . . ."

"You were in the army *then*?"

"Yeah. So what?"

"I thought you were in Toronto."

Shloime flushed. "Who're you? J. Edgar Hoover? I was in the army. You can check, if you want."

Margo squeezed Noah's arm. "Talk to me," she said.

"You could have got compassionate leave if you were in the army."

The jukebox band began a rumba.

"Do you believe in mental telepathy?" Margo asked.

"Why did you join the army?"

Shloime put down his drink and assumed a stern expression. "Liss'n, wiseguy, these are dangerous times. I'm not saying that you or all the other ginks in here are chicken, but me, I love my country." Noah hadn't expected that. Shloime noticed that Margo was impressed. "I'm being sent to Germany in two weeks," Shloime continued. "Did you know that? Liss'n, this town is stinkink wid commies. If there weren't two ladies around I'd tell you in plain English what we guys are gonna do to dem. Somebody's gotta protect Canada. I'm willing – if necessary – to lay down my life for freedom. I don't want my kids brought up in a land run by Panofskys. I wish more people would realize how serious the commie menace is," he said. "The other day a college professor in . . ."

Noah's attention faltered. Shloime's speech was an incongruous mixture of newspaper editorials, army lectures, and ghetto fear. Obviously, Shloime had found his level. He was a fully adjusted member. Had Melech Adler abandoned love for the sake of right-eousness and come to America to produce this dangerously small man? Was this boy the end-product of religious fanaticism? Noah drank. My father died for money, he thought. Position. But that was a *real* thing to believe in. "I'm a lady. If we lived in Outremont I could hold my head up." Was she his murderer?

"If I had six months to live I'd be too sad to enjoy myself," Margo said. "Even if I had a million dollars."

Shloime ordered more beer. Mary poked Noah. "Stop being such a sad-sack," she said. "Think of your girl."

"Did you hear about the moron who went to bed with a problem on his mind," Shloime said, "and woke up with the answer in his hand?"

Mary squirmed with delight. The joke seemed to assume physical proportions for her.

"Keep it clean," Margo said.

Noah began to understand Shloime's anxiety, the need for all those jokes, at last. Hadn't he warned Wolf that he would get even? *He had been the one who had phoned that night.* Noah leaned towards him. "Moore saw you do it," he said.

Shloime turned pale.

"Lay off him," Mary said.

"You look just like Paw looked the day he threw me out," Shloime said.

"Moore saw you."

"Moore saw him," Mary said. "Now we know why butter costs eighty-seven cents a pound."

The jukebox wailed and wailed.

"How did I know that the crazy fool would run into the . . ." Shloime's eyes darted about furtively. "You. Yeah, you. What about *you*? You left. You didn't care a damn what happened to the rest of us. That day you found me in de lane you couldn't get rid of me quick enough. Big favour you done me, eh? You were ashamed of me in front of dat broad. You think I couldn't tell? Me, I'm stupid. I got leprosy. Don't you get your balls in an uproar. You didn't care whether he lived or died. You – you and your commie friends. You and Panofsky. You . . ."

Margo's hollow eyes filled with terror. A scene, she thought. They'll throw me out again. She gulped down her whisky. "I'm going to the little girl's room," she said.

". . . can't prove nuttin'," Shloime said.

Noah gripped his hands together tight. The fury, the pain, raging inside him prevented him from speaking. First there were the poets, he thought. The poets, Jacob Goldenberg, had too much vanity. Then came the religious fanatics. Melech Adler is a coward and without truth. After that a branch split off. Communists. Then, a rivalry for leadership. Harry Goldenberg *vs.* Max Adler. My father, he remembered, defined me as a Nothing. "Does Max know?" he asked.

"Nobody knows."

"Are you sure Max doesn't know?"

Mary wriggled upright, her hands on her hips. "We were gettin' along just fine – perfect – until you came along. Look, mister, nobody's . . ."

"What are you gonna do?" Shloime asked.

Noah got up. "Nothing," he said.

"Will you shake on that?" Shloime asked.

"Your pal's a crybaby," Mary said, pointing at Noah. "Look at his eyes."

"No," Noah said.

"Will you gimme your word?" Shloime asked.

Mary began to snivel, mimicking Noah.

"I swear on a hundred Bibles that I never dreamed he would . . ."

"I know, I know. But . . ."

"If he doesn't stop crying he'll flood the bar," Mary said. "Look at his eyes."

"Noah, lemme go with you. She's probably got syph, anyway. I . . ."

"You little twerp," Mary said. "How dare you!"

"He didn't mean it." Noah turned to Shloime. "It's too late for that. But . . ." Noah grabbed Shloime desperately. "Get out of the army as soon as you can. Please, Shloime. What you're . . ."

"I've never been treated so good as I am in the army."

Noah pushed his chair back. He wiped his eyes hastily.

"Will you promise?" Shloime asked.

"It wasn't all your fault. It . . ."

"*Will you promise not to say anything?*"

"I said I'd do nothing. Let's leave it at that. I – do I really remind you of *Zeyda*?"

"At times."

Outside, Noah was startled by the white glare of the snow. There seemed to be an accusing purity about it. The swift night air greeted him like slaps on both cheeks. Snowflakes – Rabbi Milton "Pinky" Fishman's food for thought – floated downwards heavily. At last Noah understood about the concentration camps. About the Goldenbergs and Harvey. The Germans had told the truth when they said that they hadn't known. They couldn't cope with knowing. Neither could the Goldenbergs. Their crimes varied in dimension but not in quality. What was he to do? One man, his grandfather, had robbed Leah of innocence by asking for a light: another, his father, had returned her to paradise by dying ambiguously. Should he tell her? She's dying, he thought. *What if her attacks are a ruse? Or self-induced? How do I know that she really has a heart condition?* He hesitated, and then turned up the stairs to the Maroon Club. A girl got up before the band and sang a blues. She was tall with lots of lechery in her movements. Lyrics wiggled out of her mouth wetly. A rapt man at a ringside table seemed to aim his cigar at her. Loneliness translated into slogans is what she was paid for. Men watched. She warbled. Between her and them there was only a void. As long as neither of them crossed that void there was safety in their shared limbo. She had been hired, she could be dismissed. Singing, the girl withdrew her hips from so many imaginary thrusts. Noah felt that she had promised better than she paid. He left. Outside again, the night seemed less hostile. Here, there were honourable agreements too. The distance between you and the stars was fixed. The moon wasn't figuring to collide with the earth. You could put your trust in the Montreal Transport Company to get you home, and lasting out a night earned you another day.

Finders keepers, lovers weepers.

Those who cheated could be hunted down by legions of Shloimes armed with the fear of their commanders.

Noah walked.

It was only important that they had made a hero out of his father if it mattered that Wolf, one small man, had been swindled even by death. It does matter to me, he thought. In fact, that explains all my differences with them.

Noah slipped into the apartment quietly. He heard voices coming from Leah's bedroom. He paused.

"After I'm an M.P.," Max said, "I'm really going to do good. How could they not elect me? Me, I'm no coward. When I get to Ottawa the Jews will have a voice – a helper. . . ."

"You don't know how much he could help you, Max. He could write your speeches. He – that boy is so bright. He could do anything as long as he puts his mind . . ."

"He's Wolf's son, and that'll help. The electors won't forget."

Noah giggled softly. Standing in the darkness, he wiggled his ears and raised his eyebrows. Experimentally.

II

The congregation decided to build a combination synagogue, hall, school, and community centre on Maplewood Avenue. Most members of the congregation now owned their own duplexes in Outremont, so what was the good of the old dump on Park Avenue? Park Avenue was a ghetto! Ever since the war the *greeners* had been flocking in by the boatload. (Why in the hell couldn't they go to Israel? God knows it's costing us enough.) Max Adler, the president of the congregation, decided that they could use the basement of the old synagogue for their building campaign headquarters. So that afternoon, two days before Christmas, Max and the vice-president, Jack Goldfarb, went down into the basement with flashlights. "Christ," Max said. "I almost forgot."

In 1939 a representative of The Hebrew Book Centre had arrived from Tel Aviv and had made an eloquent speech about the pioneers in Palestine. He told the congregation that the Hebrew language had been rejuvenated by these men, and that it was the duty of Jews everywhere to read their works, for, at the same time, they would be acquiring culture and helping in the noblest cause. It got a shock when the books arrived C.O.D. five days later. "Deal with the Jews," Max had said.

So the books were stored in the basement and quickly forgotten.

"What are we gonna do with the goddam books?" Goldfarb asked.

"I'll take them off your hands," Max said.

"Not so fast, Max. They belong to all of us."

An executive meeting was called for noon the next day. Max explained that they had to get rid of the books because they needed the space. That was fine, but suddenly everybody wanted the books. Ross said that he could use the big ones in his country home. Lou Bazer wanted three feet of the smaller ones for the bookcase attachment to his bedroom set. Krashinsky wanted two dozen – any size as long as the binding was good – for his real-estate office. Max settled the argument. He grabbed two books, held them behind his back, and said: "Okay, Goldfarb. Which hand?"

The books were divided up in a little less than three hours.

Afterwards Moore drove Max back to the office. Noah was supposed to be waiting there, and Max was in high spirits. "Liss'n, Moore, why couldn't you be a nigger? Or still better a Chink? Who in the hell ever heard of an Irish chauffeur?"

"You're kidding, Max."

Max rolled a cigar on his tongue, spit out the end, and then lit it. "What's new with the A.A.? You get a good report card this month?" He leaned towards Moore. "Lemme smell your breath, you old bastard. I catch you drinking and I'll break your . . ."

"I haven't had a drop, Max."

Max's office was different from his father's old office on St. Dominique Street. It was vast, and dominated by a long, semi-circular oak desk. The panelled walls were sound-proof. A bar on rollers was disguised as a bookcase. Press a button, and the industrial mural on the wall behind the desk rolled up to reveal a screen. On the opposite wall a panel lifted and a projector rolled out. Max enjoyed showing prospective clients films of previous Ajax Trading jobs interspersed with short items like *Lesbians in Action* or *Honeymoon in Paris*. Press another button and a photograph of Melech Adler slid back to reveal a wall safe. Press still another button and a panel lifted revealing a small bedroom. Other photographs hanging on the walls included one of Max and the mayor.

Noah stared at the one that had a black frame. IN EVERLASTING MEMORY. A photograph of Wolf and a simple poem.

Max burst into the office and grinned broadly. He pulled out the bar and rolled back the "books." "I should get Moore to do this. That's what he's paid for, eh? But me, why should I wave a carrot in front of a donkey's nose?" He paused, allowing time for Noah's laugh. "Did you meet Miss Holmes coming in?"

"No."

"It takes that broad five hours to eat lunch. Bad digestion. Any way, she'll be back before six. You'll meet her." Max served drinks, and then assumed a more serious expression. "Are you gonna work for me, Noah?"

Noah had last seen that expression, heard that tone of voice, when he had been a boy. That's how they had used to swear each other into street gangs.

"That's not why I came here," Noah said.

"I'm sold on you, Noah. What's wrong? Don't you go for me?"

"Sure I do, Max, but . . ."

"I'll pay you a hundred and fifty a week for the first six months. That's when you'll be learning to count your fingers after shaking hands with a customer. After six months, if you've still got fingers left, you become my personal secretary and I'll up you to two hundred a . . . You don't seem to be listening."

"I'm listening."

"Noah. I can't trust anybody. You I could. You're not jealous like the others." Noah didn't reply immediately, so Max continued. "I'm going to go far, Noah. This is just the beginning. I . . ."

"Max, you knew that my father didn't rush into that fire after the scrolls. Nobody knew that the *Zeyda* was working on scrolls. You know damn well what my father thought was in that box."

Max pulled out a fresh cigar and rolled it on his tongue and spit out the end. He sat down behind the desk. "Hell, Christ may have died thinking that Judas was going to split with him at the eleventh hour and that they would make their getaway together. But the people . . ."

"So you've known all along."

"I did it for Paw's sake," Max said.

"Let's not start lying to each other at this point."

"All right. So I didn't do it for Paw's sake." Max flung his letter opener down on his desk. "How much do you want to *borrow*?"

"Are you serious, Max? Do you think that I've come here for money?"

"Statistics prove that nine out of ten guys who step through that door come here for that very item."

"Does my mother know about the scrolls?"

"Not unless you intend opening your big mouth."

Max flipped open the intercommunication system on his desk and asked about Miss Holmes. But she hadn't arrived yet. He turned to Noah. "That girl'd do anything for me," he said. "She loves me. She – aw, what the hell!"

"What would you do if she were pregnant, Max?"

"Mail her a hat-pin. Hey, what do you think. We've got doctors in this town, eh?"

There had been no sign of recognition. He obviously didn't know about Melech.

"I'd like to meet her," Noah said.

"You will."

"I don't want any money, but Shloime might get ideas if you ever became an M.P."

"Shloime?"

"Look, Max, are we going to crap around or . . ."

"I'll kill that old lush. I'll break every bone in his . . ."

"Moore hasn't said a word. He's kept his bargain, I guess. I saw Shloime a few nights ago. But I had hoped that at least you didn't know that Shloime was responsible for the fire. That – did you put him in the army?"

Max lifted his arms into the air and then allowed them to drop helplessly to his sides.

"You don't want a scandal, eh, Max? You're worried about the election?"

"Here." Max tossed a pamphlet across the desk. It was for the Synagogue Building Campaign. There was that picture of Wolf and that poem. The school was to be called the Wolf Adler Memorial School. "I've been watching you for some time, Noah. Do you know what would happen if the so-called true story of Wolf's death got out? The anti-Semites would have a ball. It would prove to them that the Jews only care for money. That they'll even die for it." Max stood by the window, his hands clasped behind his back. "I think you'd like that because I think you're the biggest goddam anti-Semite I've ever met."

"My father didn't die for money because he was a Jew."

"You go talk to the *Goyim*."

"I'm not talking to the *Goyim*. Or the Jews. I'm talking to you."

"Me. That's right. And I'm telling you that if the so-called true . . ."

"Wolf Adler died because his father was a coward and allowed the *Goyim* to define him. For another, his wife was a bitch and his son a blindly selfish bastard. One brother a moron and the other a scoundrel. That other being you. All right. You've all got reasons. But somewhere this ugliness has got to stop." Noah drank hastily. "Anti-Semitism is an obscene enough thing, Max, without it being used to rationalize your business perversions."

"I'm listening. Go ahead."

"If this nonsense about Wolf isn't stopped – if this pamphlet isn't withdrawn, and unless you swear not to use Wolf in your election campaign – I'll let the true story out."

"That's blackmail."

"All right. It's blackmail."

"Nobody'd believe you."

"You can't afford to take that chance."

"I can't, eh? And what about you? You're such a weakling, Noah. You're as bad as Panofsky. You'd never tell the true story because you know what it would do to your *Zeyda* – and your mother. . . ."

"I'm leaving my mother in a few days."

"You're what? She's sick. Why that would be enough to kill her."

"I don't think so. She . . . she might live another ten or twenty years. I'd have to leave her sometime. I . . ."

"I'm beginning to think you're a bigger bastard than I am."

"Will you withdraw the pamphlet?"

"No. But I'll up my offer to two-fifty a week and let the customers count *their* fingers."

Noah got up. "My mother's illness is convenient. Whenever I want to do something that she doesn't like she has an attack. That could go on for . . . You don't understand."

"You walk out and she dies. I'm willing to put money on that."

"You're willing to put money on anything."

Max walked around the desk and confronted Noah. "I can see it all now, you know. You walk out, you kill her. Bango! You're into the bottle like a pig into its own shit." Max poked him with his cigar. "You drink a bit already, don't you? But you think you can stop if you want. Yeah, sure. They all think that." He shoved the cigar back into his mouth. "You'll come crawling back, Noah. You'll be willing to take fifty bucks a week, but by that time you won't even be worth ten. But stinker that you think I am I've got a big heart and I'll take you in. I'm corrupt, eh? Who keeps the whole family in cars, you or me? Sure, I'll take you in out of the rain. Maybe I'll even be able to swing it so that you and Moore are in the same A.A. group."

There was a soft rapping at the door.

"All right," Max said. "Let's stop quarrelling. It's Miss Holmes. She . . ." Max gave Noah a hard, penetrating look. "She's somebody – the only person – that I can still trust."

Noah watched. Miss Holmes handed Max a batch of letters to be signed and Max accepted them tenderly. Noah was introduced. She didn't recognize him. But Noah's mind returned swiftly to that night in the Café Minuit. He eats out of my hand, she had told Harry, as long as I keep sugar in it.

As soon as Miss Holmes left Noah grasped Max's arm. "Max, listen, there's something you ought to know. I . . ."

Max misunderstood. He grinned with delight and grabbed Noah's hand. "You've changed your mind. You're gonna stay. Is that it?"

Noah inched back from him. "No, I . . . Max . . ."

"You sick? Sit down."

Noah broke away from him. "I'm sorry, Max."

"Sorry?"

"Sorry for you. Sorry for me, too, I guess. I – I wonder if I'm as weak as you say?"

He slipped out.

Miss Holmes waved to him as he passed her desk, but Noah didn't notice.

III

"Happy New Year," Collin yelled.

Marg Kennedy leaped on to the table and pulled a whirl of crepe paper around her. "The Hydrogen Bomb Age is now one year old." She giggled. "Stop looking up my skirts, Howard."

"The H-Bomb Age may be one year old," Howard said, "but I reached puberty long ago."

Marg tumbled off the table and into his arms.

"Happy New Year," Collin yelled again.

The telephone rang. Bill Goodman swept it up to his mouth as though he meant to devour it. "Communist Party headquarters," he said.

Jane MacEvoy shrieked. "Do you want the RCMP over?" she asked.

"Comrades, and members of the FBI," Collin said.

"It's Harold," Bill said, holding the phone in his hand. "He says that when this ship runs dry we can come aboard his raft."

"There's still a lot more to drink," Theo called out glumly, keeping his eye on Miriam and Neil.

"Tell him we'll come alongside in a few hours, Bill," Marg yelled.

"Hang a blonde out of the window," Bill said into the mouthpiece, "and keep same well lit. Otherwise, we might miss your barge in the fog." Bill hung up.

Neil McLeod pursued Miriam into the bedroom.

Theo watched. So did Marg.

Theo's mother smiled. She noticed that Neil had shut the bedroom door after him. "I enjoyed your last book of poetry so much, Howard," she said. "Do you count Auden as one of your influences?"

"I count Canadian Club as my only influence," Howard said.

"And he's usually under it," Daphne said.

Mrs. Hall watched the shut bedroom door. She's only been back with him three months, she thought. And that makes the fourth man. She looked at her watch. "What did you say, Howard?"

"I said that Canada hasn't any writers, Mrs. Hall. We'll have to get an identity first. Meanwhile, we're British without the tradition and American without the . . ."

"I don't think you're right, Howard. I . . ."

A glass crashed in the kitchen.

Jane MacEvoy cornered John Kennedy. "Neil's psychiatrist says that he's got strong homosexual tendencies because he says that he'd never wear suède shoes. He says that if Neil wasn't afraid to wear suède . . ."

"I can understand everything about queers," John said, "except their taste in men."

Marg touched Theo's arm. "Oh, don't be such an old lady. It's New Year's Eve. So what if she kisses a man in the bedroom?"

"Things haven't been the same ever since . . ."

"Believe me, Theo. She's learnt her lesson. She could have a dozen affairs now and they'd all be silly. Noah taught her to stick to her husband. So stop being so possessive. You . . ." Marg kissed him and smiled. "I can always be your consolation prize, darling."

Mrs. Hall looked at her watch again. Five minutes, she thought. Why doesn't Theo . . .

"I like Canadians and human beings, too," Howard said.

Jane MacEvoy perched on the arm of the sofa. "Of course there may be concentration camps, John, but now that Stalin's dead . . ."

"Orwell would call that double-think," John said.

Hortense pulled the curtains aside and smiled back at Edgar. "Think of all the parties and all the drinks being consumed in all those apartments. I hate parties."

"I'm superior to being superior to parties," Edgar said.

"Edgar, our marriage will be different – won't it? Theo and Miriam are so dreadfully unhappy."

"Oh, he's all right. She's man-crazy, that's all."

"It's hopeless, Edgar. You *never* understand."

Hortense moved away and Edgar stared after her dumbly.

Bill Goodman picked his nose absently. "Does that disgust you, Irene?"

Collin popped a balloon with a cigarette.

"That's phallic," Jane MacEvoy said.

"You want to see something phallic?" Collin said.

Marg noticed Mrs. Hall head for the bedroom door and, moving swiftly, managed to get there first. "Enjoying yourself, Mrs. Hall? I was just telling John that we must have you up for dinner. . . ."

Mrs. Hall glanced at her watch. A burst of laughter came from behind the bedroom door.

Edgar caught up with Hortense. "I always seem to be saying things," he said.

"Theo's impossible! I won't have you blaming Miriam just because . . ."

"I'm not blaming Miriam. But if she had to get into the sack with Harold why did she have to do it right under everybody's nose. Now she's slipped out with Neil. Theo's not a bad guy. Couldn't she have a little dignity about it?"

"I know her, Edgar. Her heart's broken. She . . ."

"Whose heart isn't broken?"

"Shall we discuss something else – *please.*"

Theo spoke to Marsha, watching the door over her shoulder. "I don't want you to think that I turned down Neil's stuff for personal reasons. But *Direction* has certain standards and . . ."

Marg seized Mrs. Hall's arm and led her over to John. "I was just telling Mrs. Hall, John, that you'd be delighted to discuss Canadian writing with her. What were you saying about Lemelin, Mrs. Hall?"

Fifteen minutes, Mrs. Hall thought. She's been in that bedroom fifteen minutes.

The record player clicked, and Fats Waller began again.

Collin turned to Bill. "I think we're going to have a big third act any minute. Neil's a bloody fool. I don't care if he's drunk, but this is Theo's house. . . ."

"Don't blame Neil, man. She was on to me once. That woman's turned into a tiger."

The bedroom door opened, and Marg whirled around to face Neil. His expression was bewildered. His shirt was soaked in whisky and his hair was wet.

"Wipe the lipstick off your face, you fool," Marg whispered.

Neil pulled out his handkerchief desperately. "That girl's mad. First she can't get to you quick enough and then . . . Why should she spill a drink in my face?"

"You should have had more sense than to . . ."

Mrs. Hall approached quickly. "Is Miriam not feeling well?" she asked icily.

"As a matter of fact," Neil began lamely, "she's . . ."

Marg backed into the bedroom and shut the door behind her.

Miriam lay face down on the bed. Her dress unzipped, she whimpered softly. Marg sat down beside her and stroked her hair gently. "I brought you a drink," she said.

Miriam gathered up bits of pillow into her fists tightly.

Mrs. Hall knocked on the door. "I'd like to get something out of my purse," she said.

Marg began to search frantically among the mess of coats and shawls and hats and bags for a purse that might feasibly belong to Mrs. Hall. "What colour is it?"

"I could find it in a jiffy if you'd let me in," Mrs. Hall called out.

IV

On that first Sunday of the winter of 1954, as under a stern sun the snows of St. Dominique Street showed glittering white in spots, Melech Adler, his mottled hands lying shrivelled on his lap, sat in the armchair in his living-room considering his past. Later, after he had taken his pills and eaten his lunch of boiled beef and potatoes, he would lie down to rest for an hour or so. Mr. Adler had ten children, six boys and four girls. One of them had died in a fire, and another was with the army in Germany. His youngest daughter, Ida, was sort of engaged. This Sunday was special. Later Max would send Moore around with the Cadillac to pick up Mr. and Mrs. Adler. The Adlers were to join their children in Max's home in Outremont for a family meeting.

Old Melech Adler sat in his chair and unfolded his newspaper and turned to the obituary column. He frowned. He recalled how long ago and during another season, Moore, the drunkard, had tried to cheat him by mixing in cast iron with the brass and weighing down sacks with earth. *After they had begun to haggle in a jocular way about prices Noah whispered to his grandfather that his father and Paquette had hidden many of the sacks. Melech, his face darkening, had asked Noah to please wait for him in the office. Melech had known that Moore's scrap was stolen. That some of it had been stolen from his own yard. But Noah hadn't obeyed him. He had begun his story over again. Melech had slapped his grandchild. But he had done that only because he wanted to protect him from the drunkard.*

He could have been the brightness of my old years. But he ran away with a *shiksa*. He's no good.

Most of the family arrived shortly after lunch.

Mr. Adler sat in a corner. Max sat in his armchair discussing school with Jonah. The other grandchildren were grouped around him, all of them making raucous bids for his attention. Now and then he gripped one of them in a huge hand, and laughing gruffly, pressed a dollar bill into his pocket.

The women sat around the table gossiping and waiting for the maid to serve tea.

Ida knew why there was going to be a meeting. She had told Max how things were between Stanley and herself, and Max had grinned boyishly and pinched her cheek and said, you'll have to get married, that's all. I want to marry him, anyway, she had said. Still better, Max had said. You don't worry about a thing. Tomorrow . . . em – Mort? Stanley, she had said. Then he had pressed one of the many buzzers on his big desk and a tall blonde woman had come in unsmilingly and had waited for his word. Miss Holmes honey, he had said, send Moore around with the Caddy for my sister, eh? After she had gone Max had turned to Ida, smiling boyishly again, and had said: Some looker, eh?

There were many things to discuss at the meeting. Noah was leaving and they would have to decide things about Leah.

Ida lolled on the bed nibbling peppermints and reading the *Good Housekeeping* magazine. She was glad that Max had given Stanley a

job because that had made him less scared about getting married:
besides, Max was his hero.

The meeting had not gone as Ida had expected. Max, for one thing,
had been called to Toronto on business at the last minute. So his
wife, Debrofsky's only daughter, had conducted the meeting. Ida
didn't like her. She was a small, bony woman with a pinched face.
Her dog, which she called Babykins, was a pedigree French poodle
that had cost a good deal of money. Debrofsky's only daughter had
a hard, unjoking way of speaking, and addressed the Adlers with
resentment, as if they, unlike Babykins, did not have a pedigree. Her
father sat behind her in an armchair. He was a yellowing man with
shrivelled eyes who was in the habit of saying: "I came to Canada
with fifty cents in my pocket" – and taking off his glasses and pointing at a picture of his factory – "and I worked hard." He wanted a
grandson before he died. Stanley had also come to the meeting. He
had sat on the piano stool twisting his fedora in his hands, avoiding
Ida's searching, sympathetic looks. When Debrofsky's only daughter had announced the engagement, Melech Adler had looked
darkly at Ida, but had said nothing. Ida had smiled hopefully at
Stanley when Debrofsky's only daughter had announced that Max
would give the young couple one thousand dollars with which to
start housekeeping. Stanley had nodded. He had been watching
Melech, the truly orthodox member of the Adler family. Stanley
thought that the old man was quite a character.

Melech Adler, who was the son of a scribe, was full of sorrow after
the meeting. He watched his wife bake raisin buns.
    "Jenny . . . *Nu*, Jenny, you – you are happy?"
    "Happy?"
    "Maybe you would like a movie sometimes. . . . Or a talk?"
    "You are not well, Melech?"

Between Melech and the grandchildren Jenny didn't get much rest.

"This is my house, Jenny. I came here fifty years ago and I knew from nothink. Scrap I collected in the lanes. I drove a horse and buggy through Griffintown and the *Goyishe* hoodlums threw stones at me. . . ." He cleared his throat, and began again. "Look at them, all over the street, new ones, *greeners*. They come around for *naduvas*. Did I beg when I came to Canada? They have it easy, the new ones. Not like we did. But their sons will be ashamed for de beards. The sons will grow up *Goyim*, like Noah. It's a bad world. You wait."

"About the *greeners* you are right. Mrs. Myerson said to me yesterday dat only de worst ones get away."

Melech stood up suddenly. He was shaking. "You heard, you heard the meeting? You think I care they don't ask me anything no more? Bah! Let them do, let them. I should worry. But when I die – probably before my time – it'll be them that put de nails in my coffin. *Them*. You hear? Some life I had." He walked around the table and grabbed Jenny's arm forcefully. "There is no justice in this world. God don't listen always. Not like He should, anyway. . . ."

"Melech, Melech. . . ."

She held her hand to her lips surreptitiously, as though to caution him against God, who was watching and listening. For the first time in his life he came close to striking her. He stared at her fiercely, his eyes burning darker, and then he retreated from the room.

"Melech, Melech, what is . . ."

V

"*Boyele?*"

"I didn't hear you come in, Maw."

"When are you leaving?"

"Tomorrow afternoon."

"Tomorrow afternoon, he says."

"Yes. How do you feel?"

"How would *you* feel?"

Noah knelt down before her and kissed her hands. "Maw, I tried to explain. I'll only be gone for a year. I haven't enough money to stay away longer. I . . ."

"Money. Wouldn't I give you money?"

"Yes. You would."

"When I think of how my father struggled to get us out of Europe. How all of us struggled. . . . Max says Europe is scum. He says they're finished. What'll you do there among all those anti-Semites?"

"I'll look around."

"Look. What for?"

"I would like to understand things better."

Leah withdrew her hands from him. "You are going to get away from me, aren't you?"

"Maw, that's not . . ."

"Are you going to begin to lie to me after all these years?"

Noah stood up. "No," he said. "But what you're thinking is only partly right. Will you listen without interrupting?"

"Who's interrupting?"

"If I stay here we'll learn to hate each other. Even now, I – I've always wanted . . . I've always loved you, Maw, but I'm beginning to . . . I can't stay. It would kill both of us. But I've always wanted to go to Europe. I'd like to . . ."

"So you couldn't wait six months? I'm sure I won't live longer than that."

"Maw, please, that's exactly what I mean. Would you like me to wait around hoping for your death?" He turned to her again. "Please stop thinking that you're going to die. I'll be back in a year's time. I'll stay with you for a while then. Meanwhile, Harry will gladly . . ."

"They don't want me."

"They want you, Maw. And many, many people with your heart condition live for ten and twenty years."

"If you decided to stay I wouldn't bother you about your drinking."

"Drinking."

"You could have as much as you want."

"Where in the hell do people get the idea that I'm a drunkard?"

"You think I'm faking, don't you? You think I only make the attacks so that I can keep you with me?"

"No, not quite. But I think that you do tend to use your condition unfairly at times."

"Why are they no longer going to call the new school the Wolf Adler Memorial School? Why did they change the name?"

"Ask Max."

"Max said I should ask you."

"Oh, I see."

"He sees. That's the sum of all my insurance policies speaking. What'll you do when you get back? Drive a taxi again?"

"Maw, I'm not your husb . . . I don't know. But I don't think so."

Leah got up. "My son has turned out a bum after all my struggles. I'm going to sleep. I don't care any longer, Noah. You're yes a taxi driver, no a taxi driver. My life is over. Finished. . . ."

Noah followed her into the hall.

"I'll write you every week, Maw."

"Write, don't write. To put a knife into my back would have been kinder. Now go. Go. Be happy."

                                    VI

Upstairs Melech Adler wandered absently through empty bedrooms that had used to belong to his children. The rooms were draughty and chill and smelled badly. Melech shivered. He tried hard to possess again, if only for a moment, the laughter and the ailments and the play that had used to fill these rooms. Bedsprings had rusted under dust-sheets. There were fading marks on the walls where graduation pictures and pennants had used to hang. In Max's old room, opening the cupboard, he stumbled on a pair of boxing-gloves and several back issues of sporting magazines. The gloves were mouldy, the pages had yellowed. Melech dropped his find to the floor and stared at his yellowed, shaking hands. He collapsed into a frayed armchair which had been covered by sheets, and stared at the walls. When Ornstein had died his children, according to the orthodox custom, had covered the mirrors with towels. They had said, according to the modern custom, that their father was better off that way. "He died quickly, Mr. Adler. No suffering." Melech Adler held his head in his hands, and sorrowed over what had become of him. He would have rested that way for hours but finally, inevitably, he noticed the white sheet he sat on. He saw the other white sheets that covered the armchair opposite him and the bureau to the right. He backed out of the room, horrified. Suddenly, he heard the radio turned on in Ida's room.

> *It's Make-Believe Ballroom time,*
> *The hour of sweet romance. . . .*

Something stirred within Melech. She is my child, he thought. He was certain that she, his daughter, would comfort him. Her door was opened. Ida, holding an absent partner, glided to and fro before the mirror. Her eyes were shut, her expression dreamy; she wallowed in a smile that said life was good, life was full. She danced naked. Dancing away from him, like the years. His eyes blurred. *Helga, Helga, forgive me.* He saw, more real than her, the rusting springs and the mattress abandoned on the floor. Fading marks on the walls and white, white sheets. Ida opened her eyes and approached the mirror as though she expected to be received by it. She saw an old, bearded man staring at her. She reached for her dressing-gown in a panic and whirled about to face her father. I caught him, she thought. Melech smiled and nodded in a friendly manner. Smiled, and saw too late that she misunderstood his intentions. His shoulders slumped. He was surprised and ashamed that his daughter could think of him in such a foul way. So he turned away, hoping to be gone before she could speak things that, once heard, could never be forgotten. But she couldn't understand that either. Besides, he was against Stanley.

"Can't I have privacy in my own room even? Spying on me, eh? I'm going and I'm glad. What are you looking? Did you ever let me do what I want? *Once*. Ever ask me how I felt? I'm going. I'm glad, you hear?"

Noah, who at that moment was parked across the street from his grandfather's house, occupied an unique position in the Adler family. He was, to begin with, Leah's son. Leah wasn't liked. He was the grandson of a man whom Melech Adler had deeply respected – Jacob Goldenberg the Zaddik. He was the son of Wolf Adler, who, as far as the others were concerned, had died for the Torah. The Adlers lived in a cage and that cage, with all its faults, had justice and safety and a kind of felicity. I wonder what will happen, he thought, now that I'm leaving? They'll need something to blame me for. Noah stared at the snow. He was immensely happy. He had spent the previous evening with Panofsky. They had sat in the kitchen drinking beer and listening to the music of Vivaldi. Even Aaron had been cheerful. He had given Noah his old suitcase. He had told him stories about Madrid. Panofsky had had lots of beer and had said that he might turn the business over to Karl next summer and come to Europe himself. Aaron had laughed. He had said that the old man was getting lecherous in his last days and that he would be fleeced by the first D.P. he met up with. Noah had laughed, too. But he had known that Panofsky would never quit City Hall Street. A new crowd is arriving, Panofsky had said. Perhaps this time things will work out better. What do I need Europe for? Noah will write us everything. Remembering, Noah grinned. The cold blue sky was without clouds. There was a dry, clean feeling to the day. Miriam had asked him what he wanted. He hadn't been able to tell her because at that time he had wanted to love her the way he had at first, and he hadn't been able to. He could tell her now, though. He could tell her that he wanted freedom and that innocent day at Lac Gandon and the first days of their love and many more evenings with Panofsky and the music of Vivaldi and more men as tall as Aaron and living with truth and, maybe, sometime soon, a wiser Noah in another cottage near a stream with a less neurotic Miriam. Oh, he wanted plenty. I'm free, he thought. Max can go to hell. You require me to be an alcoholic, he thought. But you'll never get that, Max. Not out of me, you won't. Noah blew on his hands. Remembering his mother, he felt that wire tightening around his heart again. He rubbed his hands together anxiously. She'll be fine, he thought. Now that she knows I'm really going she'll pull through. I'll write every week. Noah dug into his pocket and pulled out two envelopes. One of them contained his rail ticket to New York and his boat ticket. Tomorrow afternoon at four, he thought, I'll be on that train to New York. What can stop me? The other envelope contained Melech's letters and receipts and photographs. Giving it to him will be difficult, Noah thought. Why shouldn't I tell him that Shloime started the fire? He knows that Wolf didn't die for the Torah. He knows.

The door opened.

Noah stood before him confidently. "I'm leaving, *Zeyda*," he said. "I came to say goodbye."

Melech Adler took off his glasses and folded up his paper. "I told you long ago," he began slowly, "that you are no longer welcome here. . . ."

Noah placed the envelope on the arm of Melech's chair. "I brought you this," he said. "I'm sorry that I took it. But there were many things that I didn't know then."

Melech ignored the envelope. "I suppose you want a thank you for such a big favour? Maybe you want I should give you a blessing for giving me back what you stole from me? Look at you! A nothing. You would mix into the affairs from your *Zeyda*."

"Had I known what was in the envelope I wouldn't have taken it."

Mr. Adler got up. "You are by me de greatest shame I had. Go."

"Did my father know what was in the box?"

Melech stared. He had known that one day Noah would come to ask him that question. A wild, vengeful part of him wanted to tell Noah the truth. Ever since he had been a boy Noah had denied him the respect that was justly his. The boy was going away. They might never meet again. Melech didn't know that Noah already knew the truth about the box. He rebelled against the idea that Noah should come to respect Wolf and not him. Wolf, who had died for a cash-box. Melech walked over to the window. He tugged slowly at his beard. Had I told him about Moore that day, if I had explained it to him first, everything would have been all right. Melech pursed his lips. He remembered that from the first he had always wanted Noah to ask him a favour. He had wanted the boy to be in his debt. He turned to him. "Your Paw knew that I had in the box scrolls. About the other stuff he didn't know. Nobody knew."

Noah turned away from him. A lump formed in his throat. He understood the gift of Melech's lie, and he was speechless.

"You came here another day," Melech said, "and told me I should try to understand. What should I try to understand?"

"I started out here today with anger, *Zeyda*. I came here to tell you things that I've found out. Facts, I guess. But now – you are no longer the same man that I had in mind. I have changed too. I . . ." Noah paused. He realized gladly that Shloime had been wrong. For

Melech, in Noah's place, would have told his grandfather that his youngest son had started the fire. Melech, in his place, would have had God and would have done what was just. "You said you wanted me to be a Somebody. A Something. I've come to tell you that I have rules now. I'll be a human being. I'll . . ."

"You are going from us?"

"I am going and I'm not going. I can no more leave you, my mother, or my father's memory, than I can renounce myself. But I can refuse to take part in this . . ."

"I understand that you are going. Finished. Go. Go, become a *Goy*. But have one look first at what the *Goyim* did to your *Zeyda*. That girl in the picture had she been willing to become a Jewess, to . . . Stones they threw at me, Noah. My heart they made hard against my children. Who burned me down my office? Who murdered my first-born? *Goyim Goyim*. Now go. Go. Go join, become my enemy."

Melech Adler sat down and picked up his paper again.

Their eyes met briefly. An old man crumpled up in a chair.

Noah reached out and touched his shoulder. "Would you give me one of the scrolls, one of – one of the scrolls you copied . . .?"

"The scrolls? *You*. I'm not a scribe . . . I . . ."

"I would like to have one to remember – one that you made."

"They are not very well done, child. There are errors. My father now, he . . . I . . ."

Melech got up and opened up a drawer. He glanced wordlessly through several scrolls, selected one, and handed it to his grandson.

"I planned so much for you," Melech began faltering, "I . . . Money you could have had – anything, but . . ."

"You have given me what I wanted," Noah said.

Melech sat down again. Noah bent over and kissed him. "I'm sorry," he said.

After he had gone Melech touched his cheek and felt that kiss like a burn. He touched his cheek and felt that he had been punished.

VII

Early the next morning Leah sat in her armchair by the window waiting for Harry to come and get her. In seven hours, she thought, he'll be gone. There's nothing I can do.

"Leah – Leah, did you . . . If – if there is a light . . ."

Oh yes. Yes. Years, years, years. Noah was no picnic I can tell you that much, but . . . Her breath began to come quickly. Her father had been a poet and, having lived too long in another country, had died a character. Her husband, a – that man died a hero. Sweat streamed down her face. Her skin turned grey. *A gathering yellow fog of exploding yellow lights, and Leah reached up wearily but in vain for a fading retreating Noah before she was washed back down under many, heavy seas.* God, God. There is nothing I can do to stop him. Nothing. Her head throbbed. A vice-like pain twisted, tightened, in her chest. Tighter and tighter. An enormous weight passed down on her. Leah gasped. Stared. A fierce pain shot down her left arm and crackled in her two little fingers. Another – and fiercer – pain sped swiftly up her jaw. Tighter.

"A light . . . If you should see . . . If – *Boyele*. . . ."

Harry knocked on the door. Knocked, and knocked again. There was no answer.

VIII

About an hour later Mrs. Adler brought in a glass of lemon tea for Melech. "Noah was here?" she asked.

"Last night. So?"

"He is leaving?"

"He's going to Europe this afternoon. Finished."

"All I did was to ask."

"Ask."

Each man creates God in his own image. Melech's God, who was stern, sometimes just, and always without mercy, would reward him and punish the boy. Melech could count on that.

"I'll get you some buns."

Melech didn't protest. He picked up his prayer-book and began to read. And why not? Hadn't the Angel of Death passed over King David because he was at his prayers?

Mordecai Richler was born in Montreal in 1931. The author of ten successful novels, numerous screenplays, and several books of non-fiction, his most recent novel, *Barney's Version*, was an acclaimed bestseller and the winner of The Giller Prize, the Stephen Leacock Award for Humour, the QSPELL Award, and the Commonwealth Writers Prize for Best Novel in the Caribbean and Canada region. Richler also won two Governor General's Awards and was shortlisted twice for the Booker Prize.

Mordecai Richler died in Montreal in July 2001.